Praise for *Dead Hairy*

'We love *Dead* [...] mended as part of their 'Bri[...] ...paign

'... extremely well written – immediate, clever, smartalecky ... immensely enjoyable.' *The Irish Catholic*

'... romps ... with exuberance and sparkling dialogue ...' Mary Arrigan, *Irish Examiner*

'... great fun, loaded with laughs ... this one is a pure delight.' *Fallen Star Stories*

can't recommend it highly enough. I think it's a brilliant ok. I was roaring laughing at the first couple of pages.' endan Nolan, radio presenter and author of *Telling les*

om the first paragraph to the last, this is a laugh-aloud ead for any age, with a compelling plot and well-rounded characters.' *Inis magazine*

Jungle Tangle

Debbie Thomas

Illustrated by Stella Macdonald

MERCIER PRESS
IRISH PUBLISHER – IRISH STORY

MERCIER PRESS
Cork
www.mercierpress.ie

© Text: Debbie Thomas, 2013
© Illustrations: Stella Macdonald, 2013

ISBN: 978 1 78117 116 5

10 9 8 7 6 5 4 3 2 1

Printed and bound in the EU.

For my superstars:
Stevie, Emily, Ruby and Rosa.

And for Mum and Dad, whose love
and encouragement have a lot to
answer for.

MEET THE CREW

The Hartleys

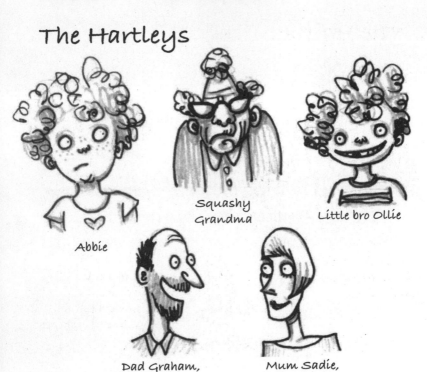

Abbie

Squashy Grandma

Little bro Ollie

Dad Graham, history nerd

Mum Sadie, ex-fusspot

The Platts

Perdita

Mum Coriander, hairdresser & world explorer

Dad Matt, Very Odd Job man & inventor

The Hairies

Chester, a shy
patch of chest hair

Winnie, Vinnie & Minnie,
mum, dad & baby
orang-utans

Fernando Feraldo,
shrunken head of
a 16th-century
Spanish conquistador

The Helpers

The Horror

Wendy Wibberly,
ex-police constable

Charlie Chumb,
zookeeper

Dr Hubris Klench,
burger-on-legs
& super-baddie

1

Hair Ticket

♫ 'Happy Birthday to You.' ♪

Everyone round the table hip-hoorayed. Abbie put a paper crown on the birthday boy. Mum, Dad and Ollie clapped. Grandma grunted.

The birthday boy tried to bow. But bowing isn't easy for a shrunken head. He lost his balance, tipped onto his nose and rolled across the table.

Abbie caught him as he fell off the edge. 'Careful. You were nearly lunch.' The table was standing by a pool in the middle of a zoo. On the far side of the pool four penguins flapped their wings and eyed the birthday boy greedily.

Abbie cupped him safely in her palm. 'And now,' she said, 'for the cake.'

The birthday boy blinked. He gasped. He craned his cut-off neck. And well he might. Coming down the path was a cake as big as a bicycle wheel. Candles were crammed on top. The sides were covered with chocolate icing.

The Platts carried the cake between them on a huge tray.

Coriander was on the left. Her three red plaits gleamed. Her green dress flapped like a bin liner in the breeze. Her husband Matt was on the right. His three black plaits flopped. His grey boiler suit sagged from his shoulders. Their daughter Perdita was in the middle. *Her* three black plaits bounced. Her orange trousers shone like carrots in cling film.

She was lighting the candles with a flaming stick. 'Four hundred and sixty … four hundred and sixty-one … four hundred and sixty-*two*. Happy birthday, Fernando!' She blew out the stick. Her parents lowered the tray onto the table.

Abbie popped the birthday boy beside the cake. She wiped her hands discreetly on her trousers. No offence to Fernando, but she still hadn't got used to touching the hard, shrivelled head of a Spanish conquistador. She grinned. There was a lot she hadn't got used to. Four months ago life had been duller than duffle coats. But ever since meeting the Platts, it had felt like a firework was strapped to her bottom.

First there had been Coriander's rescue. Abbie had found her imprisoned in the zoo by the wicked Dr Klench. With the help of three orang-utans and Chester, a trusty patch of chest hair, Abbie had freed Coriander. But returning home to the Platts' Museum of Hair, they'd been recaptured by Perdita's aunt and uncle who were in league with Dr Klench. The girls and their families – along with Fernando and the orangs – had barely escaped before the Hair Museum was destroyed.

And that was just the summer holidays.

Since then Abbie had been helping the Platts settle into their new home, the zoo. Looking after the animals with Perdita and her parents had been the biggest adventure of all. There was just one teeny problem.

School.

Perdita's arrival this term had gone down like a foot in a cowpat. It wasn't just her oddness. She was smart, too. The smartest in class. Smarter even than Marcus Strode-Boylie. Which, when you thought about it, wasn't a smart thing to be because Marcus Strode-Boylie *hated* being outsmarted, especially by a girl.

Talking of smart, thought Abbie – *not*. Dad was thumping the table with his fist. ♪ 'For *he's* a jolly good shrun-ken,' he roared. Abbie winced. He really was the brightest star in the nerdiverse.

Everyone else round the table joined in. Two penguins swam across the pool to get a better look at the cake. A third one got so excited he forgot how to swim and had to be rescued from the bottom by his aunt.

Fernando's eyes glittered. 'All thees chocky. I never see such cake een all my born days.'

'Too many born days by 'alf,' muttered Grandma.

You're just jealous, thought Abbie. Ever since Dad had suggested a birthday party for Fernando, Grandma had gone all huffy. Mind you, Dad hadn't exactly helped with comments like, 'Four hundred and sixty-two, and he's *still* got his own hair.' Grandma relied on Chester – who had become her wig as well as her best friend – to cover her balding head, and she was only seventy-three.

'Take a deep breath, Fernando,' said Dad. 'You've got to blow out the candles.'

Fernando glared at him. 'How I suppose to do that?'

Good point, thought Abbie. She'd find it hard enough to blow out that many candles, and she had lungs. Where on earth would a shrunken head find the puff?

Ollie got up from the table and crept over to Abbie. 'Shall I get Winnie?' he whispered.

Abbie looked at him. For a maddening little brother, he had his moments. 'Good idea,' she murmured. Winnie was the orang-utan mum who'd escaped the Hair Museum with her baby, Minnie, and Vinnie the dad. In all the mayhem Winnie had been injected with a potion that made her superstrong. Blowing out the candles would be a breeze for her mighty lungs. But they mustn't let Fernando see. The proud little head would never accept help.

So Abbie distracted him while Ollie went to fetch Winnie. 'You don't look a day over thirty,' she said, remembering that was just the kind of thing grown-ups like to hear on their birthdays.

It was a big mistake. 'Of course not!' wailed Fernando. 'At thirty I was shreenked by tribesmen. My ageing estop there, in Amazon jungle.'

Ollie came back leading Winnie by the hand. The orang-utan – whose hair grew mega fast, also thanks to the potion – had been shaved that morning. She looked like a rusty thistle. Abbie winked at her. Winnie stood behind Fernando.

Perdita cleared her throat. 'One, two, three …'

Fernando blew his hardest. And Winnie blew hers. A mighty wind wrinkled the tablecloth. Cream flew off cupcakes. Sausages shot across the table like supersonic slugs. Chester sailed off Grandma's head and wrapped round the neck of the penguin that had nearly drowned, almost strangling him.

'Well done, *señor*,' shouted Dad.

'You did it, Fernando!' cried Coriander.

'Good show,' murmured Matt as four hundred and sixty-two candles smoked in the air.

'Thanks,' Abbie whispered to Winnie. 'Well done,' she said loudly to Fernando.

He blushed to blackcurrant. 'You people so kind. I no deserve.'

'Go on,' cried Perdita, 'make a wish.'

Fernando's lips sagged. 'You know my weesh. To find my *señora*, the wife of my life.

> The head of my heart, the heart of my head,
> Who roll on jungle floor
> In deepest Ecuador.
> My darling leetle Carmen.
> No lady is more charmin'.'

He gave the very deep sigh of a very bad poet.

Perdita winked at Abbie, who winked at Coriander, who winked at Matt, who winked at Dad, who winked at Mum, who winked at Ollie, who winked at Grandma … who burped.

'Time for your presents,' said Perdita.

Abbie and Ollie put a small package on the table. There was an awkward silence.

'For the love of Nora!' Grandma burst out. ''Ow's 'e s'posed to open that? 'E's armless.'

'Of course he's harmless, Mother,' said Dad. 'He's our friend.'

'I said armless, brainless. 'Ere, I'll do it.' Grandma grabbed the packet and tore off the wrapping paper. The wind snatched it up and blew it towards the penguin pool. It caught in the beak of the nearly drowned, nearly strangled penguin, who nearly choked.

'Sun cream?' said Grandma, holding up a white tube. 'Whassee want that for? 'Is skin's as tough as a tangerine.'

'Have *you* got him a present, Grandma?' asked Abbie pointedly.

Grandma sniffed. 'Course I 'ave. Somethin' useful. Somethin' that'll protect that ancient brain of 'is. No point wrappin' it.' From her handbag she brought out a tiny sombrero, the sort of wide-brimmed hat that bad actors wear when they're playing Mexicans. She popped it on Fernando's head and pulled it down, squashing his birthday crown. 'Perfect!'

Abbie wouldn't quite have said that. With the brim at his chin, Fernando looked like a spinning top.

The wind lifted the hat. It frisbeed through the air and hit the head of the nearly drowned, nearly strangled, nearly choked penguin, who was nearly knocked out.

'I confuse,' said Fernando. 'All thees present, they for sunshine. But now we in Frosty Crunchers.'

A good name for November, thought Abbie.

'Here,' said Perdita, 'maybe this'll make things clear.' She took an envelope from her pocket.

Fernando frowned.

'It's an air ticket, you 'airbrain,' said Grandma.

'An hair teecket?' said Fernando. 'Why I need teecket for hair? I have plenty.' He tossed his black locks.

'She said *air*,' Coriander explained. 'It's for an aeroplane. That's a big metal bird that flies you across the world. I brought you here in one. You couldn't see it because your eyes were sewn up. But you'll see it when you go this time.'

Perdita jumped up. 'And so will we! Abbie and I are

coming too.' She did a cartwheel, landing on the foot of the nearly drowned, nearly strangled, nearly choked, nearly knocked-out penguin, who ran away and set up a home for battered seabirds.

'Only three weeks to go!' Abbie couldn't wait to get away from school. Because she'd discovered this term that there was only one thing less smart than being the smartest girl in class. And that was being her best friend. It had made Abbie as popular as measles.

Fernando still didn't get it. 'Where we fly een metal bird?'

Coriander crouched down and rested her chin on the table. 'To Ecuador,' she said, looking into his eyes. 'To find your wife.'

* * *

The second smartest pupil in the class heard footsteps on the landing. He stuffed his calculator down the back of his trousers as his dad poked his head round the door.

'How's the homework going, Marcus?'

'Nearly finished.'

Marcus's dad came into the bedroom and peered over his shoulder. 'Long division, eh? And all in your head. That's my boy.' He ruffled Marcus's fair hair. 'Make sure you check it, mind. I always checked my Maths–'

'Three times, Dad, before you gave it in.'

'And it paid off, boy, it paid off. Aimed for the stars, I did, and look where it's got me.'

Marcus looked. And saw a silver-haired man with wide

shoulders and a square chin. The sort of chin that suggested Dr Terry Strode-Boylie MSD (Massively Successful Dentist) had got what he wanted and found it wasn't quite enough.

When his father had gone Marcus rescued the calculator. He had to get everything right. That pratty Platt girl and her stupid friend needed to be taught a lesson.

* * *

Dr Hubris Klench, burger-on-legs and villain extraordinaire, rolled out of bed. He bounced a few times and came to rest on the floor. Bouncing was one of his talents. The others were eating, keeping clean and wickedness or, as he fondly called it, 'eefil-doink'.

He opened his eyes. 'Mummy?' He peered round the hotel room. But his only companions were the bed, a wardrobe and a cockroach heading for the skirting board to collect her kids from school.

'I must have been dreaminks.' Klench rubbed his eyes. 'Mummy died four years ago.' But what a dream …

Mummy had been towering over him, wagging a red-hot finger. 'Hubris,' she'd barked, 'you have been in ziss country fifteen veeks. And still you have not done vun decent crime. Useless boy. I knew ven I died you vould mess up vizzout me. Am I right or am I right?'

Klench remembered how Mummy's questions often hinted at the answer. 'Right,' he whimpered.

'Quite. So now I'm back to boss your brain and help you turn to bads again.'

Klench had nodded meekly, recalling also her fondness for rhymes.

'For starters you must lose veight,' she went on. 'Top-notch crooks must all be slim, zeir bumsies small and tumsies trim.'

'Vy, Mums?' Klench had whined.

'Viz your flabs and tummy rolls, how you slip through nets and holes? Remember, Hubes, too much fat killed cat.'

Klench hadn't quite understood. 'Vich cat?' he'd mumbled.

But Mummy wasn't a woman to be mumbled at. 'Silence! You diet or I riot ...'

Klench sat up on the floor. He gasped. Mummy was still glaring at him from the corner of his mind. That had been no dream. She was back to haunt him. He'd have no rest till he obeyed.

He patted his stomach sadly. 'You must go, my friend.' But how? Since he'd arrived in this miserable town there'd been nothing to do except eat fajitas and steal toys from penniless children. A button pinged off his pyjama shirt. 'But first let me have some breakfasts.'

2

Trouble in a Tracksuit

You'd almost think Fernando was enjoying himself. It was the day after his party. He was sitting – or was it standing? – on a stool in the bird house, giving reasons why the Ecuador trip wouldn't work. Abbie was sweeping the floor while Chester the chest hair dusted the perches. Perdita was back-combing the feathers of Mackenzie the parrot.

Fernando sighed. 'Ees too espenseeve.'

'I've told you,' said Perdita, 'money's no problem. The zoo's doing brilliantly.' She rubbed hair gel into Mackenzie's crest. 'There you go,' she said. 'Mohican Mack.'

'Mohican Mack!' shrieked the parrot, baring his tongue in a well-hard way.

Fernando tried again. 'Perhaps I get airseeck on plane.'

'We'll give you travel pills,' said Abbie.

'Perhaps I choke on peells.'

Perdita wheeled round. 'For goodness sake, do you want to find your wife or not?'

'Wife or not! Wife or not!' screeched Mackenzie.

'Of course I want. But how? My Carmen, she teeny head. My Ecuador, she beeg country. Needle een haystack ees easier peasier.'

'Easier peasier! Easier peasier!' Mackenzie agreed.

Chester stopped dusting. He dived to the floor and pulled out a needle from a pile of rubbish. Then he flew up and perched on Abbie's broom handle.

'Of course,' cried Perdita, 'the world's greatest finder! We'll bring Chess.'

Hang on, thought Abbie. *If we bring him, that means …* 'Oh no,' she said. 'Oh no-no-no.'

Chester shrugged. He dropped the needle back into the rubbish.

Perdita grinned like a mouth organ. 'You won't come without her, will you, Chess?' Chester shook his curls.

'All right,' Abbie snapped. 'But bagsy not sit by Grandma on the plane.'

'Bagsy not! Bagsy not!' screamed Mackenzie.

* * *

Maybe it won't be so bad, thought Abbie. She was flicking through her travel guide in bed that night. The pages of *Exploring Ecuador* blazed with adventure: she could almost smell the colours and taste the sounds of the mountains and rainforest. Yep, it would take more than Grandma to stop her going. Imagine the cool points she and Perdita would earn at school when they announced the trip … leaving out the shrunken-head hunt, of course.

That would shoot them both off the scale on the class freakometer.

And she could just imagine the look on Marcus's face. Abbie grabbed her tape recorder from the bedside table. 'BULLY BOY EXPLODES WITH ENVY,' she said into the microphone, picturing the headline in the local newspaper. Underneath would be a photo of smoking green rubble with fair hair: all that remained of Marcus and his jealousy.

Oh yes, Grandma's company was a small price to pay. Besides, in all the excitement of Ecuador, the dear old cabbage would probably just fade to a grumpy lump. Abbie used to think of her as Squashy Grandma. But these days she was definitely more lumpy. Elephant dung wasn't the lightest and, since Grandma had started to clean out Gina's yard at the zoo, her wobbly bits had really firmed up.

The rest of the family, too, mucked in whenever they could. Mum cooked a meal every Saturday for all the human staff: three Platts, five Hartleys, zookeeper Charlie Chumb and ex-policewoman Wendy Wibberly, who now ran the café. Ollie spent his weekends playing with the orang-utans. When he wasn't wrestling strong-mum Winnie, he was tickling lazy-dad Vinnie or playing hide-and-seek with baby Minnie.

And Dad 'helped' Matt with his Very Odd Jobs. That meant he read out bits of the book Fernando was dictating – *Heads and Tales: Confessions of a Conquistador* – while Matt oiled the gibbons' skateboards or patched up the porcupines' bouncy castle.

Which left the best work for Abbie: grooming the animals with Perdita and Coriander. Abbie loved holding the manicure case while Coriander trimmed the talons of Angelica the fish eagle. She adored rubbing moisturising cream into the skin cracks of the elephant, Gina. And, perching on a ladder to comb the endless eyelashes of Alphonse the giraffe, she felt on top of the world.

No wonder visitors were flocking in. The animals shone with health. The buildings gleamed with welcome. And thanks to Wendy, the teapots in the café topped the twinkling charts.

When Matt lowered the entrance fee to £1 for adults and free for children under thirty, the money poured in. And when Dad sent off the first draft of Fernando's book, he was offered a huge advance by a publisher who adored a gory story.

So buying an extra air ticket for Grandma was no problem. In fact, the way Dad rushed to the travel agent, you'd think it was a relief.

'Can't accept this,' snapped Grandma as he pushed the ticket towards her in the zoo café. She pushed it back across the table.

'Really, Mother, it's a pleasure.' Dad pushed it back again. 'A big one, believe me.' Grandma leaned forward to look at the ticket, knocking over her cup of tea.

'Wendy,' called Abbie. 'Spill.'

'Oh, super!' Wendy glided across from the till. She skated over the puddle in her shoes with spongy soles.

'Not sayin' I don't want to go, mind.' Grandma tapped the ticket dreamily. 'Always fancied standin' on the equator.' Chester jumped up and down on her head.

'That's sorted, then,' said Dad a bit too quickly. He beamed at Abbie. She sighed and unwrapped her third Kit Kat.

* * *

'I can't imagine how she'll cope.' Abbie was in the school changing room with Perdita the next day. They were getting ready for PE. 'Can *you* see her tramping through the jungle?'

'Definitely.' Perdita pulled her T-shirt over her three plaits. 'Your grandma's amazing. Remember how she stood up to Dr Klench when we were kidnapped?'

Abbie had to grin. The old sausage had certainly sizzled at the vast villain in the Hair Museum last summer. Even he'd appeared to be impressed. 'But that was mental energy, not physical.'

'Climbing up ninety-three stairs and bellowing? She was Olympic. And anyway, she's fitter now.'

'Still …'

'Oh, come on. You're as bad as Fernando. You'd think he'd be jumping – or at least rolling – for joy at the thought of finding his wife. But he's been nothing but moany-groany-what-if-thissy.'

The girls went out to the playground. 'Perhaps he doesn't dare get excited,' said Abbie, 'in case we don't find her. Which, let's face it, is pretty likely.'

'At least we're trying. And at least he'll see Ecuador again.'

'Who will?' Marcus Strode-Boylie strolled up.

Oh no, thought Abbie. *Trouble in a tracksuit.*

'Hi, Marcus,' said Perdita in her loud, cheery voice. 'We're talking about Fernando.' She unleashed her grin.

'Don't,' Abbie muttered. 'Can't you see he's looking for a fight?'

Apparently not. 'We're taking him to find his wife,' said Perdita. 'In the Amazon jungle. He's a shrunken head, you see.'

Disaster. Abbie whacked Perdita's arm.

'Oh, I see.' Marcus turned to Greg Fnigg, a skinny boy with a black belt in snickering. 'Hear that? Nerdy Perdy's friends with a shrunken head.'

Greg made a noise that could have come from either end. 'Takes one to know one.'

'Actually,' said Perdita generously, 'he's more Abbie's friend than mine.'

'Shut *up*!' Abbie kicked her ankle.

'He's always singing Abbie's praises,' Perdita continued enthusiastically.

'A *singing* head.' Marcus tutted. 'Now I *know* you're from the Funny Farm.'

Perdita looked puzzled. 'No, I'm from the zoo.'

Marcus and Greg hooted.

A whistle blew. 'Get in line, children,' chirped Miss Whelp. 'Running race today.'

* * *

'So, m'boy.' Terry Strode-Boylie eyeballed his son across the dinner table. 'What did you come top in today?'

Marcus chewed his steak and stared at the table. 'The usual.'

'Maths?'

'Yep.'

'English?'

'Uh-huh.'

'PE?'

'Mmm.'

Under the table Marcus's mum squeezed his hand. 'Even

if you hadn't, you know it wouldn't matter. We'd love you just as much.'

'What did you say, woman? Of course it matters!' Terry speared a meaty brick with his fork. 'Remember this, boy.' He jabbed the fork at Marcus. 'I never learned the meaning of second. I always came top, always aimed for the stars – and look where it's got me.'

Marcus looked. And saw a mouth you didn't mess with and a nose that meant business.

* * *

Hubris Klench dabbed his mouth and forced himself not to eat the napkin. He was starving. Only two omelettes for dinner. But how could he order another? Inner Mummy had told him that dieting would improve his criminal skills – so diet he must.

His stomach growled. The waiter scurried over. '*Si Señor?*'

Klench swatted him away. 'I said nothink. Go avay before I eat *you*.' Klench pushed his hands against the table. The chair legs screeched backwards.

'Exercice iss my advice,' sang Mummy. She may not still be alive, but she was very much kicking in his brain.

Klench waddled out of the hotel. On the pavement he gasped for breath. He should never have come to this country, full of heat and height. Whoever designed these mountains deserved a good smack.

The street was deserted except for two boys on the

opposite side. One was whirling a hula hoop round his waist. The other dribbled a football in the dirt.

Inner Mummy tapped Klench on the brain. 'Go on, Hubes. You know vot to do.'

He shuffled reluctantly across the road. Shaking his head, he reached into his pocket. Sighing, he pointed a gun at the boys. The football rolled into the road. The hula hoop bounced on the ground. The boys ran off squealing.

'In you get,' ordered Inner Mummy. Klench stepped miserably into the hoop.

'Now lift.'

He pulled the hoop up as far as his knees. 'I cannot do ziss!' he shrieked as the plastic dug into his flesh. 'Loosing veight iss for loosers.' He snapped the hoop and stamped it into the dirt.

For a second his mind went blank. Then darkness swelled like a storm. Thunder roared and lightning flashed through his brain.

'HUBRIS VILDEBEEST KLENCH!' roared Inner Mummy. 'Trim your hide or voe betide!'

3

Hiyaa!

Marcus Strode-Boylie lifted his foot. Perdita skipped over it. Abbie didn't and crashed into a desk.

Marcus scowled at Perdita. 'That was meant for you. For tripping me up in the race.'

'She did *not!*' Abbie rubbed her arm to numb the pain Marcus would love to know he'd caused. 'Perdita won fair and square.'

But apart from his hair, there was nothing fair about Marcus Strode-Boylie. 'She's a cheat,' he muttered to Greg Fnigg. 'Cheats at PE, cheats at Maths, cheats at everything.'

'Hang on.' Perdita frowned. 'If I cheat at everything, that means I cheat at cheating. And if I cheat at cheating that means I'm *not* cheating. Isn't that funny?'

'No. But this is.' Marcus stamped on Perdita's foot. Then Abbie stamped on his. Then Greg stamped on Abbie's. Then Abbie stamped on Greg's.

Except it wasn't Greg's. It was the teacher's – he'd slipped in between them. 'Whoa there,' gasped Mr Dabbings.

'*He* started it,' Abbie snarled.

'She hurt my foot.' Marcus made a show of rubbing it.

Mr Dabbings nodded. 'I'm sure your foot feels *very* hurt, Marcus. And sad, too. Because feet aren't for fighting, are they? Feet are for dancing and treading grapes. Now let's all join hands and say a big hello to November the twelfth.'

Abbie said a small hello. She stomped to her desk. 'Why didn't you stick up for me,' she hissed, 'when I stuck up for you?'

Perdita didn't seem to hear. 'Poor Marcus,' she said, sitting down beside Abbie. 'He finds it so hard to lose.'

'Poor *Marcus*? When he's spent the whole term making *our* lives a misery? Oh yeah, my heart goes out to him.'

Perdita nodded. 'Mine too. I wish we could help him.'

Abbie gazed up at the ceiling. *Why do I bother*, she wondered, *with a friend who understands sarcasm like a lentil understands astrophysics?*

Because, answered the ceiling, *that's why she's your friend. She couldn't be snide if she tried.*

'Hey,' said Perdita, 'look what I made you.' She plonked a furry brown pencil case on Abbie's desk.

Abbie squeaked. 'Is that–?'

'Yep.' Perdita nodded proudly. 'Yeti nostril hair. Remember that piece we saved from the museum? I couldn't think of a better use for it.'

'Wow.' Abbie recalled picking up a dusty tangle from the rubble after the Hair Museum had collapsed last summer. 'Thanks a mil.' She grinned up at the ceiling.

The ceiling grinned back. *That's the other reason. She's the craziest friend in the world.*

Mr Dabbings clapped his hands. 'Settle down now, boys and boyellas. Time for Maths. Page fifty-seven, *Count Me In.*'

Count me out, thought Abbie, opening her book with a groan. Maths was double yuck these days. There was the single yuck of – well, obviously – Maths. Then the extra yuck when Perdita finished first, got everything right and triggered more malice from Marcus.

The only *good* thing about Maths was that Mr Dabbings hated it too. 'It doesn't really matter how many nuts the squirrel gathered,' he sighed when Claire Bristles got stuck on question five. 'What's important is that he made some granola bars and shared them with his friends.'

'He collected a hundred and sixty-eight,' said Perdita. 'Twelve piles with fourteen nuts in each.'

Mr Dabbings cleared his throat. 'Correct. I was just about to say that myself.'

Abbie looked at Marcus. He was leaning over his desk, his face scrunched with spite, whispering into Greg's ear. Greg was sniggering for England.

'Remember, kids,' said Mr Dabbings, who hadn't noticed them, 'numbers are all very nice, but what's the point of *counting* nuts when there's nothing to *collect* them in? Books away, overalls on. It's pottery time.'

Yes, thought Abbie. *Goo and squelch and no more sums.*

She and Perdita were last in the queue for clay. That was

because Marcus and Greg kept letting people in ahead of them. Even Claire, a tall girl with a friendly fringe, slipped in front.

'You're pushing in,' said Abbie.

'It's OK,' said Perdita. 'I don't mind being last.'

'Could've fooled me,' said Marcus over his shoulder, 'Miss Nutty Know-All.'

Abbie wondered if clay was good for making thumb-screws. She collected her lump and returned to her desk. Perdita was soon smoothing off a perfect bowl. 'That's fantastic,' said Abbie. 'Who's it for?'

'Winnie. To keep her hair things in. She's always losing them.'

Abbie laughed. It was true: they were always finding the orang-utan's clips and combs round the zoo.

'I'll make a giant fruit bowl,' said Abbie, 'for Gina.' The elephant loved apples – and bowls were simpler than thumbscrews.

'I'll help you,' said Perdita. 'Let's get more clay.'

The girls went up to the front desk. Abbie heard a whisper behind her. Then a rustle, then a hiss, like wind whipping up a wheat field.

'Yeuucch!' said someone.

Abbie and Perdita spun round. People were giggling at their desks.

'What?' cried Abbie.

'Must be from the zoo,' said Marcus loudly.

'Ooh, I wonder which animal?' said Greg.

'Hmm. Tiger?'

Abbie's hand flew to her bottom. 'You smeared our chairs with clay!'

Perdita examined her orangey hands. 'No, Marcus, tiger dung would be darker. This looks more like elephant.'

'You *complete* …' Abbie tore off her overall and hurled it at Marcus. It missed by miles.

'Hey!' Mr Dabbings put down the bison he was knitting for the North American display. 'Calm, Abigail.' He patted the air with his hands. 'Now, count to three and tell us how you're feeling.'

Abbie swallowed. Her throat was bursting, her face on fire.

Mr Dabbings put a hand to his ear. 'Not quite hearing you there, Abigail. But my *guess* is you're feeling sad. We all feel sad sometimes, don't we, kids? And it makes us, well … *sad.*' A snigger went round. 'How about you, Perdita?'

'Oh, I'm fine.' She grinned. 'Actually, Marcus just gave me a great idea. No one seems to know much about zoos here. So why don't you all come and visit? A school trip. My parents would love it. And so would the animals.'

The class froze. Abbie gasped. And Mr Dabbings's sideburns wriggled with joy.

* * *

'Why is Marcus so *awful*?' Abbie was slumped at the kitchen table after school. 'I mean, what's his problem?'

Mum took a spoonful of crumbs from a pot and sprinkled

32

them over a pie. 'Who knows, darling? But the more you show you're upset, the more it'll encourage him.'

'I wanted to cry. But I didn't.'

Mum reached over and stroked Abbie's chaos of curls. 'Well done. How did Perdita react?'

'She didn't seem to care at all. And can you believe it – she's invited the whole class to the zoo!' Abbie covered her face with her hands. 'She's already the class joke. Imagine when they see parrots with mohicans and hippos in bubble bath.'

Mum finished sprinkling. 'Don't worry. I bet most of them have visited already.'

'No, they haven't.' Abbie's hands plonked wearily onto the table. 'They'd boil their bums in butter before supporting Perdita.'

'Well then, they've got a treat in store.' Mum smoothed the crumbs over the pie with the back of the spoon.

Abbie snorted. 'They're bound to find some way to hate it.'

Mum waved the spoon like a mamma on a pizza advert. 'Thassa notta your problem.'

Abbie sighed. You'd think Mum would understand. Four months ago she'd have ironed raisins to impress the neighbours. Still, on the plus side, it showed how much she'd lightened up. Since meeting the Platts she'd learned to care so much less about other people's opinions and so much more about having fun.

'Here.' Mum scooped up more crumbs. 'Try some.'

Abbie licked the spoon. 'Yum. What are they?'

'Toasted toenails. Coriander says they're full of vitamins.'

* * *

'ANOTHER DISASTER LOOMS.' Abbie was sitting on her bed after dinner, confiding in her tape recorder. Over the term her microphone had become more of a sympathetic ear than the practice ground for a budding reporter. She still wanted to be a journalist, of course. It was just that with school, homework and zoo duties she hadn't actually got round to writing anything lately.

'Perdita Platt's plan to show her class round the zoo,' she said, 'is the latest in a string of brain-bashingly bad ideas.' Abbie paused. Maybe 'brain-bashingly' was a bit harsh. What were the other ideas again?

1. Taking a shrunken head to find its shrunken love in the world's biggest rainforest.
2. Bringing a grumpy gran and her whizzy wig along for the ride.
3. Leaving Mum, Dad and Ollie to help Matt run the zoo.

'... A string of brain-bashingly bad, mind-mashingly *mad* ideas.'

Abbie switched off the tape recorder. The door opened.

'Great news.' Dad danced into her room. 'I've just been on the phone to the *Hiyaa!* show. They want to interview me about my ... er, Fernando's ... er, *our* book.' He did a jig on the carpet. 'Wotcha thinka that then? Your dad's a celeb!' He bowed out backwards, whistling the *Hiyaa!* theme tune.

Abbie switched on the tape recorder again. '... A string of brain-bashingly bad, mind-mashingly mad, skull-smashingly *sad* ideas.'

* * *

It was worse than sad. It was Dad. Sitting there in front of the world at 7.30 on Thursday morning. His bald patch gleamed. His bow tie beamed.

Opposite him sat Caz Cazoo and Wippy Winkel. 'Hi*yaaa!*' they yelled as the theme music faded.

'Plonkers,' muttered Grandma, watching the telly from the sitting-room sofa. Abbie guessed that she didn't just mean the presenters. And she was right. Why had Dad insisted on that spotty bow tie? It looked like a disease.

'This morning,' Caz gasped from the screen, in her so-excited-I've-forgotten-to-breathe voice, 'we're *thrilled* to have a sneak preview of a book that really sticks its *neck* out.' She held up the book. Fernando was understandably sensitive about his appearance and had refused to be photographed for the cover. Instead there was a painting of men in armour shooting men in loincloths.

'*Heads and Tales: Confessions of a Conquistador,*' breathed Caz, 'will be *head*-ing for the bookshelves soon. Joining us is the co-author, Graham Hartley, a man who's a-*head* of his time!'

35

Fernando, who was perching on Grandma's lap, snorted at the telly. 'He not the Ahead. *I* the Ahead.'

Wippy Winkel winked from the screen. 'Yes, viewers,' he said. 'Graham's account of a conquering conk will soon be hitting the *head*-lines!' He slapped his shiny green trousers.

Fernando wobbled dangerously on Grandma's lap. 'Ees *my* head! *My* lines!'

'Quiet,' said Mum. She gazed adoringly at the telly.

'History-teacher Graham,' gasped Caz, 'has written a biography of Fernando Feraldo, a sixteenth-century Spanish conquistador who *lost his head* in Ecuador.' She hooted with laughter, nearly falling off the TV sofa. 'Graham, how did you go about your research? Reading the book I was

just amazed by ...' she looked at the notes on her lap ...
'the astonishing depth of scholarship, the insight into the
conquistador brain, the tireless attention to–'

'She 'asn't read a word of it,' said Grandma.

Dad sank back in his TV chair. 'Well, Caz, I'd just like
to say what a treat it is to be on your show. Free croissants,
unlimited coffee ... and I never knew Wippy wore lipst–'

'Tell us,' Wippy said sharply, 'how can Fernando Feraldo
be the co-author? He died more than four hundred years
ago.'

Dad sucked his cheeks in. 'We-e-ell, I felt I owed it to
him. His story was so vivid, so alive – almost as if he were
here today, speaking to me.'

In the sitting room Fernando leapt off Grandma's lap. 'I
am here! I *am* espeaking!' he roared, bouncing on the carpet.
'I tell whole story! Your father, he lie to take glory. Your
father,' he snarled at Abbie, 'will pay for greedy deed.'

* * *

'Dad,' yelled Marcus, 'come and see this!'

Terry Strode-Boylie gulped his morning coffee and
went into the lounge. He didn't let Marcus watch TV in
the evening because it ate into homework time. But fifteen
minutes after breakfast was OK, as long as Marcus had
cleaned his teeth – brushed, flossed and gargled – combed
his hair, checked his homework and practised his tuba (not
a popular instrument: Terry had chosen it to boost Marcus's
chances of getting into the county youth orchestra).

Terry stared at the telly. 'That bloke. I've seen him at the school gates.'

'It's Abigail Hartley's dad.'

Terry frowned. 'What the devil's he doing on the box?'

'He's written a book, Dad.'

'What?' Terry Strode-Boylie's children's book, *The Adventures of Philip the Filling*, had just been rejected by the sixty-fourth publisher. 'Damn cheek!'

Marcus's mum crept in. 'Don't worry, dear.' She squeezed his arm. 'He probably paid someone to publish it.'

Terry straightened his tie. 'That must be it. Now turn off that twaddle, boy, and polish your shoes.'

* * *

Hubris Klench chewed the jacket sleeve he'd sprinkled with sugar while Inner Mummy was looking the other way. He waddled sadly along the pavement. 'But I cannot cut calories,' he mumbled, pushing an old man into the road.

'Zen you must *burn* zem,' ordered Inner Mummy. 'If eating less brings you stress, zen ride your bike or take a hike.'

'But bike vill break and hike vill ache.' A car horn tooted as Klench shoved another pensioner off the pavement.

'Look down street,' said Mummy. 'You see zat travel agency? Inside you vill buy ticket to Baños. Ziss lovely town in central highlands has natural sprinks and other outdoor thinks.'

Klench sighed, wishing that Mummy hadn't got a degree in tourism when she was alive.

Reaching the travel agency, he squeezed through the revolving door. And with the money he'd just picked from the pockets of those elderly pedestrians, he bought a bus ticket to Baños.

4

Fernando's Revenge

Dad opened the front door. Everyone was waiting for him in the hall.

'One, two, three …' Mum and Ollie clapped wildly. Abbie clapped mildly. Grandma rolled her eyes and went into the kitchen.

'You were brilliant, Graham.' Mum hugged him. 'Did you get their autographs?' She was a huge fan of Caz Cazoo who, she said, had skin to die for.

'It's *my* autograph you should be asking for,' said Dad, loosening his bow tie. 'And by the way, Caz's make-up's as thick as cement. Here, kids, I nicked these from the canteen.' He handed Abbie and Ollie a paper cup each with *Hiyaa!* scrawled between the grinning faces of the presenters.

'Wow.' Ollie hugged his cup. 'I'll take it to school for Show and Tell.'

Abbie whisked hers behind her back and crumpled Caz and Wippy to a walnut. If Cringeworth was a town, Dad would be mayor.

'Tell us all about it,' said Mum. She took Dad's hand. Abbie followed them into the kitchen.

'Where's me free croissant, then?' said Grandma as Dad sat down at the table. She shoved a mug of coffee towards him.

'Sorry, Mother. Only for TV stars, I'm afraid. It *was* delicious.' Dad raised his mug. Grandma raised her eyebrows.

'I hope the Platts were watching,' said Dad. 'You reminded them I was on, didn't you, darling?'

'Of course.' Mum rubbed his arm proudly. 'I phoned them as soon as you left.'

Dad took a gulp of coffee. 'Yeuuchh!' He flung the mug onto the floor. Dangling from his mouth was a tangle of hair. Dangling from the hair was a mangle of face. And dangling from its nose was a clothes peg. Dad spat it all onto the table.

'Ha!' shrieked Fernando. 'Serve you right! The Gradba she block by doze. Thed she hide be id coffee.'

Grandma wagged her finger at Dad. 'Naughty boy. Pinchin' the limelight, tellin' 'is story as if it was your own.' She unclipped Fernando's clothes peg. 'You all right, chuck?' She felt his forehead. 'Bit warm after that coffee. Shall I run you under the cold tap?'

'No!' Fernando snorted. 'Remember I was shreenked. Remember I was boiled. Remember hot stones, they rolled around my head. For me, hot coffee ees piece of cake.'

'I'm sorry,' said Dad, wiping hair from his lips. 'I was

only trying to protect your privacy. You've always said that fame's the last thing you want.'

* * *

It was the last thing Abbie wanted too. Three hours later she was leaning miserably against a wall in the playground. If one more person came up and told her what a plonker her dad had looked in that bow tie, she'd … she'd …

Barry Poff came up: a short boy with a nose full of radio crackle. 'Your dad looked a plo–'

'I'll … I'll …' said Abbie, raising her fist.

But she didn't. What was the point? Snorty Poff was right. 'Leave me alone,' she growled.

He did. And for the rest of the day so did everyone else. Even Perdita, after Abbie snapped at her. Which was just fine. Because, thanks to her, more poop was about to hit the soup. Tomorrow the class was visiting the zoo.

* * *

Marcus saw his dad's Jaguar pull up by the school gates. He sauntered across the yard. 'Hi, Dad.' With a cool half-wave to Greg Fnigg he opened the back door of the car.

'Wait.' Dr Strode-Boylie got out of the front. Marcus followed him back through the gates. In the yard Mr Dabbings was chatting to Abigail Hartley's dad.

'… fascinating interview,' the teacher was saying. 'I'd love to read your book in class, Mr H, if it wasn't for all the entrails. Kids are so sensitive to entrails, aren't they?'

42

'Not this one.' Mr Hartley put a matey arm round his daughter. 'You love a good dose of blood and guts, don't you, Abbs?' She scowled.

Marcus's dad barged in. 'Tell me, Hartley,' he said, jabbing Graham's chest, 'what did it cost you to publish?'

'*Cost* me?' Abbie's dad laughed. 'No no, the publisher's *paying* me. A whopping great advance, as it happens.' Grinning all over his bow tie, he held out his hand. 'I'm Graham. Don't think we've–'

'In the car, boy!' barked Terry. He turned round and shoved Marcus out through the gates.

The Jag growled off. Marcus looked back through the rear window. Abigail was standing at the gate. Catching her eye, he turned round quickly.

* * *

Hubris Klench stumbled off the bus. He raised an arm and sniffed at the damp patch in his armpit. 'Sveat!' he gasped. 'I must vosh.'

'No need,' said Inner Mummy. 'Ve are in lovely Baños. Zat is Spanish vord for "bath". In ziss town are five pools of volcanic vorters. By jumpink in and havink svim, you vill be clean and quite soon lean. Zen you vill be supercrook, fit to hide in any nook.'

Klench shuddered at the thought of undressing in public. 'But Mums,' he tried feebly, 'I have no svimmink trunks.'

'Then get some,' she barked. 'Down ze street is shop of sports. Go inside and steal some shorts.'

5

Poop and Paint

'Don't push, don't shove. Make way with love,' sang Mr Dabbings as he waved the class through the zoo barrier.

Abbie dragged through last. Why hadn't she painted red spots on her face this morning? Why hadn't she held her forehead on the radiator to get a temperature or made puking sounds from the bathroom?

Because she had to come and defend her friends – and not just the human ones. Even if the Platts were immune to the mockery of the class, the animals might not be. What about Gina with her all-hearing ears? Or the tapirs and their snouty shyness?

Perdita and Coriander were waiting for the class inside the gate, in front of the zoo pond. Behind them ducks ducked and flamingoes flamingoed.

'Welcome, everyone,' said Coriander, beaming. In her billowy red dress and green poncho she looked like a thrilled tomato. 'I recognise most of you. And you might've seen me at the school gates.'

'How could we miss you?' muttered Marcus Strode-Boylie. 'Weirdo.' A giggle went round.

How dare he? Abbie shot Marcus with invisible bullets. She recalled his small, pinched face looking through the back window of the Jag yesterday. *Bet he never speaks to his dad like that.*

Mr Dabbings ignored the laughter. 'All righty,' he said, clapping his hand-knitted gloves, 'I'm sure we'll have a great day, as long as we remember to be *kind* and *thoughtful.*' There was a squeal from Ursula Slightly, a tiny, pale girl, as chunky Henry Holler stamped on her foot.

'Now,' said Coriander, who hadn't noticed, 'because you're missing school today,' (there were cheers) 'you must be feeling sad' (and jeers). 'So I've organised a few lessons,' (there were moans) 'starting with English' (and groans). 'Nothing too hard,' (there were phews) 'just a quick spelling test' (and boos). She winked at Perdita, who skipped off down a path.

'Thought this was a day off,' rumbled Terrifica Batts, a large girl with lively nostrils.

'Might as well be at school,' mumbled Rukia Zukia, whose ponytail was neat and whose pencils were sharp.

'Nerdy Perd's idea of fun,' grumbled Greg Fnigg.

Abbie glared at Coriander. Brilliant start. What on earth was she playing at?

Perdita returned. Mackenzie the parrot perched on her shoulder. A tartan cap perched on Mackenzie.

'Ready?' said Perdita. The parrot squawked.

'You mean *we* test the *parrot*?' gasped Mr Dabbings. 'That's amazing!'

'A-mazing! A-mazing!' screeched Mackenzie, flying onto the teacher's golden head.

Mr Dabbings froze. He looked up, wrinkling his forehead till his eyebrows had eyebrows. 'OK,' he said nervously, 'how do you spell "nut"?'

Mackenzie clicked his tongue. 'N-u-t.'

Mr Dabbings gulped. 'How about "Ca*shew*"?'

'Bless you!' screeched the parrot.

When the laughter had died down, Marcus sneered. 'So what? Anyone can teach a parrot to spell. That's not English, that's copying. *English* is making things up, like poems and stories.'

Mackenzie flew from Mr Dabbings and landed on Marcus's head. He glared round the class then shrieked:

'A foolish young boy, so I've heard,

Finds it hard to believe that a bird

Could make up a poem,

Well watch while I show 'im,

'Coz actions speak louder than words.'

He did a sloppy white action on Marcus's head and cackled off to a branch.

'Yeeaggh!' yelled Marcus.

'Deep breath, Marcus,' said Mr Dabbings. 'Now, everyone, Marcus is going to share with us how he's feeling.'

'How d'you think?' Marcus shouted. 'Pooped on!'

Mr Dabbings nodded sympathetically. 'Marcus has

just described his emotions very well, children. And we
understand his pain, don't we? Because being used as a
lavatory isn't fun.' There were giggles, grunts and a gasp
from Ursula Slightly as Henry Holler yanked her ponytail.

'Shall we move on?' said Coriander hurriedly. She
handed Marcus a tissue and headed down a path to the left
of the pond.

The children chattered behind. They stopped at the tapir

pen to stroke the two snouts peeping over the fence. Abbie grinned. Matt's nose-shortening mirrors, hanging from the trees, had done wonders for the tapirs' confidence.

Claire Bristles flashed her a smile. 'This is fun,' she whispered. Abbie's heart leapt. Could the class be warming to the zoo?

Ahead of them on the path, Rukia Zukia squealed. Everyone ran to join her.

On the left was a sandy area. In the middle stood Gina the elephant, surrounded by paint pots with brushes stuck inside. In front of her was a huge easel and canvas. With a brush held expertly in her trunk, Gina was painting a picture of pink buns.

The children wowed. The ellie bowed.

'There's no fence!' squeaked Ursula, crouching behind Terrifica Batts.

'Don't worry, dear,' said Coriander, 'Gina wouldn't hurt a fly. And she'd never leave this area. She's got plenty of entertainment. Same with all the animals. They're so happy there's no need for cages.'

Mr Dabbings nodded approvingly.

'Except for the ones who might eat the others,' said Perdita. 'Like Silvio the tiger. And the crocodile – though Edie won't hurt you if you treat her with respect.'

'So why do the tapirs have a fence?' said Greg Fnigg. 'They look pretty harmless.'

'That's to keep *us* out,' said Perdita, 'because they're so shy.'

Coriander pointed to a tree where aprons were dangling from a branch. 'Who wants to paint with Gina?' she said.

Henry Holler needed no encouragement. He snatched an apron and ran to a pot of yellow paint. Pulling out a brush, he painted a pile of chips next to Gina's buns. 'That's *my* favourite food,' he shouted.

Jeremy Boing, a keen boy with huge feet, painted a cone of mint ice-cream. Rukia Zukia did a chocolate bar with perfect right angles. Snorty Poff slapped on a giant cheeseburger. Terrifica Batts did a leg of lamb and Abbie painted bacon.

Mr Dabbings did a blob of rainbow sick. 'Ratatouille!' he cried happily. Even Ursula Slightly joined in, though her white bread without crusts was hard to see on the white canvas.

Only Marcus, Greg and a few other boys hung back. Marcus was managing a look of scorn. But the sneering mouths of the others were battling with their envious eyes.

Abbie looked at Perdita, who was painting a bowl of lice crispies. She'd been right to invite the class. They were loving it.

'Sorry for sulking,' Abbie whispered. 'Best friends?'

'Best friends!' yelled Perdita. 'Chocolate sprinkles!' she added, flicking brown paint on the crispies.

'Hey,' cried Jeremy Boing, 'you flicked me!' He flicked her back. And that was it. Perdita flicked Abbie. Abbie flicked Claire. Claire flicked Snorty Poff, who flicked Greg Fnigg.

Greg couldn't resist it. He grabbed a brush and flicked cool Robbie Rudge. He flicked moody Jack Doody, who flicked Henry Holler, who flicked Mr Dabbings.

Everyone froze.

Mr Dabbings looked at his hand-knitted, paint-spattered jacket.

Then he took a brush and flicked Coriander. She jumped back, laughing, and stepped in a pot of purple.

Gina trumpeted and stepped in the orange. Then everyone stepped in everything and did rainbow footprints in the sand.

Gina looked at Marcus with her kind wrinkly eyes. She dipped her trunk in a pot.

'Yaww!' yelled Marcus as the elephant sprayed him with red paint.

'Yeww!' he howled as everyone stopped and stared.

'Yiww!' he wailed as Mr Dabbings rushed over.

'Yoww!' he bellowed, pushing the teacher's knitted hanky away.

'Yuww,' he spluttered, running out of vowels.

'Easy lad,' soothed Mr Dabbings. 'Tell us how you feel.'

'How d'you think?' shouted Marcus. 'Red!'

Mr Dabbings smiled. 'Marcus has expressed himself very clearly, kids. And *we* feel red too, don't we? Because being squirted by an elephant is pretty embarrassing.'

Coriander put her arm round Marcus. 'Sorry, dear. Gina just wanted you to join in the fun.'

Marcus shoved her away.

'Maybe it's time for lunch,' she said. 'Perdita, would you take the class to the café while I help Marcus clean up?'

* * *

Dr Terry Strode-Boylie frowned over his patient's gaping mouth. 'There's a lot of decay, Mrs De Ponge. You're going to need three fillings.'

'Aah.'

He scraped her second left molar a little harder than necessary. Whopping great advance, indeed! Who did that Hartley think he was?

'Aaah,' gasped Mrs De Ponge.

'Whopping great adva– I mean holes, Mrs De P.' Not that whopping. And actually only one hole. But he was the dentist and she was rich. Besides, her breath smelt. Bet Hartley's breath smelt under all that beard.

Terry glanced along the bookshelf on the surgery wall. *The Anatomy of Ulcers ... The Philosophy of Flossing ... Top Ten Dental Disasters ...* He imagined his book slotting in between. *The Adventures of Philip the Filling* – such a delightful read for children awaiting dental treatment. Why couldn't publishers see that? It wasn't fair. Terry scowled and yanked.

'Aaaaaaaaah!'

* * *

Klench stared at the toffee dangling from a hook at a street stall. It looked like a sticky ponytail. He swallowed. 'Just vun,' he begged silently. 'I have not eaten since lunch.'

'Lunch voss ten minutes ago,' barked Inner Mummy. 'And vot did I tell you? Healthy snackss or Mummy smackss.'

Klench chewed his cheeks. 'But, Mummy, ziss toffee is famous Melcocha, speciality off zese parts. I must try.'

'I vorn you, vast boy – loose zose layers or say your prayers.'

Klench took a deep breath. 'Our Fazzer who art in Heaven …' he began defiantly. He snatched a string of toffee. His teeth sank into sugary bliss.

Mummy raised her inner hand to smack … then stopped. 'Vait!'

'Vot?'

'Zat.' Inner Mummy pointed to a newspaper on the counter.

While the stall owner was serving another customer, Klench snatched the paper and scuttled down the street. He stopped in a doorway and examined the front page. There was a photo of a building surrounded by jungle. It was huge and white, with a swimming pool on one side.

He pointed to the headline above. 'Vot's it say, clever Mums?'

Thanks to her degree in Spanish she translated easily. '*Hotel Becomes Vite Elephant.*'

'But Mums, zere are no elephants in South America.'

Mummy tutted. 'Off course not, silly billy boy. It meanss hotel cannot be used. Like you, it is vaste of space. *Newly built Hotel Armadillo,*' she read, '*stands empty in ze junkle. No customers are prepared to visit ziss remote spot. Hmm.*'

A smile crept across her inner face. 'Empty hotel … remote spot … sounds like ideal place for vickedness. Are you thinkink vot I am thinkink, my Hube?'

He frowned.

'Here,' said Inner Mummy, 'I give you clue: I, V, H, M, V, C, B, Z, H, A, R, I, A, T, C, F, R, C, W, V, T, D, Z, S, Z, P, V, N, R, Z.'

Klench was good at word games. 'Ah, I bet zat stands for: If Ve Had Money Ve Could Buy Ziss Hotel And Run It Ass Treatment Centre For Rich Criminalss Who Vont To Disguise Zemselves So Zat Police Vill Not Recognise Zem.'

'Vay good, my chocky pud. Face liftinks, leg stretchinks, nips and tucks, pinches and plucks.'

'And not only zat.' Klench was getting excited now. 'If I am in junkle, perhaps I can capture animals for smugglink again.' He smiled at the neatness of the plan. Last summer, endangered animals had been smuggled to him at the zoo in England. He'd kidnapped that hairdresser woman to smarten them up for selling on as pets. But the project had been thwarted when a meddling girl with crazy curls had rescued the woman. Now he could resume the business from the other end, trapping the animals and selling them directly, without the complication of a zoo.

'Most absolutelies.' Mummy patted him on the inner head. 'Now zere is phone number. You must ring and buy hotel. But before you do zat, you must raise funds. And before you do *zat*, you must go for daily svim. Remember – you vork out or Mums vill shout.'

6

Fun and Blames

The children gathered at the café entrance. Wendy was waiting in her green overall with silver buttons.

The teacher held out his glove to Wendy. 'Branston Dabbings,' he said. 'Goodness, what lovely buttons.'

Wendy blushed. 'Wendy Wibberly. I like your gloves. Especially the six fingers.'

Mr Dabbings's sideburns trembled. 'Bit of a mistake. I knitted them myself. Please call me Bran.'

The children filed into the café.

'She's really gone to town,' Abbie whispered to Perdita. Wendy had draped a banner across the window.

You really are very welcome

it said in shiny red letters on a gold background and, underneath,

indeed

Claire Bristles and Ursula Slightly came over. 'Can we sit with you?' said Claire.

'Sure,' said Abbie, trying to sound cool while her heart did a handstand. It was the first time anyone had asked all term. Jeremy Boing came too and Craig Nibbles, a small boy who blinked a lot. Henry Holler looked hopeful until Ursula put her rucksack on the seat beside her and squeaked, 'No room.'

The grown-ups sat at a nearby table. Abbie looked at Mr Dabbings. He was staring at Wendy as she poured coffee. Catching Abbie's eye, he looked away quickly. Then he bent over his rucksack, took out a Thermos flask and unwrapped a knitted scarf from its neck.

Grinning, Abbie opened her lunch box. The grin vanished. Mum's idea of a fun picnic was a tuna sandwich, three crackers, an apple and fourteen raisins.

'Do you want my crisps?' said Ursula. 'Salt and vinegar burns my lips.'

Abbie beamed. Today was turning out gazilliantly.

After lunch they did PE. There was ostrich racing for the sporty: Jeremy Boing, Terrifica Batts, Robbie Rudge and Greg Fnigg. Coriander offered an ostrich to Marcus, but he just scowled and sulked on the sidelines, his face and hair still red. The giant birds flounced to and fro like huffy aunts, while the children sat on their backs and clung on for dear life.

'Don't try this at home, dears,' Coriander warned.

There was tortoise racing for the timid. Ursula and

Craig lured Clement and Persephone across the grass with vegetables. Clement won by a turnip.

And there was spider racing for the icky. Snorty Poff and Henry Holler each held the hairy leg of a tarantula – the harmless sort, Perdita assured them. She blew a whistle and the boys let go. Babs beat Hilda to the finishing post, a dead fly.

Claire won Giraffe Hoopla. She threw five foam rings over Alphonse's neck. The gentle beast was so busy munching the leaves of a tree, he didn't even notice.

Then they played Hungry Hippo. The class gathered by a pool of foaming water.

'Forty-eight bottles of bubble bath in there,' said Perdita. 'Grab some sugar cane, everyone.' She pointed to a bucket filled with thick brown sticks. 'See who can throw it into Hepzibah's mouth.'

'Where *is* her mouth?' asked Jeremy Boing. Only the hippo's ears poked above the bubbles.

Coriander began to hum, low and slow. Hepzibah's head rose from the water. She gave a grunting, creaking yawn.

'Wow,' gasped Rukia. 'It's like you called her. Can you talk to animals?'

Eyes went wide. Murmurs went round.

'Awesome.'

'Magic.'

'Dr Doolittle.'

Coriander raised her hand. 'No,' she laughed, 'nothing like that. It's just that I've travelled all over the place,

57

collecting rare specimens of hair. And I guess I've collected sounds too. My song attracted Hepzibah, reminded her of Africa – of mudbanks and grasslands and hot red earth.'

That seemed to satisfy the class, although Abbie knew it was more than that. She'd watched last summer as Coriander's humming had calmed a crocodile and charmed a tiger into letting her clean his teeth.

The children took it in turns to throw. Hepzibah caught every stick in her monstrous jaws.

'We don't usually let visitors feed the animals,' said Coriander. 'But this is a special day.' You could see it was special for the hippo too. The water frothed as she chomped and gaped for more.

'Heppie adores sugar,' said Perdita. 'She'll do anything for a mouthful.'

'Those teeth,' squeaked Ursula. 'Are you *sure* there shouldn't be a fence round the pool?'

Coriander patted her arm. 'Don't worry, dear. You're perfectly safe. She only comes out at night to feed.'

Craig shuddered. 'On what?'

Coriander laughed. 'Grass. She's our lawn mower. As long as you treat her with respect there's nothing to be frightened of.'

Terrifica Batts pointed to the path ahead. 'Cu-*yoot*!' An orang-utan was bounding towards them. Behind her trailed a metre of auburn hair.

'Winnie!' cried Abbie. She ran from the bridge to hug the orang. The rest of the class stood round, cooing and oohing.

Behind Winnie's hair came a man with enormous ears and wearing green overalls.

'This is Charlie Chumb, our zookeeper,' said Coriander.

'Hi, Charlie,' said Mr Dabbings.

'Pleased to, er ...' Charlie nodded shyly. 'Let me introduce, um ...'

'Winnie,' Perdita finished for him. The orang raised her hand.

'High five,' said Mr Dabbings, though he was holding up six. He slapped her palm with his glove.

'What's with her hair?' asked Jeremy.

'Long story,' said Abbie, deciding that the class had had enough excitement for the day. Now wasn't the time to explain how Winnie had been injected with Samson juice, which made her hair grow long and her muscles strong.

Winnie peered round the faces. Then she lunged at Marcus and lifted him in her mighty arms.

'Oh dear. She thinks you're an orang,' laughed Coriander, 'with your red hair.'

Marcus wasn't laughing. 'Get *off*!' he howled as Winnie hugged him tight.

'Let *go*!' he screamed as she smothered him in smackaroos.

Ever obliging, she did. He collapsed on the ground in a weepy heap.

'Easy, Marcus, easy.' Mr Dabbings grasped his shoulders. 'Try and put your feelings into words.'

'Mnnff,' Marcus sobbed. 'Gckk. Hhnng.'

Mr Dabbings frowned. 'Not the best English. But we understand, don't we, children? Marcus is making it clear that being dumped by an ape is *not* uplifting.'

'Oh dear,' said Coriander, grabbing Winnie's hand before she could cause any more trouble, 'I think we'll call it a day.'

'No!' cried Snorty Poff.

'I want to see the tiger!' hollered Henry.

'Next time,' laughed Coriander. 'Now, I hope you've enjoyed the trip' (there were 'Yays') 'because *we* certainly have' (and 'Hoorays'). 'Come again soon' (there were 'Greats') 'with your parents' (and 'Can't waits').

Wendy came to wave them off. Abbie noticed she'd changed into her *pink* overall with *gold* buttons.

'Goodness, what a lovely uniform,' said Mr Dabbings – though it was Wendy's face he was looking at.

* * *

'Outrageous!' bellowed Terry Strode-Boylie, stomping round the lounge.

'You poor boy,' said Marcus's mum. She stroked his hair, still undeniably pink after its fourth wash.

'Pooped on by a parrot, squirted by an elephant, mauled by an ape – it's an insult to the family name.' Which, recalled Mrs Strode-Boylie, had been the rather more humble 'Strodboil' until Terry had changed it. But now wasn't the moment to remind him.

'And stop snivelling. I can't abide mucus, Marcus.'

Marcus's mum kissed his cheek. 'More hot chocolate, darling?'

He nodded, wiping his nose on her sleeve. 'They don't cage their animals, Dad.'

'*What?*'

'The elephant and the hippo – they can wander anywhere.'

'You're joking! Those are wild beasts. That's a safety hazard, a health hazard, a fire hazard, a wind hazard.'

'What's a wind hazard, Dad?'

Puffed up with rage, Terry Strode-Boylie demonstrated. 'Genevieve!' He gave his wife a shocked look.

She knew the routine; it happened often enough. 'Pardon me,' she mumbled obediently.

* * *

The evening was warm and still. Mountains pierced the sky like the fingers of a gigantic hand, cupping Baños safely in their palm.

Or not so safely.

The town's tubbiest tourist waddled down the street. He glanced scornfully at the other foreigners, wandering arm in arm or chatting at café tables in their T-shirts and shorts. How good it felt to be back in his tight white suit after those dreadful elasticated swimming trunks. And even better to be out of that stinky volcanic pool with its snot-coloured water and giggling bathers …

'Vot you starink at?' he'd snapped at three little boys who'd stopped their game of piggy-in-the-middle.

'A *real* piggy,' the smallest one had squealed in Spanish (Inner Mummy had rather unkindly translated). Klench had done a mean little jump in the pool, nearly drowning the boys …

Now, just as he was wondering how to sneak a snack without Mummy noticing, he saw a shop on the right.

Merv's Mini Marvels

said a little sign above a low wooden door. Underneath it said:

Tiny treasures from terrible times

Klench – who could resist the word 'treasures' no more than he could resist a doughnut the size of Wales – stopped. 'Hmm,' he murmured. 'Here perhaps I can steal small treasure. Zen I can sell it and buy Hotel Armadillo.'

'Super plan, my chubby man,' agreed Inner Mummy.

Klench pushed the door, breathed in and squeezed in.

It was dark and musty inside, crammed with wooden tables and shelves. Scattered on top were all sorts of knick-knacks: chipped pots, leather sandals, old books and tarnished brooches. It looked like any old junk except for its size. Every item could fit inside a handbag.

'Can I help you?' piped a voice.

Klench screwed up his already screwed-up eyes. Through

the gloom he made out a face. A man was resting his chin on the shop counter.

'Vy do you speak Inklish,' said Klench suspiciously, 'ven you are in Ecuador?'

'Because I *am* English. Came here on holiday ten years ago and forgot to go home. Why do you speak in an accent I can't quite place when *you* are in Ecuador?'

'Becoss I am from *place* you can't quite place,' said Klench. 'Now stand up pleasse so I can check you are not Inklish policeman come to arrest me for eefil-doinks, vich I have not done.'

'I *am* standing up,' said the man. He reached a hand across the desk. 'Merv Periwink, pint-sized collector of

pint-sized plunder. Dinky Inca trinkets and conquistador curios to stow in your suitcase.'

Klench eyed Merv thoughtfully. 'You have small head,' he said, 'vich means small brain. Zat vill be vay helpful to me.'

Merv smiled happily. 'Glad to oblige, mate.'

'Now, small Merv, I seek small treasure. Somethink most pricey and compact. Somethink I could pinch vizzout you noticink. Somethink to make me vay rich if I voss bad man, vich I am not.'

'Mmm …' Merv stroked his teeny moustache. 'What about that Inca hanky on the table next to you. It's woven from llama wool.'

Klench shook his head. 'It vill not fetch much prices.'

'Well … how about this silver sword from the doll's house of a conquistador's daughter?'

'Zat iss better,' agreed Klench. 'But it sits on your desk. I could not distract you for lonk enough to snatch it if I vonted to, vich I do not.'

'Mmm, see your point, mate.' Merv rubbed his mini chin. 'Well – there's always that golden Inca box on your right, with an engraving of the sun on the lid and – oh yes – a shrunken head inside.'

'Aha!' Klench unscrewed his extra-screwed-up eyes till they were merely screwed up again. 'Now you are talkink. Pleasse look out off vindow, vhere you vill see a flyink potato vearink orinch knickers.'

'Where?' Merv craned his teeny neck. 'I can't see it.'

Thirty seconds later Klench was running down the street on his very short legs.

Behind him ran Merv on his even shorter ones. 'Stop thief!' he yelled. 'Bring back me treasure!'

Klench stopped. 'You mean ziss box viz shrunken head inside, vich I could take to police becoss it iss crime for you to sell such an object?'

Merv stopped. 'Really?' He scratched his head. 'Ten years in Ecuador and I never knew that.'

'That iss becoss you are vay stupid man.' Klench chuckled. 'And if you tell anyone about ziss stealink, or try to stop me from sellink ziss box so I can buy hotel in junkle, you vill be even more stupid – becoss I vill spill beans on your shrunken-head crime.' And off he capered, with the box in his hand and the song in his heart that came from ruining someone's day.

7

Zoo Crazy

It was Saturday evening at the zoo. The Hartleys and Platts were sitting round the picnic table with Wendy and Charlie. Because of the cold weather they'd chosen the reptile house for the weekly staff dinner.

In front of them, through the open door of her cage, lay Edie the crocodile.

'Sounds like the class visit was a roaring success,' said Dad. He slurped a spoonful of tomato soup.

'There was certainly lots of roaring,' said Perdita, 'from Marcus.' She threw a breadstick to Edie, who snapped it between her jaws.

'Poor Marcus,' said Coriander. 'Not his day, was it? I felt so sorry for him.'

'Me too,' said Perdita. ''Specially when his dad picked him up from school. Did you see them, Abbie?'

'Who didn't?' The whole class had watched Dr Strode-Boylie explode at his red-faced, tear-stained, mud-spattered son. They'd all stared while he bundled Marcus into the car.

And they'd all listened while he roared at Marcus to 'Take those filthy trousers off before you ruin the seat!'

'It was brilliant,' she giggled.

'Abbie, dear.' Coriander frowned. 'How would *you* feel, going through a day like that only to be shouted at by your dad?'

Abbie grabbed a bread roll from the table. 'What *is* it with you Platts? Why do you always stand up for Marcus? He's the *biggest* pain in the *biggest* bum and *you* know it!' She ripped the roll in half.

Coriander stirred her soup. 'Have you ever wondered *why* he's a pain, Abbie? People often *cause* pain because they're *in* pain. Let's try to understand him.'

'I do. I understand he's just horrible!'

'No one's *just* horrible,' said Perdita. 'Everyone has good bits too.'

Abbie's eyebrows went highbrow. *Here we go. Touchy-feely, understandy, love-and-lentils la-la-la.* 'You're as bad as Mr Dabbings,' she said.

Coriander beamed. 'Now *there's* a compliment. What a nice man.' She winked across the table at Wendy. 'Don't you think so, dear?'

Wendy spluttered soup over Charlie's arm. 'Oops,' she gasped. 'Sorry.'

'Don't, um … it'll come off in the – you know,' he mumbled as Wendy pulled a handkerchief from her pocket and wiped his sleeve.

Abbie's irritation gave way to surprise. The initials B. D.

were embroidered in the corner. 'Hey, is that Mr Dabbings's hanky?'

Wendy blinked. 'He, um, gave it to me before he left the zoo.'

Matt smiled across the table at Coriander. 'Reminds me of the time I gave you that self-cleaning hanky I'd invented. Remember how you blushed and offered to plait my fringe? That's when I knew you were the girl for me.'

Dad smiled across the table at Mum. 'Reminds *me* of the time I gave you that pack of tissues I'd bought. Remember how you blushed and offered to iron my History essay? That's when I knew you were the girl for me.'

'Slush and nonsense,' said Grandma, which makes an interesting sound when you're slurping soup at the same time.

Wendy was staring at the table, her cheeks the colour of an over-keen sunset. Abbie grinned. Could this be the start of something?

You bet. On Monday morning Mr Dabbings bounded into the classroom with 'I love Wendy' written all over his face.

OK, not actually written. But the way his sideburns quivered as he unpacked his rucksack was a dead giveaway.

OK, not a dead one. But the way he exclaimed, 'Let's thank Perdita with joyful hands,' said it all.

OK, not all. But the way he hummed ♪ 'All things bright and beautiful, all creatures great and small', while stroking a familiar golden button, made it clear he wasn't thinking of *all* creatures but *one* in particular.

The rest of the class had gone zoo-crazy too. At break time Terrifica Batts led a procession to the horse chestnut tree, where Abbie and Perdita were collecting conkers for a tournament between Ollie and the orang-utans.

'Friday was supes, girls,' said Terrifica. 'We've brought some thank-you presents.' She handed Perdita three pots of pink body glitter. 'To paint Gina's trunk.'

Claire gave Abbie a bead necklace for Alphonse. 'It's two metres long.'

Ursula had brought a scarf the colour of porridge – 'My favourite colour' – to go with Mackenzie's tartan cap.

Snorty had filled a matchbox with flies' legs for the tarantulas.

Jeremy gave five pairs of shin pads for the ostriches' football practice.

'Wow! Thanks, guys.' Perdita grinned all over her teeth. 'They'll *love* these, won't they Abbie?'

Abbie couldn't speak. After a term of scoffing and gossip – this? Was the class beginning to *get* Perdita? Were they all starting to see what a way-out whizz she was?

Not all. Marcus strolled up. 'Sucking up, are we?'

Behind him Greg made slurpy noises. Friday's fun was forgotten. His sneer was back.

Marcus tutted. 'Just because Perdita's got a gweat big zoo-zoo full of cuddwy cweatures and cwazy pawents.'

Perdita turned her grin on him. 'You're nearly right, Marcus. The zoo *is* big and the animals *are* cuddly. But my parents aren't crazy. You should come and meet them

69

properly some time. How about the week after next? We'll be in Ecuador and I bet my dad would love some help round the zoo. Why not come over one Saturday and join everyone for the staff dinner?'

Abbie shook her head in despair. When would Perdita get it that Marcus would hate her forever – or at least as long as she beat him in class?

* * *

Sergeant Bernard Bolt picked up the phone. '*Brad*-leigh Police Station. Can I help you?' He stressed the 'Brad' for two reasons:

1. To make Bradleigh sound like a bigger town than it was. Bolt's recent transfer from Garton Village Police Station had been a real step up and he wanted the world to know it.
2. To confuse him with Brad Pitt. This only worked if the caller was thick.

Sergeant Bolt was out of luck.

'*Doctor* Terence Strode-Boylie here,' boomed a very un-thick voice. 'I wish to report an emergency. Bradleigh Zoo, recently taken over by the Pratts – I mean Platts –'

'How *are* they? I've been meaning to pop in.' Sergeant Bolt beamed at the mention of the family who'd brought him a moment of glory last summer when he'd stormed their museum like a Hollywood cop.

'Well, you should *pop in* right now, my man! That place is a disaster-in-waiting. Are you aware that the animals are free to roam?'

Sergeant Bolt chuckled. 'Indeed I am. Young Minnie the ape urinated all over my trousers last time I visited.'

'What? You mean you *know* about this?'

'Of course.' Bolt cleared his throat. He didn't like this geezer's tone. Time for a spot of menace. '*I*, sir, am an officer of the law. There is nothing in *Brad*-leigh that I do *not* know about.'

But Terry Strode-Boylie was a master of menace. 'This is an outrage! Get me your boss.'

'Certainly. One moment, please.' Bolt pulled out his shirt and stuffed the phone receiver underneath. He wiggled it over his hairy stomach to make a crackling sound then brought it back to his mouth. 'I've – ahem – informed my superior of your complaint. He asked me to convey that he is *fully* aware of the zoo arrangements and that, if you trouble us again, you will be fined for wasting police time.'

The phone spluttered. 'Do you know who you're talking to? I'm a Massively Successful Dentist, you know.'

'And I, sir, am Brad Pitt. Goodbye.'

* * *

Hubris Klench lay on his bed in the Baños hotel. ♪ 'Vistle vile you cheat,' he sang, ♫ 'stealink iss so sveet …' He took a sip of lemonade and told Inner Mummy it was sparkling water.

She was so proud of his theft she let it pass. 'You acted

quick, my clever chick. Merv vill not chase you now. You must sell golden Inca box schnip-schnap. But vot about ze small head?'

Klench frowned. 'Perhaps I can sell zat also, to vicked pals in criminal vorld. But first I must examine.' He opened the mint-green suitcase that lay next to him on the bed. He unpacked a mint-green toilet bag. From one of its labelled pockets he took out a pair of mint-green rubber gloves. He pulled them over his neat little hands. Then he opened the golden box on the bedside table.

'Most diskustink,' he murmured.

The head, the size of a tennis ball, sat in a cloud of black hair. Its skin was dark grey and wrinkled. Its eyes and mouth were sewn shut. Wisps of grey string dangled from them. With its pursed lips and sticky-up nose it looked huffy and proud, as if it had died in a sulk.

Klench tweaked the nose, unable to resist cruelty even to a dead head. 'So ugly – you vill fetch good price.' He ran a gloved finger across the head's bumpy lips.

Then a thought slid into his brain like a knife into lard. 'Vait a sec.' From the toilet bag he took out a pair of nail scissors. 'I vunder …' He snipped the twine from the eyes and mouth of the head. The lips lolled.

Inner Mummy turned green. 'Vot you doink?'

'Vell, Mums, I vunce met shrunken head vich could talk. Perhaps ziss vun too has voice. If so, it vill fetch *vast* sumss.' Klench lifted the head till it was level with his face. 'Speak, freak.'

Not a flicker.

'Vot's up, ugly mug?'

Not a sausage.

'Howdie-do, face-like-poo?'

Not a dicky bird.

Inner Mummy yawned. 'Give it up, my podgy pup.'

Klench punched the head. 'Vy you not talk like Fernando?' he shrieked, hurling it at the floor.

'Fernandohhhhh!' the head shrieked back.

8

Abigail Absinthe

The zoo trip had split the class in two. On one side was the Zoo Crew, those wowed by the visit. On the other side were the Boylie Boys – Greg and a few others – who stuck by Marcus and sneered their way through the week.

Keenest of the Zoo Crew was Mr Dabbings. On Tuesday he made the class write parrot poems to Mackenzie. On Wednesday they worked out the average speed of a tortoise that takes an hour to cross a four-metre lawn. On Thursday he replaced the North American display with Alphonse's African savannah.

And on Friday in Art – button collages – he sidled up to Abbie and Perdita. 'Lovely round circles, girls,' he murmured.

Abbie wondered what other shape circles could be.

'I was just thinking,' he tucked a golden curl behind his ear, 'maybe I could, um …' he rubbed a sideburn … 'tomorrow, say …'

'Come over and pretend to be interested in the zoo when

actually it's Wendy you're interested in?' asked Perdita, gluing on a button. 'Of course. You're very welcome.'

'No. I mean, sort of. I mean …' Mr Dabbings's sideburns blushed. 'Oh, all righty, yes.'

When he'd gone Abbie spluttered all over her buttons. 'You could have been more subtle. Poor Mr D.'

Perdita looked puzzled. 'Why? He's always telling us to express our feelings. I was just expressing his.'

* * *

Abbie spent Saturday morning cleaning out the chameleons' playground with Coriander. With only four days to go before they left for Ecuador, they wanted to leave things spick and span for Matt.

Mr Dabbings appeared at the door of the reptile house. 'Hi there.' He waved a woolly glove. Each finger was a colour of the rainbow.

Coriander waved back. She dropped her cloth. It landed on a stone. The stone scuttled away. 'Oh, there you are, Hue!' She laughed. 'I was wondering where you'd got to.' She crossed the playground to meet Mr Dabbings. 'Sorry, Toney,' she said, tripping over a branch that wiggled its tail.

Mr Dabbings was looking nervously through the open door of Edie's cage. The crocodile was looking un-nervously back.

'Don't worry,' laughed Coriander, 'if you love her, she'll love you.'

'That's what worries me,' mumbled Mr Dabbings.

'Gosh, Mr D, you look thirsty.' Coriander winked at Abbie. 'Why don't we pop over to the café?'

Abbie grinned. She finished wiping the chameleons' climbing frame and followed them out of the reptile house.

In the café Wendy was polishing the chocolate wrappers. 'Oh,' she gasped as they came in. Abbie hadn't told her that Mr Dabbings was planning to visit, in case he didn't turn up. Wendy wasn't good at disappointment.

'Hello,' said the teacher. 'I was just passing and, um …'

'He needed a drink,' finished Coriander.

'Great,' said Wendy, 'I mean, right. Toffee or Cea? I mean –'

'Do you have nettle pop?' said Mr Dabbings.

'Er, no. But there are some nettles by the bird house. I could go and pick them.'

'Allow me,' said Mr Dabbings gallantly. 'I have gloves on.' He held up his left hand. Wendy giggled at the seven fingers. They headed out together.

'They're acting like school kids,' said Abbie disdainfully, forgetting for a moment that she actually *was* one.

'We'll leave them to it.' Coriander smiled. 'Now, come and have a muffin and tell me what you've packed.'

When Wendy and Mr Dabbings returned Abbie had written lists on four serviettes. The headings were Underwear, Overwear, Medical Supplies and Emergency Rations. While Mr Dabbings and Wendy crushed nettles, Coriander the World Wanderer advised Abbie on what to add ('More toothpaste, dear. Cleaning your teeth is the high point of the day in the rainforest') and what to leave out ('No chocolate. It'll melt over everything'). And, while Wendy and Mr Dabbings sipped and gazed at each other, Abbie decided that, chocolate or not, she was the luckiest girl in the world.

* * *

Monday was the girls' last day at school. Abbie fidgeted through Maths and fiddled through English. When the final bell rang she and Perdita ran for the door.

'Waity-ho.' Mr Dabbings raised a hand. 'Before you go, girls ...' He brought out a card from his desk. On the front was a map of South America with Ecuador marked

I'll miss you
Claire Bristles XX

(Me too. Ursula Slightly x)

CATCH ME A PIRANHA
HENRY HOLLER

Rather you than me
Craig Nibbles

Boing!
Jeremy

Hnnff
Barry Doff

Pack neatly
Rukia Zukia

Chin up,
shoulders back, girls!
Terrifica Batts

TO ADVENTUROUS
ABIGAIL AND
PLUCKY PERDITA,
HAVE AN
ECUADORABLE
TRIP!

Hug the rainforest from me
Branston Dabbings

Ciao dudes
Robbie Rudge

in the top left. Llamas, gold necklaces and ponchos had been drawn all over it. Some of the class had signed inside. 'Recycled paper, of course,' said the teacher. 'Sorry I couldn't persuade everyone to sign.' Abbie didn't mind. It was the best card she'd ever had.

She showed it proudly to the family that evening. They were in the sitting room after dinner. Dad was jotting down some fabulous facts about the Inca people who used to live in Ecuador. Grandma was sitting on the sofa. She had the local newspaper on her knees and was frowning at the crossword. Fernando sat next to her. He still hadn't got over Dad's performance on the *Hiyaa!* show and kept correcting him. Mum was perched on the arm of the sofa, chewing her lip in a not-going-to-cry sort of way. Ollie was on the floor, Sellotaping toilet-roll tubes together to make South American pan pipes.

Grandma tutted. 'I'll never manage them Ecuador papers. The crossword clues'll be Greek to me.'

'Spanish actually, Mother,' said Dad.

'I know that!' she snapped. 'I'm not just a pretty face, you know. Three down – attractive appearance. P somethin', F somethin'.'

'Pretty face?' said Abbie.

Grandma sniffed. 'Obviously.' She filled it in. Then she gave up on the crossword and leafed through the rest of *The Bradleigh Bellow*.

''Ere!' she said suddenly, looking up at Abbie. 'I've 'ad a brainwave. You could write articles for *The Bellow*. You want to be a journalist, don't you? Well now's yer chance. You can describe Ecuador for the folks back 'ome. Paint a picture in words, scribble a scene in sentences.' Grandma threw out her arms, knocking Fernando off the sofa.

'No!' He bounced on the carpet. 'You cannot esplash me over pages. I will be laugheeng stock. I will be estolen for science.'

'She doesn't have to mention you,' said Dad. 'She can just describe Ecuador – the sights, the sounds, the smells. Talking of smells, did you know that Inca women rinsed their hair in wee to make it shiny?'

'Not reense – *soak*,' Fernando corrected. 'Now you must all be quiet while I theenk about thees plan.' He rolled around the carpet, muttering.

'Hokay,' he sighed at last, coming to rest at Abbie's feet. 'You can write. But not of me.'

Abbie picked him up and kissed his cheek – which, when you think about it, was an act of true friendship.

* * *

At eleven o'clock next morning Abbie and Grandma were sitting on a lumpy sofa in the office of the local newspaper. On the other side of a huge desk sat the editor of *The Bradleigh Bellow*.

Corky Shocka was a hard-nosed hack with short grey hair. She listened while Abbie explained the idea. Then she leaned back in her chair and steepled her fingers. 'Interesting,' she said. 'How old are you?'

'Never you mind, cheeky,' snapped Grandma.

'She meant me,' said Abbie. 'Eleven.'

'Hmmm.' Corky scratched her hard nose with a finger. 'I can see the potential.' She wrote in the air: 'Letter from the Equator, by junior journo Abigail Absinthe.'

'My surname's Hartley.'

'Oh no it isn't. Not for this. We need spice. We need danger. We need an alcoholic drink that killed famous people.' Corky scratched a finger with her hard nose. 'Ouch! Four articles, three hundred words a shot. Think you can do it?'

Abbie nodded so hard her eyebrows felt sick.

* * *

That night Mum came up to tuck her in. She sat on the bed and smoothed Abbie's curls. 'What am I going to do without you?' Her voice trembled like a finalist's in a quiz show who's going win fifty million pounds if she gets the next answer right and a biro if she doesn't.

'Make the dinner? Phone your friends? Breathe?' suggested Abbie.

Mum didn't smile. 'I mean *apart* from that. I must be mad letting you fly across the world with a shrunken wig, a grandma head and a mother friend.'

Abbie couldn't quite put her finger on it but she sensed that Mum was upset. 'Don't worry.' She squeezed her hand. 'Coriander'll look after us.'

'I know. I wouldn't dream of letting you go if I didn't trust her completely. It's just … I'm going to miss you so much.' Mum's lower lip quivered like a worm who's watching her daughter crawl towards a blackbird that's popped into the garden for a takeaway.

'I'm going to miss you too,' said Abbie, biting her lip so it wouldn't do the worm thing.

'Phone us when you can. And email, won't you?'

'Of course. But remember there's no signal in the jungle.'

Mum kissed her. 'You're a brave and brilliant girl. I'd never have the guts to do this. Be careful, darling. I love you.' She hugged Abbie tightly, like a mother who's agreed to let her daughter travel across the world to find a very small head in a very big rainforest but is having second thoughts.

'I will. Night, then,' said Abbie quickly, before Mum's second thoughts became third ones.

* * *

''Night, then.' Genevieve Strode-Boylie kissed Marcus's forehead. 'I'm sure your dad'll be over it by the morning.'

'You've been saying that all week.' Marcus rolled over to face the wall. 'And he's not over it at all. He's getting crosser and crosser.'

'It's hard for him, darling,' said Genevieve. 'After that zoo trip, he feels the family name's been dragged in the …'

She sighed. Who cared about the family name? Surely the *family* was more important? Shaking her head, she turned off the bedside light.

* * *

Klench couldn't believe his luck. All it had taken was a few photos of the box and a short description emailed to Wotsitworth.com. He'd received an e-certificate within a few hours from an expert evaluator who confirmed that, yes, it was genuine Incan and worth a very, very pretty packet. There had been a wobbly moment when Klench had doubted that the packet was pretty enough to buy a hotel. But now the owner, sitting across the table, was nodding at the certificate and moaning softly.

'You mean you agree?' said Klench.

The man nodded wearily again.

'You mean you vont no more proofs it iss real deal?'

The owner shook his head.

'No second opinions?'

The owner shrugged listlessly.

Klench couldn't understand how anyone could care so little about so huge an exchange. But this man didn't seem to care about anything. He was staring miserably into space as if he'd forgotten Klench was there.

'Deal.' Klench banged the table. 'You take me to hotel. Zen I give you box.'

The owner murmured his agreement. Then, putting his head in his hands, he moaned and moaned.

9

Toodle Pip

Getting into the car next morning, Abbie felt as trembly and second-thoughty as Mum had looked the night before. She waved. Mum and Ollie were crying on the doorstep. Mum had refused to come to Heathrow – she couldn't bear airport goodbyes – and Ollie had school.

'I'm taking your photo in for Show and Tell,' he shouted. 'Every day.'

'See you soon.' Abbie blew kisses. 'I love you.'

'I love you too.' Mum blew them back. 'And don't talk to any strange llamas.'

Dad drove off. Mum and Ollie shrank into sobbing blobs. Abbie sniffed.

Dad put a hand on her knee. 'It's only two weeks,' he said, rather trembly himself.

Two weeks. That's fourteen little boxes of Coco Pops, thought Abbie.

'That's fourteen crosswords,' said Grandma from the back seat. 'For the love of Eric, *will* you settle down?'

Abbie looked round. Chester was tickling Grandma's glasses.

'Oh, I *see*,' said Grandma. 'Chester wants to know if you took yer travel pills, Fernando.'

'*Si*,' said the head, who was perched on Grandma's lap. 'Now I no pukey in fly bird.'

They drew up at the zoo. Winnie was waiting at the entrance. She unpacked their suitcases from Dad's car and carried them to Matt's battered green van.

In front of the pond, a crowd had gathered to see them off. In the front row Babs and Hilda both stood on one hairy leg and waved their other seven. Clement and Persephone bowed their ancient heads. Hue, the chameleon, tried to stow away by turning silver on the front of Perdita's tracksuit. She only noticed when he wouldn't zip up.

In the middle row the seals flipped their flippers and the penguins flapped their flappers.

At the back, Alphonse fluttered his eyelashes and Gina curled her trunk into a heart shape.

At the gate Coriander put her arms round Minnie. Vinnie put his arms round Coriander. Then Winnie put her arms round Vinnie and lifted them all in an eight-arm love squash.

Mackenzie flew onto Perdita's head. 'Cheerio!' he screeched. 'Off you nip to the equator. Toodle pip and see you later.'

He flapped over to the gatepost and wolf-whistled everyone into the van.

Matt drove. Coriander sat next to him. The others squeezed in behind.

All the way to Heathrow Dad banged on about the Incas. 'They didn't have money, you know. They paid their taxes by doing lots of work for the emperor – things like farming and building.'

'But gold they had, and seelver. And we conquistadores, we take that metal to make into coins. We seedy greedy graspers.'

'So the Incas had no cents – and *you* had no sense!' Dad hooted. For once Abbie didn't groan. At least he was trying to jolly things along.

There was silence in the front. Matt was rubbing a finger over his teeth. Abbie hadn't seen him do that since Coriander had been kidnapped last summer. He must be so scared of letting her go again. But she had five companions this time – and three of them had legs. What could possibly go wrong?

They parked at the airport and loaded their cases onto trolleys.

Grandma popped Fernando into her handbag. 'Keep down,' she said. 'Don't want the world and 'is wife gawpin' at you. And keep off me travel sweets.'

Coriander took Matt's hand. 'Let's say goodbye here,' she murmured. The Platts entwined in a nine-plait cuddle.

'Look after each other,' said Matt in a choking voice.

'We will,' said Perdita and Coriander. Matt's glasses streamed with tears. He pressed something behind his ear. Tiny windscreen wipers swept across each lens.

The Hartleys entwined in a three-heart huddle.

'Look after each other,' said Dad in a choking voice.

'We will,' said Abbie and Grandma. Dad's cheeks gleamed with tears. He pressed something behind his ear. Nothing happened.

'And now, please, we go,' said Grandma's handbag. 'My pants they have ants for find my wife.'

They checked in their luggage. Before going through security Abbie took Fernando out of the handbag. She stuffed him up her sleeve just in time to avoid the X-ray machine and some embarrassing questions.

And then it was hot chocolate, 'I Spy' and 'Spot the Funniest Bot' while they waited in the departure lounge. Abbie had to think very hard *not* to think how Mum, Dad and Ollie would be thinking of her.

An hour later, walking up the steps to the plane, she took her last sniff of home.

* * *

Dr Strode-Boylie ripped out the letters page of *The Times*. He screwed it into a ball and hurled it at the floor. 'Why haven't they printed my letter of complaint? That unfenced zoo – it's a national scandal!'

Genevieve patted his arm. 'Maybe that's the problem, dear,' she said quietly. 'It *isn't* national. Maybe you should lower your sights: try a local newspaper, like *The Bradleigh Bellow*.'

'Lower my sights? I've spent fifty years with my sights on the stars, woman. And look where it's got me!'

Genevieve looked. And saw a man whose sights were very low indeed, beneath the silver scowl of his eyebrows.

* * *

'Put me down, peeg!' Carmen Feraldo, shrunken wife of Fernando and prisoner of Hubris Klench, tried to bite through her captor's rubber glove. But after four centuries without exercise, her teeth didn't make a dent. 'My husband, he keell you for treat me so bad!'

Klench chuckled and dropped Carmen on the desk in front of him. He gazed round the huge lobby of his new possession, the Hotel Armadillo. 'Your husband,' he said, 'cannot hear you. Ass I explained, he iss in Inkland.'

After Carmen had shrieked in the Baños hotel, Klench had told her all about meeting Fernando last summer. Well, not quite all. He'd told her how he'd kicked and bullied Fernando, not how Fernando had saved the day.

'Zere zere.' Klench now pinched Carmen's ear. Then

he unscrewed the pot of glue sitting on his desk. He smiled. This was no ordinary adhesive but Bitter Albert's Superdooperglooper Glue, a gift from a former fellow prisoner who'd once used it to stick a warder's hands together.

'Sticks like ze Billyo,' sang Klench, brushing her neck with glue. 'Now I can show you offs to guests – and sell you to highest bidder.' He giggled. His criminal clients would be queuing up to buy this freaky knick-knack. 'Until zen, you can be my receptionist.' He squeezed Carmen into a hole that he had drilled in the desk.

'Villano!' she squealed as her neck wedged tight.

He yanked her hair fondly. 'You are too kind.' Ignoring her curses, he sat down at the desk. At last he could relax. The journey had been terrible – all that dirt and exercise. But now it was over. That miserable fool who'd led him here was long gone with the Inca box, and the hotel was his. The new staff were already hired: young men from local jungle villages who were prepared to cook, clean and work their guts out for practically no pay. Six of them had been sweating out front all day, clearing a space for helicopters to land.

'Right on schedules,' he murmured, looking at a timetable on the desk. Tomorrow morning the three doctors whom he'd contacted through his criminal network would be flying in, ready to operate on rich crooks in search of disguises.

'Let me go, *el Bruto*!' Carmen tried to wriggle free. But she was stuck fast to the desk. 'I never estand for thees!'

'You never stand for anythink, I think!' Klench gave her playful poke in the eye. 'Now shut ups and practise your smilinks. First guest vill arrive in two days. You must velcome him nice. He is vay rich man.' He rubbed his hands. He couldn't wait. Carmen would wow that crooked cowboy out of his diamond-studded socks.

10

Plane Awful

The food was dreadful. It was the best part of the flight.

The trouble started on take-off. Grandma was sitting next to the aisle ('I'll need to go a lot') next to Perdita (what a star) next to Abbie at the window. Coriander sat behind Grandma.

The plane roared into the sky.

''Oo wants a sweetie?' Grandma took the tin out of her handbag, which she'd refused to stow in the overhead locker.

'*Si*,' squeaked Fernando inside. The man across the aisle frowned, as if he'd just heard a handbag squeak.

Grandma lowered a toffee into the bag. There was a choking sound. The man across the aisle stared, as if he'd just heard a handbag make a choking sound.

Grandma reached into her bag and took out a half-chewed toffee. 'Sorry, Fernando. Too tough to swallow?' The man across the aisle gaped, as if he'd just heard a handbag being apologised to.

Grandma popped the half-chewed toffee in her mouth. It

pulled her false teeth down from her gum. The man across the aisle asked to move.

'You'd better keep quiet,' Abbie murmured to the handbag, 'or the staff might confiscate you.'

'For why?' replied the bag. 'I not eellegal. I have passport.' (Coriander had stuck his photo in a little red book to make him feel important.) 'You ashame of me or sometheeng?' The bag began to sing a loud Spanish marching song. Abbie sighed. She leaned across Perdita, took Grandma's bag, stood up and shoved it in the overhead locker. Poor Fernando – but what could you do?

Then there were silly little sandwiches and Grandma spilling her drink over Perdita. Who took it very well, of course. 'Mmm, I smell all orangey.'

The girls were too excited to read their books. So Perdita taught Abbie the Dreadlocks Game (changing every word that began with d to 'dreadlocks'). And when that got too dull, Abbie taught Perdita the Pudding Game (guessing what type of dessert the other passengers would be). And when that got too mouth-watering, Coriander told them about her last trip to Ecuador, when she'd found Fernando and his wife in the jungle.

'I wasn't *looking* for shrunken heads.' Coriander spoke softly, so that Fernando overhead wouldn't be reminded of losing his wife. 'I was after the Fringed Bees of Logroño.'

'The *what*?' said Abbie. She'd never get used to the wonders of Coriander's former job, travelling the world to collect rare samples of hair.

'Logroño is in the eastern rainforest. The bees there grow long fringes over their eyes. Then they can't see a thing, so they crash into trees and die. Matt made me a tiny pair of scissors so I could save their lives. Never found any bees, though. Just … you know,' she pointed upwards, 'on the forest floor.'

'Where *exactly* did Fernando's wife fall out of your bag?' whispered Abbie.

Coriander shrugged. 'I'm not sure. Somewhere near Logroño. We'll have to go there and retrace my steps in the rainforest.'

Hot, wet jungle seeped into Abbie's mind. She shivered deliciously. 'What's it like?'

'Steamy, crowded, noisy–'

'Bingo!' While they were talking, Grandma had been playing by herself, calling out the numbers *and* filling them in. Strangely enough, she'd won.

A flight attendant rushed up. 'Everything OK, madam?'

'I've got a full 'ouse,' said Grandma. 'Where's me prize?'

The attendant frowned. 'I'm afraid we don't provide, er …'

Grandma jabbed the attendant in the stomach. 'I won fair and square, young lady.'

Abbie dreamed of stuffing Grandma in the overhead locker with Fernando.

'*I'll* play with you,' said Perdita, neatly avoiding a scene. 'Abbie, you can call the numbers.'

So Abbie spent the rest of the flight to Spain, their first

stop, writing numbers on scraps of paper, stuffing them down the sides of her knee-length flight socks and then pulling them out one by one. 'What a bore, thirty-four. Waste of time, eighty-nine. Oh what *fun*, sixty-one.'

Then there was the four-hour wait in Madrid airport. Fernando managed to keep quiet till they got off the plane. But when Grandma told him where they were, he hurled himself against the sides of the handbag till it bulged like a cheek full of sweets. 'España, my beloved country! Four hundred feefty year I have not seen her. Fiesta, siesta, Castilla, Sevilla – the sights, the sounds, the esmells. Let me out!'

'Sorry, chuck, no can do,' said Grandma kindly but firmly. Abbie had to admit she had a way with heartbroken heads. 'There'd be a right rumpus. Why don't we describe it to you? I bet Spain's changed a bit since your time.'

The handbag sighed. 'Hokay. What choice I have?'

So they took it in turns to find a private spot and whisper into the bag – which wasn't as easy as it sounds since the only private spot they found in the transit lounge was the loo.

On top of this, Fernando found all the changes very upsetting. Sitting on a toilet seat for the third time, Abbie tried a new approach. Instead of taking him out and showing him the bathroom tiles, she kept the handbag shut.

'Oh, look,' she cried, pulling the flush. 'There goes a happy, er ... peasant chucking a bucket of water over himself in the, um ... plaza.' *I wish Dad was here*, she thought. *He'd be able to fill me in on sixteenth-century Spain.*

'What thees peasant wear on head?' came Fernando's suspicious voice from the handbag.

'Oh, you know, a floppy-ish sort of, um, hat,' said Abbie, remembering pictures of Henry the Eighth. He was from the sixteenth century, wasn't he?

By the time their flight was called it was past midnight. Everyone who had legs stumbled onto the plane and fell into their seats. Everyone who didn't was already snoring on Grandma's head and in her bag.

Abbie was woken by a face in her face. 'Breakfast, *señorita*?'

She stared at the perfect parting and wondered why Mum had dyed her hair black. Then she remembered where she was. 'Oh. Yes please.'

It sounded good: 'Omelette and cheeps.' It looked bad: a sad yellow rag with soggy yellow twigs. It tasted worse.

'Ooh, me back!' Grandma jolted awake. Chester, who was still half asleep, lurched off her head and landed in Abbie's omelette. That woke him up. He shook himself off, spraying egg and chips everywhere, then flew back onto Grandma's head.

'Me back's killin' me,' said Grandma. 'Last time *I* spend a night in a plane.'

So we'll have to leave you in Ecuador, then, thought Abbie. *Isn't that a shame?* What she said was, 'Would you like my omelette, Grandma?'

So Grandma tucked into two breakfasts. She just had

time to spear the last Chester-coated chip before the plane began its descent into Ecuador.

* * *

Marcus scrawled the answer. He scraped his chair backwards so that everyone would know he'd finished. He sauntered up to the front. 'Done,' he said, slapping his Maths book down on Mr Dabbings's desk. It felt good to finish first again, now that Pratters had gone.

Mr Dabbings looked up. 'Thanks, Marcus. Oh, butter-beans, look at the time! Pens down, kids. It's eleven o'clock. The girls should be arriving in Ecuador right now. Time for our Happy Landing Harmony.' He picked up the guitar that was leaning against his desk and slung the knitted strap over his shoulder.

Marcus turned back to the class and rolled his eyes. The teacher played a tinny chord.

'Hap-py Land-ing,' sang Mr Dabbings on bottom G.

'Hap-py Land-ing,' Henry bellowed on B.

'Hap-py Land-ing,' chorused Terrifica, Snorty and Jeremy on D.

And, on top G, 'Hap-py Land-ing,' sang Claire, Rukia, Craig (and Ursula, though no one noticed).

'Idiots,' muttered Marcus, heading back to his seat.

'Idiot,' echoed Mr Dabbings thoughtfully. 'An interesting word, Marcus, though not a *kind* one. Remember now, our tongues were made for *kindness*. So you'll *kindly* use yours to apologise.'

Marcus glared at the giggling class. 'Sorry!' he snapped. He slumped back in his chair and stared at the floor. Even Dabbers was telling him off. Face it: he was no longer cool at school.

* * *

Klench stood at the entrance of the Hotel Armadillo. The first guest had climbed out of his private helicopter and was striding across the clearing. His gold-toed boots gleamed in the evening sunlight.

Klench bowed in the doorway. 'Greetinks.'

'Howdy.' The tall man tilted his cowboy hat. 'Brag Swaggenham.' He wore a fringed suede jacket and denim jeans. His belt buckle glittered with rubies.

Clicking his heels, Klench ushered his guest through the door.

Brag Swaggenham waved a hand round the hotel lobby, as if claiming for himself the mirrored walls, the lampshades made from armadillo shells and the fountains where Cupids sprayed water from rude bits. The jewels of his many rings winked. 'Like yer style, if not yer body, buddy.'

Klench scowled. 'For vich treatment you have comes?' he asked icily.

Brag held up his hands and sprang backwards, as if under arrest. 'Fingerprint redesign. So the cops can't pin that ol' fire on me.'

Klench raised an enquiring eyebrow.

'Last year,' said Brag, 'In-doh-nesia. Remember? It was headline news.'

Klench gasped. 'You mean zat blaze vich destroyed whole island – zat voss you?' He stared at Brag in admiration.

Twelve villages burned to the ground; eight species of jungle vine wiped out. 'Vy you do it?'

Brag grinned. The diamonds in his back teeth sparkled. 'Underground oil. Couldn't be doin' with forest folks and stoopid flowers in the way.' He shrugged. 'Shame we never found no oil. An' shame they found mah fingerprints on the matchbox.'

Klench nodded in what was the nearest he could get to sympathy.

Brag waggled his hands in the air. 'So that's why ah need a new set o' prints. Think ah'll have mah fingers stretched too, so ah can fit more rings on. And while ah'm here, I might just explore this ol' jungle for oil.'

A snort came from the reception desk. 'Eh stupido! Why you want more? My husband, he always want more – more gold, more seelver. For thees we die.'

Brag Swaggenham whistled. 'Gee. *Love* the special effects.' He crossed the lobby to the desk. 'Where's the wires?' Grabbing Carmen's ears, he tried to unscrew her.

'Aieee!' she screeched as Bitter Albert's Superdooper-glooper Glue held her fast.

Klench came over to the desk and pinged a bell. A moment later a man came down a staircase at the right of the lobby. He wore a white doctor's coat. His face was tanned to toffee. His hair was banana yellow.

'Dr Banoffee,' said Klench, 'pleasse take Mr Brag for pre-treatment chattinks.'

11

Doctor's Orders

Email: corkyshocka@bradleighbellow.net
Subject: Letter from the Equator

FIERY FUMES AND
GOLD MEDDLES
By Abigail Absinthe

Flying into Quito, the capital of Ecuador,
is like landing in a giant mouth. The
mountains rise on all sides like broken teeth
and buildings speckle the lower slopes like
fillings.

When I stepped off the plane this morning,
my eyes wouldn't stop watering. The light
is dazzling here, nearly 3000 metres above
the sea, and the sun scorches down. As we
wandered round the old city centre, the back
of my neck felt on fire.

Quito is the second highest capital in
the world, nestling in the second highest

mountain range, the Andes. The grumpiest peak is Mount Pichincha, a volcano that grumbles above the clouds, ready to blow its top any minute.

The Ecuadorians don't look worried, though. In fact they look pretty relaxed about everything – and so colourful. In the Plaza San Francisco, the oldest square in Quito, there was a lady in the brightest red shawl you've ever seen, selling the brightest blue cloth you've ever seen and grinning with the brightest yellow teeth. She wore a black felt hat and had a long plait. On her back was a bundle of blanket that turned out to be a baby. We found this out when Grandma Hartley-Absinthe smiled and the blanket burst into tears. The lady's one of the Quechua people who lived here with the Incas before the Spanish grabbed Ecuador. I don't mean *she* lived here, of course, but her relatives way back did.

And wow did the Spanish grab. Inside the San Francisco church the walls are coated with gold. There are gold statues, gold screens and gold pillars. The conquistadores pinched all this gold from the Incas, who used it to make plates and cups and things. Imagine a 24-carat bowl of cornflakes!

Abbie stopped typing. She leaned back in her chair in the Internet café and yawned. It had been an exhausting morning. Not because of the flight. Not because of the jet lag. Not even because of the sightseeing. Well, sort of because of that …

Inside the San Francisco church Fernando had started sobbing. Luckily he was on Perdita's palm, covered by a hanky. That meant his tears could be mopped up and muffled at the same time, preventing funny looks from other tourists.

'Thees church not complete when I die,' he'd whispered with what would have been a lump in what would have been his throat. 'Always I want to see thees masterpiece, thees place to honour God. But now what I see? Only greedy wallpaper.'

'There, there.' Even Perdita had whispered in the dark splendour of the church. 'Don't be hard on yourself.'

But Abbie could see Fernando's point. Gazing at the exquisite altar with its statues of Jesus and Mary, she wondered why people would kill each other to grab a stack of metal and give it as a gift to God, who hated people killing each other.

'All a bit grand for me,' Grandma had declared. Abbie agreed. Overawed by the smell of incense and the careful creak of shoes on the wooden floor, she'd followed Grandma outside. An old lady had been sitting by the entrance. She peered at them from a face that needed ironing. Mumbling something in Spanish she'd held out a cup. Grandma had fished out her purse from her bag. Bending down she'd pressed a ten-dollar bill into the lady's hand.

The lady's face had smoothed into a grin. '*Muchos gracias, señora.*'

'You're welc– aaaaahh.' There was a cracking sound. 'Me back!'

… Which was why Grandma was now at the doctor's getting painkillers. The others had gone with her while Abbie slipped off to the café to write her first article for *The Bradleigh Bellow.*

She reread it. All that history. Dad would be proud of her.

Dad. A lost puppy whined in her stomach. *Mum. Ollie. Coco Pops.*

Abbie pressed 'Send' and wrote a quick email home. Then she paid the bill and rushed off to join the others for lunch before the whine became a bark.

* * *

Grandma glared across the restaurant table. 'So what did the doctor say, then?'

Coriander was the only one who'd understood his Spanish. 'Well …' She ran a careful tongue over her lips. 'He advised that we go to the town of Baños. So you can, um, swing from a bridge. On a rope.'

'*What*?' Grandma dropped her spoon in her soup. 'You must be jokin'! I'd rather eat a guinea pig.'

Which everyone had just refused to do. The waiter had come to their table and pointed to the back of the restaurant. Abbie had gasped at the line of guinea pigs roasting gently on spits. It wasn't that she was vegetarian. It was just the sight of those little paws going round and round.

'Just say "*No gracias*" politely,' murmured Coriander. 'It's a speciality here, called Cuy. People have kept guinea pigs in their homes for food since Incan times.'

Abbie opted for *tortillas de papa* – potato cakes with cheese – and fried eggs. Which, when you thought about it, were baby chicks who'd never even *seen* the world, let alone roasted in it. For two and a half seconds she went off her food. Then she tucked in heartily.

'That doc wants 'is 'ead read if 'e thinks I'll dangle from a bridge,' said Grandma, fishing out the spoon from her bowl and licking the handle.

'But he said it'll straighten your spine,' said Coriander.

'I'll come with you,' said Perdita cheerfully. 'Sounds fun.'

Abbie grinned. Who else would offer to swing from a bridge with a grumpy old grumbug? Perdita might have annoyed the pants off her at times this term, but she was still the best friend ever.

'Aahh,' groaned Grandma. 'Well, I s'pose it's worth a try. Anythin' to get me out of this agony.'

'It'll mean a slight detour,' said Coriander. She opened a guidebook on the table. 'We'll get to Logroño a day later.'

A wail came from Grandma's handbag. 'But my Carmen! So close we are and steell you delay. How I can wait?'

'You'll 'ave to,' moaned Grandma, 'if I'm to go traipsin' round the rainforest.'

'And remember,' said Abbie, 'we don't know exactly *where*

your wife fell out. There's a lot of jungle round Logroño. It could take a while to find her.' *If we ever do*, she thought.

The handbag sulked.

'Where did you say we go for this swingin'?' Grandma swept Chester off her head to wipe up the soup she'd spilled on the tablecloth.

'Baños.' Coriander found the page in the guidebook. '"This lovely town in the central highlands has natural springs and other outdoor things."'

After lunch Abbie, Perdita and Coriander headed for the new part of Quito to stock up for the jungle. When Fernando begged to come too, Abbie put him in her rucksack. In the back of the taxi she checked that the driver's eyes were on the road ahead. Then she popped Fernando on her palm so that he could look out of the window.

'What happen to my country of conquer?' he whispered as taxi horns hooted, buses parped and office blocks towered around them. 'Where the trees, the flowers? Now beeg smelly mess.'

At the shops Coriander bought binoculars for bird-spotting and pens for clothes-dotting. 'That's in case we meet a jaguar,' she said. 'We'll draw spots on ourselves so that he thinks we're jaguars too.' Abbie marvelled at the patience of a carnivore who'd wait while she coloured herself in.

Meanwhile Grandma was back in the Hotel Cóndor, where they'd booked in for the night. She spent the afternoon playing 'I spy' with Chester. It went like this:

1. Grandma's turn. She said her 'Somethin'-beginnin'-with.' Then Chester flew onto the Something. It worked well until she chose A for Aeroplane and Chester knocked himself out against the window.
2. Chester's turn. He curled into the shape of his first letter. If Grandma guessed the word correctly, he jumped back onto her head. If she didn't, he landed on whatever was the right answer. That was fine until Grandma said that his 'T' for Trouser Press should have been 'TP' and accused him of cheating. And, as any fool knows, you *never* accuse chest hair of cheating. Chester dived behind a pot plant and stayed there.

So Grandma watched a TV quiz game in Spanish and couldn't answer a thing.

By the time the others got back, Grandma and Chester were crabbier than crabs who've been picked for dinner from one of those restaurant tanks. Because of that, and the early bus ride to Baños the following morning, everyone had dinner and went straight to bed.

* * *

On the top floor of the Hotel Armadillo, Brag Swaggenham lay on an operating table. 'What's with the buckets?' he asked nervously, glancing down either side.

'They're to catch your rings,' said Dr Banoffee. 'The anaesthetic will start working any second now. When your fingers go numb the rings will slide off.'

'Now don't you go nicking 'em,' said Brag as the first diamond band clanged into a bucket. 'Ah've got twenny-three – and twenny-three ah'm keeping.'

'Don't worry.' Dr Banoffee bared his yellow teeth. 'With the money you're paying, I could buy a *hundred* and twenty-three. Now straighten your arms, please. I need to tie you down.'

Brag's eyes widened. 'You what? Ah'm anaesthetised – surely ah shouldn't feel a thing.'

'True,' agreed the doctor, tying a rope round his arm. 'But we can't be sure. Redesigning fingerprints is ground-breaking science. And finger-stretching is cutting-edge medicine.' He laid a hand on Brag's arm. 'One moment, please, while I fetch the Groundbreaker and the Cutting Edge.'

Three minutes later Brag Swaggenham, brutal oil baron and tough-guy supreme, was screaming for his mummy.

* * *

'Hey, look!' Marcus nearly choked on his porridge.

'Don't speak with your mouth full, boy. I don't appreciate seeing your oatie canines over my toast.'

'Sorry, Dad. It's just … that article's written by Abigail Hartley.'

Terry Strode-Boylie snatched *The Bradleigh Bellow* from his son. 'What do you mean?'

'Remember I told you she's gone to Ecuador with Perdita Platt? Well this letter's from Quito.'

'Don't be ridiculous. The writer's surname is Absinthe.'

'But look. It says, "when Grandma *Hartley*-Absinthe smiled and the blanket burst into tears". Abigail must be using a false name.'

'A pseudonym, you mean. Can you spell that?'

'S-U …'

Terry glared at his son and scribbled the word on the edge of the paper. 'I'll test you later. What the *blazes* is a girl in your class doing writing for the newspaper? You're far better at English than she is.' He raised a warning eyebrow. 'I *hope.*'

'Course he is, dear,' said Genevieve, squeezing Marcus's arm.

'Good,' said his dad. 'Because after school *you're* going to write an article. And *we're* going to take it to *The Bradleigh Bellow*. And *they're* going to print it.'

Marcus wiggled his spoon miserably round his porridge. 'But what do I write about, Dad?'

Terry scanned Abbie's article. 'They're obviously into gold. Write about winning the gold medal in the Swimathon.'

'He didn't, dear,' said Genevieve. 'He won stainless steel.'

Terry's silver eyebrows bunched in fury. '*I* didn't build the family name by telling the truth, woman! And it paid off. Look at me now.'

Genevieve looked. And saw a man with thunder in his eyes and jam on his tie.

12

Gulp!

Email: corkyshocka@bradleighbellow.net
Subject: Letter from the Equator

OLD SWINGER
By Abigail Absinthe

Grandma Hartley-Absinthe spends most Friday mornings at the library. But she spent this one swinging from a rope high above a river.

We've come to Baños in the central highlands so that Grandma can go 'puenting'. That's when you leap off a bridge while attached to a rope – like a bungee jump that swings instead of bounces. It's all the rage here.

Even so, tour agent José Molina wasn't keen to let Grandma go. 'When you are

seventy-three, you are not twenty-one,' he
said. But hearing it was the doctor's orders,
and seeing the dollars in Grandma's hand,
Molina understood. 'When you are seventy-
three you have more money than sense.'

So at ten o'clock she was standing on
a bridge above a river, wearing a harness
strapped to a rope.

Tour assistant Eduardo Huerta checked all
the fastenings were secure. He looked very
pale. But Grandma was grinning from gum to
gum (she'd removed her false teeth and wig
in case they fell into the river).

Grandma did the thumbs up at Perdita
Platt, who was strapped to another rope next
to her. Together they counted to throe and
dived head first.

With cries of 'Bingo!' and 'Dreadlocks!' the
plucky pair swung below the bridge. They
came to rest a few minutes later above the
raging Rio Blanco.

'She fantastico grandmama,' said Huerta.
'I wish she mine.'

Replacing her wig, Grandma Hartley-
Absinthe recommended puenting to all
pensioners.

'I feel twenty years younger,' she said,
sucking her teeth back in. 'Not a twinge in
me back. I could salsa the day away.'

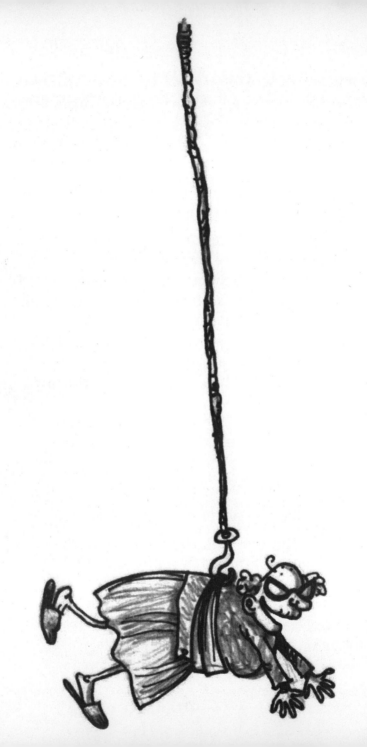

Which is exactly what she was doing right now, while Abbie wrote her second email to *The Bellow*. Coriander and Chester had gone with Grandma to wiggle their hips and shake their curls. Perdita and Fernando had stayed with Abbie in their Baños hotel.

'Finished?' asked Perdita, looking over Abbie's shoulder. 'Let's go and look round town. I want to get some souvenirs for the class.'

Guilt did its own little salsa in Abbie's stomach. Trust Perdita to think of presents. She'd probably buy something for everyone, even Marcus. 'There's no room in our luggage,' she snapped.

'Just little things,' said Perdita. 'Come on, Grumpy Guts.' She jabbed Abbie in the ribs, which didn't help at all.

Strolling along the warm streets of Baños, Abbie couldn't help but cheer up. The breeze breathed life into her bare arms after their woolly imprisonment in England. Shops and stalls lined the pavements, their brightly painted fronts peeling. The air was sweet with the scent of huge red flowers that lined the road. They passed a man lounging in a chair. A boy knelt at his feet and polished his shoes till they gleamed like coals.

A lady in a long skirt fat with petticoats stopped them. She took out a round cheese from her basket. '*Delicioso*,' she said, waving it in Abbie's face.

'*No gracias*,' Abbie gasped as sour goat galloped up her nostrils.

At a street stall the girls bought lemonade and packets of

crisps that were pegged along a string like washing. Abbie gazed hungrily at thick ropes of toffee that dangled from the wall. But seeing the flakes of green paint stuck to them she lost her appetite.

She looked up at the mountains that protected Baños on all sides. Taking a deep breath, she opened Grandma's handbag. 'It's so beautiful, Fernando.' She lifted him onto her palm, shielding him from sight with her fingers.

He glared round the street where tourists strolled in shorts and bikini tops. 'These people,' he hissed, 'why they wear notheeng? No helmet, no armour, no beard. *Ay caramba*, they naked like *bebé*!' He dived back into the bag. Giggling, the girls walked on.

'Hey,' said Perdita, swigging her lemonade, 'look at that shop. Bet we'll find little presents in there.' Before Abbie could answer she'd dived through the doorway. Abbie followed, banging her head on the low beam.

Her eyes took a moment to adjust. She peered through the gloom at the tables cluttered with tiny bric-a-brac. 'Dad would love this old junk,' she murmured.

'Old it may be. Junk it ain't,' squeaked a voice. A little head popped above the counter.

'Oh, sorry,' Abbie mumbled, grateful for the darkness that hid her blush. 'It's just that my dad's a History teacher and he loves old stuff.'

'Well you've come to the right place, Miss. Merv's my name; old stuff's my game. Inca knick-knacks, Conquista-dornaments …'

Grandma's handbag gasped.

The tiny man's teeny ears heard nothing. 'Feel free to browse,' he said. 'But remember, I'll be watching you. Just 'coz it can fit in your pocket doesn't mean you can fit it in your pocket. Or something.'

'Excuse me,' said Perdita, all high-and-mighty, 'we are *not* thieves.'

'Excuse *me*,' said Merv, all low-and-mighty, 'but you never can tell. I lost me two greatest treasures ten days ago – to a *very* smart-looking bloke.'

'Oh dear,' said Perdita whose heart was bigger than her huff. 'I'm sorry.'

'Not half as sorry as me, Miss. Waddled in here, all suit and tie and la-di-da. Distracted me with some yarn about flying veg. And next thing I knew, he'd pinched a golden box from the table and was off down the street. Genuine Incan it was – had an engraving of the sun on the lid. Worth a pretty penny, I can tell you.'

'Why didn't you keep it safe, then, inside a display case?' said Abbie.

Merv looked at her in admiration. 'Never thought of that.'

'What was the other treasure?' asked Perdita.

Merv sighed. 'I say treasure … horrible thing, really. But it meant a lot to me. It was inside the box.' He shook his head. 'Gets lonely in here, see. I used to chat to it, tell it about me day. Not that it could understand, of course. But there was something about it.' He laughed sheepishly. 'Oh, you'll think I'm off me tiddly trolley.'

'No we won't,' Abbie lied.

'Well, I used to pretend it was ... listening. Had this look on its face, see.'

'Face?'

'Yeah.' Merv came out from behind the counter. He stood on tiptoe and whispered into the girls' shoulders, 'Promise you won't tell? Apparently it's illegal to sell 'em.'

'Promise,' whispered Abbie and Perdita.

'It was one of those shrunken – BLIMEY O'*REILLY*!'

Grandma's bag leapt off Abbie's arm and bounced on the floor. Abbie snatched it up. Before Merv had time to shriek in capitals again, she gabbled, 'A shrunken head? Where did it come from?'

'I, er, dunno.' Merv was gaping like a goldfish. 'Some bloke brought it in. Found it in the jungle somewhere east.'

'What did it look like?' asked Perdita, as Grandma's bag whooped in Abbie's arms.

'Er ...' Merv backed towards the counter. 'Black hair, small chin, stuck-up nose.'

'Ah beautiful nose, ah cutieful snout,' sang the handbag. 'My Carmen, I esneeff you out!' Merv shot behind the counter.

Time for introductions, thought Abbie. 'This ...' she opened Grandma's bag, 'is Fernando.' She lifted him out by his hair. 'Say hello to Mr, um ...'

'Peri–, Peri–' stammered Merv.

'Señor Periperi,' said Fernando solemnly. 'Four century ago I lose my life. Today I find again, thank to you.' He made

116

a kissy face at Merv. The tiny man whimpered behind the counter.

Time for explanations. So Abbie told him the whole story: how Fernando had lost his wife and why they'd come to Ecuador.

'Of course,' said Perdita, 'we can't be sure that was *Carmen*'s head. There could be lots of them kicking round Ecuador.'

'How they keeck?' snapped Fernando, bouncing indignantly on Abbie's palm. 'Of *course* she my Carmen. Thees I know, because thees *nose* I know … no, thees nose I *knows* … no, I *knows* thees nose … no! Oh, thees Eenglish I no know, but thees *nose* I *know.*'

Abbie stroked his hair. 'We understand. But Perdita's right. We can't be sure it's Carmen.' She thought for a minute. 'Mr Periperi, can you remember what the man who stole the head looked like?'

Merv shuddered. 'I'll never forget him, Miss. Like I said, he wore a suit. White, it was. And he was fat as a football. Piggy little eyes. Pale skin, shiny like a sausage. Bright yellow hair. Strangest accent, too – wouldn't tell me where he was from.'

Abbie gulped.

Perdita gulped.

Fernando forgot he had no throat and gulped too.

'You don't remember how he parted his hair, by any chance?' said Perdita in her smallest voice, which medium-sized.

117

'Right down the centre, Miss, straight as anything. It was the most memorable thing about him – apart from his clothes and his shape and his eyes and his skin and his accent.'

Abbie scooped her voice from her stomach. 'Do you know where he went?'

'Didn't leave his contact details.' Merv looked hurt, as if that was the least a thief could do. 'Just said he'd spill the beans on me keeping a shrunken head if I spilled the beans on him stealing it. Oh cripers.' Merv clapped his tiddly hand over his diddly mouth. 'I've just done that.'

'Don't worry, Mr P,' cried Perdita, 'your secret's safe with us.' Grabbing Abbie's hand she ran out of the shop. Then she ran back in and bought twenty-four gift-wrapped Incan toothpicks.

* * *

♪ 'Forty-five *go-hold* rings,' crooned Brag Swaggenham, even though Christmas was still two weeks away. 'That's what I'll have on mah pinkies soon.' He waved his bandaged hand at a young woman sitting at the hotel bar. She didn't see him wince with pain. That was because she had a bandage round her eyes.

'What's with the headband?' asked Brag.

The woman fumbled for her drink. 'Eye levelling,' she said weakly. 'My left eye's always been higher. Dr Ecclescake says it'll be level with my right when I take this off.' She sighed with a quaint mixture of delight and agony. 'Then the cops can't prove I'm the Pittsburgh Pearl Pincher.'

'Sure sounds sore,' said Brag.

'Sure is,' said the woman.

Dr Klench sidled up. 'Pleasse not to mention pain,' he hissed. 'You vill upset uzzer customers who are now vaitink for treatments.' He waved round the hotel lounge where tanned men and women chatted and sipped from crystal glasses.

'Sure,' chorused Brag and the woman. She tried to wink. He tried to thumbs-up. Then they tried it the other way round, which worked much better.

Klench waddled off to the lobby. 'Business is boomink, Mums,' he murmured.

'Not boomink enough, my pastry puff. Alvays ze clients complain about pain. Zat you must fix. And ziss too.' She pinched the inside of his stomach. 'Still fat as a vat.'

A tear squeezed from Klench's eye. Inner Mummy was never satisfied. Here they were offering a wonderful service to the criminal world and she was *still* nagging. When would she grasp that her dream of a slim son was pork pie in the sky? While she'd been snoozing in his brain, he'd visited the hotel psychiatrist. And Dr Squidgychocolatelog had told him that the problem was clear. Inner Mummy wanted to control him. No matter if he was thin or fat, she'd always put him down, ruin his confidence, so that she could rule in his brain. Until he stood up to her, he'd never be free.

Klench gulped. He'd rather give money to a *poor* person than stand up to Mummy.

* * *

'What d'you *mean* it doesn't grab you?' A bead of spit flew from Terry Strode-Boylie's mouth. It sailed across the desk and landed on the hard nose of Corky Shocka.

Wiping it off, she pushed Marcus's article about the Swimathon back across the desk. 'It's not juicy,' she yawned. 'Not spicy. Not vindaloo with extra chilli. It's not *news*.' Marcus grabbed the article and scrunched it into a ball, blushing madly.

'News? You think *this* is news?' Terry shoved the second Letter from the Equator into Corky's face.

'Absolutely. I've had phone calls, texts, emails. The readers love it.'

'*News* indeed!' Terry's finger jabbed the air like a drunken woodpecker. 'Well what about *my* news? Why haven't you printed my letter of complaint about the zoo?'

'Pompous, long-winded and boring. Now, if you'll excuse me, I've got to file my nose.'

13

On the Trail

'It *could* be,' said Coriander that evening.

Fernando was insisting for the umpteenth time that the head stolen from Merv's shop was Carmen. He was perched in the sink in Abbie and Perdita's hotel room. The cold tap was running to calm him down.

'It *could* be,' she agreed when Abbie said that finding the head, whether Carmen or not, would be impossible.

'It *couldn't* be!' she gasped when Perdita described the thief. Her hands flew to her face. 'What's *he* doing here?'

Abbie thought back to their last news of Hubris Klench. After holding them hostage in the Platts' Hair Museum last summer, the wicked wobbler had simply disappeared. The police had combed the country armed with charge upon charge against him. There was animal smuggling, weapons dealing and money laundering (trust Klench to wash his cash). There were armed robberies of banks, businesses and bakeries. And there were the thousands of Chinese burns he'd inflicted on small children and pensioners.

But the police hunt had been fruitless. Klench had vanished in a puff of pastry. He could have escaped anywhere. And Abbie had to admit that the Amazon jungle, dark and dense, was as good an anywhere as – well – anywhere.

You could see that Coriander was admitting it too. Her peachy cheeks paled to potato. Her round face sagged to oval. Her double chin doubled. It was hardly surprising, considering that she was the one Klench had kidnapped last summer. She was the one who knew him best.

There was a long silence. Abbie pictured a beach ball in a suit rolling through the jungle. A fight broke out in her stomach. Fear shouted rude things at Courage, who was cheering at the thought of chasing Klench and defeating him once and for all. Courage shouted rude things back. Fear burst into tears and wanted its mum. Courage said sorry, it had got carried away and needed time to think.

Finally Abbie said, 'Even if it *was* Klench and Carmen, we've no idea where they went.'

Fernando gave a sob. A lonely tear squeezed from his eye. It met the tap water already streaming down his cheeks and was surrounded by friends for the rest of its journey to the sea, where it decided it couldn't take crowds and evaporated.

There was another long silence.

Then Grandma leapt up – and we're talking leapt. She boinged in the air like one of those little toys on springs that stick when you lick, then suddenly flick. '*Course* we can find out where they went! 'Ow many ways can a bod leave this town?'

Coriander frowned. 'Well, there's no airport or train station. Bus or car, I s'pose.'

'Or bicycle,' said Perdita.

Grandma rolled her eyes. Even they were more sprightly since her bridge-jumping. 'As if Klench could ride a bike! No, we'll start at the bus station. 'Oo could forget sellin' a ticket to *that* lump o' lard?'

Abbie stared at Grandma. The brainy old boot was right. If Klench had caught a bus, *someone* would remember him.

The question was: did they *want* someone to?

Grandma clearly did, the way she was rubbing her hands. So did Fernando, who was grinning from ear to crumbly ear. Coriander clearly didn't, the way she was twisting a plait round her finger. Nor did Perdita, who was scraping her chin with her teeth.

And what about Abbie? In her stomach, Fear crept up and bonked Courage on the head. Courage fell over – and was caught in the arms of Anger. How *dare* Klench get the better of them again? How *dare* the very mention of him scare them off their quest? Courage and Anger took a deep breath … and punched Fear's lights out.

* * *

Grandma was right. Someone *did* remember Klench. Someone with wobbly teeth that jiggled as he giggled in the ticket booth of Baños bus station next morning. '*Si*

Señora.' He nodded as Coriander ran out of Spanish trying to describe Klench. 'I never forget thees belly on legs.'

'Told you so!' crowed Grandma, jiggling her own false teeth in triumph.

'He buy two seat,' the ticket man said. 'One for each – how you say? – butt*ock.'*

'Where did he go?' asked Abbie.

'He go …' The teeth went still. 'Ah *si*! He go east. To Puyo.'

'Are you sure?' mumbled Coriander miserably. 'Maybe you've remembered wrongly.'

The man shook his head till his teeth rattled. 'Puyo. For sure.'

'What are we waitin' for?' bellowed Grandma. 'Four tickets to Puyo, *por favor*, ducks.'

* * *

The bus growled down the mountain road. On the left rose a wall of grey rock, shiny-wet as if wrapped in cling film. Ferns and mosses crouched in its cracks while waterfalls flung spray through the window. *Good job we sat on the right*, thought Abbie. *Though on second thoughts …* Along the right side of the road ran a low wall. Beyond it was misty blankness. Anything could be out there – or nothing. For a terrifying moment Abbie felt as if she was in a drawing that God had forgotten to finish.

Then the mist thinned. Abbie gulped. Beside her a canyon plunged downwards. Clouds pottered beneath her. A river rushed along the valley floor.

'Wow!' said Perdita, lunging across her to look out the window. 'Cloud forest, river gorge – it's like a Geography lesson.'

Abbie clutched the seat in front and wished it *was* a Geography lesson. She pictured Mr Dabbings meandering between desks, being the middle course of a river. Snorty Poff was on sound effects and Jeremy boinged about like pebbles in the current.

The bus was having a good old boing itself. And strangely enough that calmed Abbie's fear. As they bounced round the mountain, breakfast bounced round her stomach. Panic gave way to sickness. She closed her eyes and dreamed of break-dancing omelettes.

She was woken by Perdita's elbow. 'Or kids,' it seemed to be saying.

Yawning awake, Abbie realised it wasn't Perdita's elbow talking but her mouth. And it wasn't children but flowers she was on about. Giant orchids lined the road, their brilliant petals lolling like tongues.

'Welcome to the jungle,' said Perdita. Abbie took off her jacket. The air in the bus had thickened and warmed.

'Ooh me 'ead,' said Grandma. 'I'm sweatin' like a sausage. You'll 'ave to sit somewhere else, Chess.'

'No, he won't,' said Coriander next to her. It was the first time she'd spoken since getting on the bus. After hearing about Klench in Baños she seemed to have deflated like a leaking tyre. 'Just pop this on.'

Abbie turned round to look. Chester jumped into Grandma's lap.

Coriander took a lumpy handkerchief from her pocket. She spread it over Grandma's head. 'Numbskull,' she said.

'There's no need for insults,' snapped Grandma.

Coriander smiled. 'Not you. The hanky. It numbs your skull with cold. You can put Chester on top. The Numbskull will cool you both down. Matt invented it for the Dazzle Ducks of Dubai.'

'The what? Never 'eard of 'em.'

'That's not surprising.' Coriander sighed. 'Tragic story. They had these wonderful silver head feathers. They were the envy of the seabirds in the Persian Gulf. Sooty Gulls used to swoop down and peck them to death out of pure jealousy. There were fewer than a hundred Dazzlers left when I was called in.'

'To do what?' said Abbie.

'Make wigs. To hide their feathers. But it didn't work. My wigs made their heads overheat. So Matt invented Numbskulls. They're just hankies with lumps of dry ice sewn in. He lined the wigs with them.'

'So the ducks were cooled and the Sooty Gulls were fooled. What's so tragic about that?' said Grandma.

Coriander shook her head. 'The wigs looked like Kinky

Kelp, a seaweed found only in the Persian Gulf. Which is exactly what Sooty Gulls use to line their nests. So the gulls pecked them off the ducks' heads and – hey presto – it was back to square one. Or rather square none. The Dazzlers became extinct.'

Grandma smacked Chester back onto her head. 'Woe betide anyone 'oo tries to peck *my* pal.'

'Don't worry, Grandma,' said Abbie. 'Chester doesn't look like seaweed.' *And I pity any gull who messes with you,* she thought.

The bus wheezed into Puyo. Bushes and flowers gave way to white houses with flat roofs. The sky was solid grey. The bus pulled into the station. Passengers stumbled off, fanning themselves. The hot air smelt of fumes and damp decay.

'I'll get the bags,' said Grandma. 'You check on Fernando. 'E slept all the way.' She gave Abbie her handbag and went to the boot at the back of the bus.

'Air,' gasped a faint voice. Abbie opened the bag. She didn't dare bring Fernando out with all the people milling around. Coriander came to the rescue with a second Numbskull, which she lowered into the bag to cool him down.

'Aaah,' sighed Fernando gazing up. 'I thank you for hankyou. For hanky I thanky. Thanks for hanks. Now, where we are, and what we do?' He looked at Coriander. Who looked at Perdita. Who looked at Abbie. Who looked at Grandma. Who returned with the bags and said, 'What are *you* lookin' at?' She dumped three rucksacks on the ground and patted her own luggage, a shopping bag on wheels. '*I dunno what to do.*'

Nor did anyone else. Beyond getting to Puyo, no one had made any plans.

Coriander kicked a stone. 'Even if Klench *did* come here,' she said, 'how do we know he brought the shrunken head? And even if he *did* bring it, how do we know it was Carmen? And even if it *was* Carmen, how do we know where they went next? We'll never find them.'

A snarl came from Grandma's bag. 'Of course eet my Carmen! And of course you find her. You must. You lose her een first place.'

Fair point, thought Abbie, remembering how Carmen had fallen out of Coriander's bag almost a year ago.

'But,' Coriander bit her lip, 'what if we find Klench too? He knows we'd hand him over to the police. He'd do anything – and I mean anything – to stop us.'

True, thought Abbie. *She knows better than anyone what he's capable of.*

Grandma jumped to her feet. 'You mean to say I've done me back in on a plane, swung from a bridge, sweated me wig off *and* missed me Bingo, just so you can all wimp out now?'

Absolutely, thought Abbie. *The old sprout's come a long way.*

'But,' Perdita scraped her chin with her teeth, 'what if Klench kidnaps us again? It would kill Dad.'

She's right. Poor old Matt would be a gibbering jelly … or even worse, an un-gibbering one.

Now what? Carry on searching or go home? The question hung in the air. It was two against two. Chester didn't count because he always sided with Grandma. Time for the deciding vote.

Everyone looked at Abbie.

* * *

Klench stood behind the reception desk of the Hotel Armadillo. He listened to the scribble of voices from the lounge. The chatter of new guests mingled pleasantly with the moans of those who'd been treated. Now and then a scream pierced the air. Klench looked down at his timetable. That must be the gangster who arrived yesterday, enjoying his neck-shortening session. Klench chuckled to himself.

At least, he'd thought it was to himself. 'Stop laughink!' barked Inner Mummy. 'Can't you hear guests are in agonies? I tell you, trouble is brewink. Zey vill give you endless grief, unless you find zem pain relief.'

* * *

'I wouldn't go in there, dear,' whispered Genevieve Strode-Boylie. 'Your father's in a bit of a mood.'

Marcus rested his hand on the doorknob of his dad's office. 'But I want to show him my Maths test. I got everything right.'

'I don't think that'll help right now, Marcus. Leave him at his desk. He's colouring in a set of false teeth. You know how that calms him down.' Genevieve's weak smile suggested she didn't believe for one second that denture decorating would soothe her husband.

They went into the kitchen. Genevieve unlocked a drawer and took out a packet of Jelly Babies. She held it out to Marcus.

'But Dad says they ruin your–'

'Dad's not here.' She winked.

Marcus took one and sat at the table. 'He's been in a mood for days, Mum.'

'I know. It's been one thing after another. First Mr Hartley appearing on telly. Then your zoo trip and that "insult to the family name" nons– I mean business. Then his letter not getting into the paper. Then two more rejections of his book.' Genevieve sighed. 'I just wish he could stop competing. That he could count *his* blessings instead of other people's. He's got enough, for goodness sake – smart job, smart house and a son to be proud of.' She reached across the table and ruffled Marcus's hair.

'Thanks, Mum.' Marcus chewed his sweet. If only that were true. If only he hadn't let his dad down. If only he hadn't messed up at the zoo. If only his Swimathon article had got into the paper. If only he could spell pseudo-thingy.

Hang on. Who was to blame for all this? Who owned the zoo? Whose articles *had* got into the paper?

Marcus took two more sweets. He squeezed one between each forefinger and thumb. 'Die, dorks!' he muttered, biting off the heads of Jelly Baby Platt and Jelly Baby Hartley.

14

Cakes and Clues

'Not another Incan pot for storing beer. I could spit!' groaned Abbie.

'Which is exactly what they did,' said Coriander. 'The Inca women chewed corn then spat it into the pot and left it to ferment. The beer's called chicha. They still brew it in the jungle.'

'Can you brew it from toffee?' Grandma was chomping one as she peered at the pot.

Abbie yawned. Her idea to visit Puyo's Museum of Archaeology had seemed brilliant at the time. If Klench *had* come to Puyo, this would be the obvious place to bring his Incan box. But when Coriander had asked the man on reception about Klench, he'd stared as if she was from Planet Pull-the-Other-One. *If* she'd asked him about Klench, of course. Abbie couldn't help wondering if someone who wasn't keen on finding someone else would make much effort to describe that someone else. But she didn't know enough Spanish to check.

She did, however, know a golden box when she saw one. And so far they hadn't. All they'd seen were pots. Pots and pots of pots.

'This is useless.' Perdita sighed. 'Let's go.'

Walking back to the hotel where they'd left their luggage, Abbie felt a rush of irritation. Coriander and Perdita had given up. Oh sure, they were *pretending* to look for leads. But really they were waiting until Abbie gave up too. Then they could all go home without looking like scaredy cats.

Well, you can wait away, she thought fiercely. *We're not quitting yet. We owe it to Fernando.*

She stopped on the pavement. 'I want to look round Puyo,' she said. 'See you back at the hotel.'

She wandered down the cobbled street. There was no one about. Shops with bright awnings lined the pavement. Above their flat roofs, electricity wires scribbled on the white sky. A car crawled past, as if struggling against the heavy air.

Abbie pulled out her T-shirt, dark with sweat, and fanned it over her stomach. She pictured Klench scuttling along in his tight white suit. *Where would he have gone? Who might remember him?*

She passed a clothes shop. No chance. Nothing would fit.

A post office. No friends to write to.

A souvenir stall. Klench buying presents? Please!

A bicycle-hire shop. That'd be the day.

She flopped down on a bench. What was she doing here?

The Platts had lost their nerve; the trail was dead. 'Stupid Puyo,' she mumbled. 'Stupid Ecuador. Stupid adventure.'

A tear slipped down her cheek. A raindrop plopped on her head. Another tear slipped. Another drop plopped. And before she knew it there was slipping and plopping all over the place. As her tears spilled, the sky poured out its sympathy. Oh the comfort, the relief, the sheer wonderful misery of the rain! Abbie threw back her head and welcomed it on her tongue, down her neck, into her bones.

Then it stopped, just like that, as if a tap had turned off in the sky. Abbie sniffed. Sat up. Snatched a handful of T-shirt. Squeezed. Felt better. Felt itchy. Felt peckish.

She looked at her watch. Five o'clock. Dinner was two hours away. Her stomach growled.

She got up and wandered back towards the hotel. The tiny leaves of bushes along the pavement glittered with rain. A fresh, sweet scent rose from their pink flowers.

Very fresh. And very sweet.

Getting fresher and sweeter all the time.

Abbie stopped. Down a side street on the left was a shop. Across its orange awning was the word Panaderia.

The smell translated for her. A bakery.

A bakery?

It was worth a try.

'Queen,' said the man behind the counter when Abbie asked if he spoke English.

'BBC,' he replied when she asked if a fat man in a white suit had ever come into his shop.

Abbie tried a different approach. She took a large bun from a tray and a small bun from a basket. She put the small bun on top of the large one. Then she took a yellow napkin from the counter and crowned the small bun.

The baker stared at the model. 'Teletubby,' he gasped.

He recognised it! 'Here?' said Abbie. 'In the last two weeks?'

'*Si si!*' cried the man. Pointing to a plate of pies he shouted, 'Big Ben!'

Abbie guessed that meant Klench had bought a lot of them. 'Where did he go – um – *dónde vamos?*' She waved up and down the street.

'Bobby on beat. London Underground. Tipitopitapas,' said the man.

Abbie frowned.

The baker pointed to the Klench model. 'Marble Arch. Tipitopitapas.'

You what?

'Left right left right. Tipitopitapas.'

Directions! Maybe Klench asked directions to a place called Tipitopitapas.

'*Muchas gracias,*' Abbie shouted. She grabbed an apple turnover from a tray and shoved a two-dollar bill across the counter.

'Crown Jewels!' the baker called gratefully as she ran out of the shop without waiting for change.

* * *

Back at the hotel the receptionist was idly flicking paper clips across the lobby. He looked up from his desk as Abbie rushed in.

'Excuse me,' she gasped. 'Do you know a place called Tipitopitapas?'

The receptionist yawned. 'That is café-bar.' He reached under the desk and brought out a street map of Puyo. He pointed with a paper clip to a spot by the river. 'There. Oh, your friends say to tell you they in lounge.'

'Thank you.' Abbie ran across the lobby. A paper clip bounced off her head.

The others were sitting round a table playing Snap, or trying to. Fernando was watching from an ashtray. Every time Coriander put down a card he yelled 'Esnap!' to stop her winning. Revenge, no doubt, for her reluctance to look for Carmen.

Abbie plonked on the sofa next to Perdita. 'Guess what?' she said breathlessly. 'I know where Klench went!' She told them about the bakery.

'So? 'E visited a bar called Tipitopitapas. Big deal,' said Grandma. 'Snap.'

'No, it's not,' said Perdita, 'it's a six and a Jack.'

'Picky picky,' said Grandma.

'Well,' said Abbie, 'at least it proves that Klench came to Puyo.' She turned to Coriander. 'I'm going to that bar. You're the only one who speaks Spanish. You've got to come with me.'

'But ...' Coriander put down a card miserably.

135

'But what?' said Abbie. 'We're only finding out where he went. It's not like we're inviting him for Christmas.'

'But what if we *do* find out?' said Perdita. 'Look, Mum and I just phoned Dad. And when I told him about Klench he burst into tears.'

Olympic wimp, thought Abbie. 'Why are you Platts so scared?' she said. 'There's six of us against one of him. What can he do to us?'

Coriander twisted a plait round her finger. 'Look what he did to *me*, locking me up for three months. Look how he starved the zoo animals. Look at the pain he's caused.'

The pain he's caused ... now that sounded familiar. 'Ha!' snorted Abbie as Marcus Strode-Boylie sneered into her mind. 'What was it you said the other day? People who *cause* pain are usually *in* pain. No one's *just* horrible.'

Coriander stared at her cards. 'Except Klench,' she mumbled. 'I'd forgotten about him.'

'You can forget about 'im now,' said Grandma. She jabbed a finger at Coriander. 'And you can think about poor Fernando instead. Snapped off 'is shoulders, snapped into a bag, snapped apart from 'is wife ... Snap!'

'No,' said Perdita, 'it's an Ace and a Quee–' The look on Grandma's face shut her up.

Coriander put her head in her hands. She sat there for a long time. Then she looked up. 'You're right. I have to do it. For Fernando. I'll come to the bar. I'll do what I can. But I won't face Klench again.'

* * *

At nine o'clock next morning it was already hot. Abbie and Coriander walked in silence along the cobbled streets. The sky was soft and grey, like damp tissue. A fine mist rose from the river on their right. A not-so-fine smell rose with it.

They passed a fisherman crouching on the riverbank and a skinny dog nosing through litter. Finally they reached a row of cafés and shops. At the first café two old men looked up from their coffees and smiled. Abbie smiled back.

But Coriander stared grimly ahead. 'There.' She pointed to the last building in the row.

BAR TIPITOPITAPAS

it said across the ragged awning. Outside stood two round tables with collapsed umbrellas.

'Come on.' Abbie took Coriander's arm and steered her through the open door.

They peered into the gloom. On the left was a dark wooden bar. A few plastic tables were scattered around. The floor was a fly fiesta. A sad beery smell curled up Abbie's nose. The place was empty except for a man in the corner. He was slumped at a table, staring into a glass of golden liquid and moaning to himself.

Abbie nudged Coriander. 'Ask him where the waiter is,' she said.

The man looked up. His eyes watered; his skin was grey.

'I am waiter. And since my wife leave I am waitress too. I do all job here. Oh oh.' He gulped his drink. 'Manager and manageress. Barman and barmess.' He gave a laughter-free laugh.

'Oh,' said Abbie in a sympathetic way.

'Oh oh,' agreed the man.

'The thing is,' said Abbie, 'we're looking for someone. We think he might have come in here about two weeks ago.'

'Two weeks? Oh oh.'

'Someone fat. With yellow hair.'

'Fat? Yellow? For sure, oh oh. He meet me here.'

Coriander grasped Abbie's arm. The man's face crumpled like a dirty dishcloth. A tear dripped onto the table. He waved at them to sit down, apparently keen to share his sorrows. He held out a hand. 'Antonio Monio.'

'I'm Tilly,' said Abbie quickly, 'and this is Mrs Budds.' No way was she going to give their real names to a man who'd shaken Klench's horrid little paw. She and Coriander pulled up two chairs, brushing off the crumbs.

'I tell you my story. But first …' Antonio heaved himself up from the table. He went to the bar, reached behind it for something and returned. '*Cigarro*?'

'Oh oh,' gasped Abbie and Coriander. Antonio Monio was holding out a golden box with an engraving of the sun on the lid.

* * *

'Good griefs!' Klench blinked up from the reception desk. 'You startled me.'

A man stood in front of him. He wore a short-sleeved khaki shirt and long shorts.

Klench glanced at his mint-green watch. 'You are right on times. But how come I not hear your helicopter?'

'Helicopter?' The man raised his eyebrows. 'A hunter

139

likes to walk.' His voice was low and quiet. 'Took less than a day from Puyo.'

Klench nodded curtly to hide how impressed he was. 'Vell, let us see if your poachink matches your timekeepink. You may start schnip-schnap.'

The man grunted through his grizzled beard. 'A hunter likes to work at night.'

'Of course.' Klench cleared his throat. 'I vos forgettink.' He glanced at the rifle slung over the man's shoulder. 'But please to leave zat here. You vill not be killink. I am sure you understand zat a dead pet iss a bad pet.' He giggled at his little joke.

The man fixed Klench with cold grey eyes. 'I'm sure *you* understand that I need my dart gun to stun the big ones.'

'Ah.' Klench shifted from one foot to the other. 'Just checkink.'

The man caught sight of Carmen on the desk. 'Hey, that's some trophy.' He whistled. 'You do that yourself?'

'Of course,' Klench lied, knowing that she wouldn't correct him. Ever since Brag had tried to unscrew her, the head had played dead around the guests. 'Now, Mr ...'

The man stared at him.

Coughing, Klench reached under the desk and brought out a bunch of keys. 'Zese are for cages, vich are ready in vine cellar under kitchen.' He rang a bell on the desk. A door on his left opened. A nervous-looking youth came through. He wore the brown uniform of the hotel staff. 'Ziss is Nanto. He vill feed animals for you. But do not give him keys to cages. And you must sleep in vine cellar.' Klench smiled at the hunter. 'You can never trust a servant – not even ziss yunk fool.' He clipped Nanto round the ear. 'Take Mr … Mr …?'

The man stared again. 'Call me Mr … Hunter.'

* * *

Marcus jabbed the white ball with the pool cue. It bounced off the side of the table and potted a stripy ball. 'Yes!'

He flung the cue on the table. So what? Dad wasn't there to witness his skill. He hadn't set foot in the games room for a week. He was still in the mother of moods.

Marcus grasped the cue again. What could he do to cheer Dad up and sort out whacko Platt and fartley Hartley once and for all? He stabbed a ball. It hit the side of the table, flew over the edge, landed on to the carpet and rolled out of the open door.

He gasped. *Of course!*

But how on earth would he pull it off?

15

No Posseeble

'But why hasn't he sold it?' said Perdita. 'Using it for cigars – he must be crazy!'

They were sitting in the hotel lounge. Abbie and Coriander had rushed back from Bar Tipitopitapas to tell the others Antonio's tale. How he'd built the Hotel Armadillo, a luxury jungle retreat. How he'd hoped rich tourists would flock there after a thrilling trek through the forest. How his wife had warned him that rich tourists aren't into roughing it. How, after eight months without a single booking, she'd left him. How he'd sunk into despair. And how no one would buy his five-star flop ... until Klench phoned.

'So Mr Moany-Pants got the box,' said Grandma. 'If it's so valuable, why didn't 'e just sell it and buy another luxury place?' She popped a peanut into her mouth.

Coriander sighed. 'He can't be bothered. Poor man, it seems he's given up on life. He got a job at the Tipitopitapas bar so he can sit there all day feeling sorry for himself.

'I wish we could help him,' said Abbie. She drained her glass of bright green, sweet-as-heaven juice.

'Who care about Moanie Man?' squeaked Fernando. He was perching on Abbie's lap. 'Where my Carmen? Where Klench take her?'

'We still can't be sure he *did* take her,' said Coriander.

'But we do know where he went,' said Abbie. 'Though we've no idea why.'

'What does Klench want with a posh 'otel in the middle of nowhere?' asked Grandma.

'That,' said Coriander firmly, 'is for the police to find out.'

* * *

But the policeman behind the desk at Puyo station wasn't interested. 'So,' he said, raising a fierce eyebrow, 'you hear of fat man in white suit? And you theenk perhaps he beeg-shot baddie? And you want us to search jungle for find? No posseeble. There are many fat mans in world. And many wear white suit.'

'But the description is just like Klench!' Abbie cried. 'He's got this funny accent and pale face and–'

'You have funny accent and pale face,' said the policeman sharply. 'If you wear white suit and stuff cushion under shirt, perhaps I arrest you too.'

'Please,' Coriander begged. 'He's committed all sorts of crimes in all sorts of countries.'

'But not in Ecuador. Now excuse me, I very busy man.' The policeman picked up a pen.

'Can't you at least check?' said Perdita. 'You've got a helicopter sitting out the front doing nothing. You could fly over the jungle, look at the hotel.'

The policeman tapped the pen. 'I tell you, I very busy.'

'Take us to your boss then,' said Grandma.

The policeman eyed her coldly. 'I am boss. When you find me a crime, I find you the time. Now I have urgent meeting. *Adios Señoras.*' He got up and marched through a door. From the gurgles that followed, Abbie guessed that his urgent meeting was with the kettle.

'Puffed-up pooper!' shouted Grandma. Abbie prayed the policeman's ears and English weren't that good.

They headed slowly back to the hotel.

'That's that then,' said Perdita. 'Klench goes free and we go home.'

Abbie kicked a stone along the pavement. 'There must be something else we can do!'

Coriander put her hand on Abbie's arm. 'Not without the police,' she said, soft-but-oh-so-firmly.

Abbie pushed her away. 'Don't you see? If we give up now, Klench'll never be caught. He'll wander the world till kingdom come.'

Coriander stared at Abbie. 'Oh dear,' she sighed, 'you're right. He must be caught. But we can't do the catching. There has to be another way.'

'Hang on!' Abbie clapped her hands. 'There is another way! The policeman said Klench hasn't broken the law in Ecuador. But I bet he has. I bet he's breaking it right now,

144

doing something terrible at that hotel. If we can prove it, then the police have no choice – they'll have to go after him.'

'So,' said Grandma, ''ow *do* we prove it?'

'We hide in the jungle and spy on the hotel. When we find out what Klench is up to, we get some evidence, then come back and tell the police. They'll have to go after him then.'

Perdita frowned. 'What if he's not up to anything? What if he's just retired from crime to run a hotel?'

No one answered. But the look on their faces said, Klench retire from crime? Guinea pigs might fly.

Back at the hotel Fernando was waiting for them in the wardrobe of Grandma's room. They brought him out and told him what had happened.

'Oh no,' he said when they described the unhelpful policeman.

'Oh *si*,' he said when they explained the plan about spying.

'Oh no,' he said when Abbie showed him the map Antonio Monio had given her. It was a solid green square  with a cross in the middle. 'How we ever find thees hotel?'

Coriander smiled. 'Don't worry, I've got a great compass.' She winked at Perdita.

Abbie smiled too. What a relief to see the Platts perking up. It must be the prospect of a jungle jaunt. Coriander loved her wildlife. And once she was happy, so was Perdita. Plus the thought of getting Klench arrested was enough to brighten anyone's day.

After lunch they repacked their rucksacks with jungle essentials. The receptionist had agreed to store the rest of their luggage at the hotel.

When she'd stuffed in her last pair of knickers, Abbie went down to the lobby and phoned home.

'Hello?' came a crackly voice.

'Hi, Mum.'

''Arling! 'Ow are you?'

'Fine. We're in a hotel at the edge of the jungle. Mum, the line's not good.'

''Issing you 'ery much. Any more 'ews on Carm–?'

'We're on her trail. Look, Mum, we're going into the jungle tomorrow. It's too much to explain. I'll be out of touch for a few days. Don't worry.'

'What's this 'bout Klen–?'

'Never mind. Please tell Matt we'll keep miles away from him.' It was sort of true. If you were an ant, fifty metres was miles.

'Be caref' 'arling. We 'ove you so mu–'

'You too, Mum. You're breaking up. I'd better go.'

Was it sniffs or static that crackled in her ears? Abbie put the phone down. She grabbed a tissue and dabbed at the stupid leak in her eyes.

* * *

Klench puffed upstairs to the third floor of the Hotel Armadillo. He paused on the landing in front of a white door.

'Go on,' urged Inner Mummy.

'Are you sure?' he mumbled. 'How can I boss zem about, Mums? I am Doctor of Eefil-Doink, not medicines.'

'But *I* sure am, you hunk of ham.'

Klench nodded meekly. How could he forget her degrees in pathology, pharmacology, cardiology and bullyology? He opened the door. Fumes of disinfectant scoured his nostrils. Fortified by his favourite scent, he strode forward. 'Doctors,' he squeaked.

Three faces looked up from their microscope, fingernail-scrubbing and tool-sharpening.

'Ve need to talk,' said Klench. 'About pain. Guests are complaininck zat treatments are too hurtsy. You must bump up anaesthetic.'

Dr Banoffee put down a knife with spikes on the blade. He smoothed his hair. 'We can't,' he cooed in a creamy voice. 'If we increase the dose it'll kill them. And if they're dead, they're less likely to pay us.'

Dr Squidgychocolatelog laughed sweetly. 'Basic psychology.'

Mummy boxed Klench on the inner ear. 'Tell zem zey

147

must make a plan – or you've got probs, you jumbo flan.'

'Make a plan, you jumbo flan,' said Klench.

Doctors Ecclescake, Banoffee and Squidgychocolatelog frowned. 'Who are you calling flan?' they chorused.

* * *

Terry Strode-Boylie tapped his watch. 'Bedtime.'

'OK, Dad.' Marcus got up from his chair.

Genevieve rose from the sofa and kissed Marcus on the forehead. 'Sleep well, darling. Love you.'

'You too, Mum. Dad.'

Terry grunted into his book.

Dad can't even say goodnight, thought Marcus, climbing the stairs slowly. If only he could finalise the plan, fit the last piece of the jigsaw. Then Dad would be the proudest parent on the planet.

16

Into the Jungle

Email: corkyshocka@bradleighbellow.net
Subject: Letter from the Equator

JUNGLE TRUNDLE
By Abigail Absinthe

If you need a shopping bag on wheels, you can't beat the Trundeluxe. I know this because Grandma's just tried to – by testing it in the rainforest. And after an hour of wheeling over roots, leaves and uber-grumpy ants, it's still in one piece. Now it's passed the test, we'll be using the trolley to carry four hammocks and a cooking pot on our jungle trek.

It's going to be a sweaty few days. Before our test-run this morning my T-shirt was turquoise. After twenty minutes in the rainforest it was navy blue.

Imagine you're a piece of onion floating in soup. That's how you feel in the jungle, shiny and slimy, held up and pressed down at the same time by the heat. At every step your boots either sink into moss or trip over roots. The smell of the forest is like a million Indian takeaways rolling up your nose – sweet and bitter, sour and spicy, mouldy and sharp.

We saw bugs as big as mugs, flies the size of your eyes and leeches fat as peaches. Best of all are the butterflies. Think of the bluest blue you can then add twelve. That's the colour of the outer wings of the morpho butterfly, designed to dazzle predators. Folded up, though, they're dull brown. Their camouflage is so good that predators look at tree trunks absolutely plastered with morphos and say to each other, 'No lunch there, mate.' Poor things. You wonder if they ever get a decent meal.

I'm writing this from a hotel in Puyo on the edge of the rainforest. The internet hasn't reached the jungle yet, so it'll be a while before I write again.

Abbie pressed 'Send' for the last time in who knew how long. 'Gracias,' she said to the receptionist who'd let her use the hotel computer.

'Enjoy jungle,' he called, flicking a farewell paper clip at her back. She ran out of the hotel and jumped into the jeep where everyone else was waiting.

A few hours later they were roaring down a river. Herons rose in long-legged alarm as the speedboat ripped through their day. Trees like giant broccoli crowded the muddy banks.

'Isn't this brill?' yelled Perdita, throwing her arms out. Abbie nodded, opening her mouth to welcome the wind right down to her toes.

''Ang on there, Chess!' Grandma clapped her hand over her head.

Coriander tapped the boatman on the shoulder and pointed ahead. On the left was a wooden jetty. The boatman nodded. He steered the boat towards it and turned off the engine.

There was a signpost on the jetty.

HOTEL ARMADILLO

it said in peeling paint. An arrow pointed down a path into the jungle. *For all those rich tourists who never came,* thought Abbie.

Everyone lugged their rucksacks and the shopping trolley off the boat. Coriander paid the boatman. They stood on the jetty and waved until the boat was out of sight. As the engine's roar faded another one grew: the hissing, crackling din of the jungle. Everyone stared at the dark opening. How many legs, wings, beaks and voices were working up that steamy rumpus? How many snakes were lurking and jaguars lounging, their fangs and claws awaiting intruders?

Coriander bent over her rucksack. From a pocket she brought out a slim metal box that fitted in her hand. On one side was a screen. She pressed a button on the back. Two eyes, a nose and a mouth appeared on the screen.

'Well hi-de-hi and hey-de-hey!' came a chirpy voice. 'Great to see the light of day.'

'Whassat?' said Grandma. Coriander put a finger to her lips.

The screen eyes blinked round. 'Greetings folks, it's good to meet. Hang on while I find my feet.'

Everyone stared as two metal legs popped out of the box. At their ends were little feet and toes.

Coriander stood it on the jetty. 'Told you I had a great

compass,' she said. 'This is Gav the Nav. Matt made him specially for our jungle trip.'

'Not that you will,' chuckled the screen. 'Trip, I mean. Now *I'm* here to mark the path, we'll skip along and have a laugh.'

The gadget whirled round three times then faced the forest opening. 'Don't be anxious, don't be stressed. Gav has found the way north-west.'

'Does 'e rhyme all the time?' said Grandma.

Coriander blushed. 'Matt knows I love barn dances.'

'Hitch your rucksack on your back,' chanted Gav, 'and do-si-do along the track.' He scuttled into the forest, surprisingly quickly for a box on legs.

''E's annoyin' me already.' Grandma took Fernando out of her handbag and perched him on top of her shopping trolley.

'For sure,' he agreed.

Gav was waiting a few metres ahead. He tapped a foot impatiently while everyone smeared on insect repellent. 'Come along now, get the beat. Grab your gear and move your feet.'

The party followed him into the jungle. He darted in front, his toes a flash of silver in the gloom.

It was clear from the sawn-off tree stumps that a path had once been cut here. But the jungle was taking over again. At every step Abbie had to push away huge leaves and hairy vines. She guessed the normal rules of growth didn't apply: everything sprouted twice as fast in this rich wetness. It was like a speeded-up nature programme. With all the rustling and snapping and the sweat blurring her eyes, she could almost see the plants budding, ripening and rotting around her.

'Spin your partner, Strip the Willow. Straight on for The Armadillo,' sang Gav, hopping onto a log.

'Eef straight on,' snapped Fernando, 'let's turn heem *off*.' He glared at Gav.

Coriander nodded. 'I suppose there is a path. Maybe we should save the battery.' She picked Gav up and pressed the Off button. His legs shot into the box.

'Some people feel they must compete,' came Gav's huffy dying voice, 'just because they don't ... have ... feet.' His face vanished from the screen.

'Phew!' Grandma sighed, flopping down on a tree stump. 'Tea break.'

Abbie agreed it was time for a rest, though tea was the last thing she wanted in this steam bath. She sat on a log next to Perdita and took a water bottle from her rucksack.

'Just sips,' said Coriander. 'Antonio Monio said we'll come to a river this afternoon. We can camp there and fill up on water. But it's a few hours away yet.'

'Plus you don't want to go to the loo too often,' said Perdita, grinning. 'You never know what might be underneath.'

'Thanks,' said Abbie, pushing her off the log.

They carried on along the trail. Coriander led the way, then Perdita, then Abbie. Grandma came last, wheeling her shopping bag with Fernando perched on top. Conversation died as they fell into step with the squeak of the Trundeluxe wheels.

Abbie sank into a green dream. Light green, dark green, every in-between green. Apple green, bottle green, bean green. Pea green, sea green, looking-up-a-tree green. How could they all squeeze into one colour? If this was painting by numbers, you'd need a thousand just for green.

A branch fell onto the path. Abbie looked up. A furry bum-bag was hanging from a tree.

'Sloth!' cried Perdita, clapping her hands. 'And look, there's a baby on its stomach.' Abbie squealed with delight. Four eyes peered from china-doll faces, not at all scared – though perhaps a little annoyed – at the disturbance.

'This place is fantastic,' she said, giving Perdita a sweaty hug. 'It's so ... so–'

'Sticky?' Grandma grumbled behind her. 'Mouldy? Gloomy-rotten-stinky?'

Yes, thought Abbie, *all those things*. That was it exactly: a great glorious mess. Not just green but a thousand greens. Not just stinky but a stack of stinks. Not just hot but steamy-sopping-stifling. She imagined God going wild in his playroom, splashing and mixing the craziest sights, sounds and smells, and then hurling them into the Amazon. Even the sweat was thrilling. It pricked her stomach with tiny shocks, as if a million ants were tap-dancing under her T-shirt.

Fernando too was perking up, now that Gav had perked down. 'Aah.' He tilted his head back on the shopping bag, which was moving a lot slower without Gav setting the pace. 'The esmell of rotten leaf – I remember how I roll with my Carmen on forest floor. The howl of howler monkey – I remember how we howl through our sewn-up mouths.'

'Cut the poetry,' muttered Grandma, 'or I'll sew yours up again.'

Abbie could see that Grandma wasn't taking to the jungle. Despite the Numbskull she'd slipped under Chester, sweat was pouring down her face. He gave up wigging and slid down to stand on her shoulder and fan her cheeks.

They walked on.

And on.

And on.

The little sun that struggled through the trees began to dim.

Eventually Coriander said, 'Can you hear the river? We should be there by now.'

Above the shrieking of the forest, the squeaking of the trolley and the creaking of Grandma, it was hard to hear anything.

'Oh dear,' said Coriander. 'I hope we haven't gone wrong.' Coriander fished Gav out of her rucksack.

'Bow to your partner, turn to the right. There's a spot to spend the night.'

'Silence, bald *bandito*!' yelled Fernando.

'Keep your cool, footless fool!' piped Gav. Coriander turned him off quickly. Sure enough, down a right fork, the jungle opened onto the muddy bank of a small river.

'Perfect,' said Coriander.

Abbie and Perdita unzipped Grandma's bag. They hung the hammocks between trees and draped mosquito nets above them. Coriander lit a fire. Then she wandered around showing the girls which nuts and fruit to collect. *Thank goodness she knows*, thought Abbie, as Coriander picked a yellow fruit encased in papery leaves, which she called uvilla, and a cluster of dark red camu camu. *I'd probably poison everyone.*

Coriander went down to the river and scooped water into the cooking pot. While it was heating over the fire, she knelt down and dug up a knobbly brown root. 'Yuca,' she said, peeling the outer skin with a knife. 'It's a staple food here – full of energy.' She chopped the white flesh into cubes and dropped them into the boiling water. The girls threw in the fruit and nuts.

Grandma peered into the pot. 'Call that dinner? I could murder a steak.'

'You'll have to,' said Coriander sharply. 'Because the only steak round here is playing tag over your head. And you'll have to kill *me* before you kill them.' They looked up. Two toffee-coloured monkeys were whooping between branches.

'Capuchins.' Coriander began to hum: a breezy, teasy tune of throw and catch. The monkeys cocked their old men's heads. Then they plucked nuts from the branches and lobbed them into the cooking pot.

'Thanks,' called Coriander. She tossed two bananas into

the tree. Two skins flew down and landed on Grandma's shoulders.

Dinner tasted soft and earthy and slightly sweet: a cross between strawberries and forest floor. Afterwards they sat round the fire and watched the inky rags of bats flicker across the stars. Lilies glowed like ghosts on the river.

Abbie heard, then saw, a frog croaking its little lungs out on the bank. 'Cute,' she said, bending over the yellow-black creature.

'I wouldn't get too close, dear,' said Coriander. 'That's a poison-dart frog. Its venom is deadly.' She yawned. 'Well, I'm off to bed. Remember to check your hammocks for tarantulas. Sweet dreams.'

Thanks a bunch. Abbie climbed into her hammock and tied the cords of the mosquito net tightly. The jungle bellowed around her. She fell asleep and dreamed of poisonous frogs in white suits barn-dancing with tarantulas.

* * *

Klench looked across the lobby. 'Vot you got for me tonight?'

Mr Hunter was dragging a sack over the floor. 'Jaguar cubs.'

'Ah, splendid. Zey make most popular cutesie pets. But ooh …' Klench winced at the trail of scratch marks. 'Please to mind my floor.'

Mr Hunter eyed at him stonily. 'I'm here for hunting, not housework.'

Klench gulped. 'Of course.' He hurried round from the

desk and opened a door at the side of the lobby. 'A cage is ready in vine cellar.'

* * *

The bell went for the end of school.

'Now then, Jims and Jimeldas,' said Mr Dabbings. 'For homework tonight, please ask your mums and dads if they've got anything that needs polishing. Remember the super, um, super*visor* of the zoo café?' A snigger went round. 'Well, she's a fantastic pers–, er, polisher. And she said she'd love some extra work. I'm, ahem, helping her out while Perdita and Abigail are away.'

Marcus looked up from his homework book. 'You're what, sir?'

Mr Dabbings coughed. 'Lending a hand, Marcus, because that's what hands are for. Now, bring your stuff in tomorrow and I'll take it to the zoo. Knives, spoons, sugar bowls and the like.'

Marcus smacked his palm against his forehead. *Of course! That's it!*

He wrote his homework down. Then he underlined it. Twice.

17

I Spy

A shriek woke Abbie next morning. She blinked through her mosquito net. Was it one of those purple-throated fruit crows she'd read about in the guidebook? Or perhaps a harpy eagle, snatching Fernando in its talons for breakfast?

No, it was Grandma falling out of her hammock. 'Bingo!' she yelled, clinging to some delicious dream. 'Where the jiggery am I?'

'In heaven,' Perdita called. She was up a tree plucking fruits that looked like lumpy sunsets. 'Have a papaya.' She threw one in Abbie's direction and climbed down. 'Coming for a swim?'

Abbie untied the mosquito net and swung out of her hammock. It would be great to cool her sweaty clothes. After less than a day in the jungle she ponged to Peru.

The water wrapped her body, calm and cool. Her feet sank into mud. Something brushed against her leg. 'Er, what fish do you get in here?' she asked.

'There's pacu – that's a big fish that eats fruit,' said

Coriander, floating on her back. 'And catfish. Oh, and piranha of course.'

Abbie shrieked and waded towards the bank as fast as she could, which, through all that mud, wasn't very.

'Relax.' Coriander laughed. 'They hardly ever attack humans. They get a very bad press, you know.'

'Really?' Abbie stopped.

'Oh yes. Beneath those teeth they're poppets. It's the caimans you've got to watch out for.'

'What's a caiman?'

'That.'

Now Abbie was out of the water faster than you could say, 'You-mean-that-long-crocodile-thing-with-more-teeth-than-I've-had-Yorkie-bars-who's-resting-its-snout-on-the-water-and-giving-me-a-look-that-says-it-hasn't-eaten-for-days-and-really-fancies-a-leg-steak-from-a-well-built-girl-who-doesn't-know-her-crocs-from-her-alligators?'

Coriander smiled. She held out her hand and hummed a tune of floppy fish and lazy bathing. The caiman sliced through the water and nuzzled her shoulder with its snout.

Abbie marvelled from the bank. With Coriander here, no jaws, claws, paws or roars need ever scare them. They had nothing to fear in the jungle – except man.

One in particular.

After a breakfast of a fruit with star-shaped leaves that Coriander called false peanut because of its rich, creamy taste, they set off again. They kept the river on their right.

Walking was easier today. Splinters of blue sky broke through the trees and the air felt clearer – which wasn't to say clear, just soup with less gloop.

Even Grandma seemed happier, belting out sea shanties as she lumbered behind. She'd given up on the Numbskull, which she said was too itchy in the jungle. Chester too had abandoned her head. He sat on top of the shopping bag, making a cushion for Fernando, who, except for a tense moment when the path forked and Gav was switched on, was almost jaunty.

'Oh, Carmen, my wench,

When we wrench you from Klench,

My life begeen again.'

No one had the heart to point out that Coriander had forbidden any wrenching.

They passed three chattering squirrel monkeys and a giant anteater before stopping for lunch.

♪ 'What shall we do with the drunken sailor?' sang Grandma, plonking down on an earthy hummock. ♫ 'Early in the morn– OUCH!' She jumped up.

'You're sitting on a termite mound,' said Coriander. Amber insects emerged from the hill. They streamed to the top for the funeral of their twelve cousins who'd died under Grandma.

Lunch was nuts, seeds and cream crackers from Abbie's rucksack. Then they hit the trail again.

Two toucans later they stopped for a barley sugar.

After three scarlet macaws they shared a packet of biscuits.

Five humming birds further on Abbie's legs began to ache.

On their ninety-fourth caterpillar the forest began to darken.

And, as the four thousand two hundred and fifty-ninth soldier ant tramped across their path, Perdita whispered, 'Look.' She pointed along the path.

Twenty metres ahead the trees stopped. Beyond that was light. Not fading sunlight, not pearly moonlight. Bright, white, electric light.

Abbie gasped. There was a circular clearing in the jungle. The rim was marked by little ground lights. The river snaked round to the right. And on the far side stood the fanciest building she'd ever seen.

It looked like a giant wedding cake, white and fussy. Spotlights along the ground lit up the façade. At the bottom stood frilly pillars and arches. In the middle were balconies with fancy curved railings. And at the top, below the low roof, ran swirls of complicated plasterwork. To the left of the building lay a floodlit swimming pool. In front was a courtyard dotted with statues.

Coriander put a finger to her lips. Quietly she took off her rucksack. 'We'll set up camp off the path,' she whispered. 'The jungle will hide us.'

From a pocket in her rucksack she took out four penknives. She held one up and pressed a button on the handle. A circular blade popped out and whirred round.

'Pensaws,' said Coriander, handing them round. 'Now let's get hacking.'

The little blades sawed through vines and stems. Chester swept away the cuttings. Twenty minutes later they'd cleared enough foliage to hang the hammocks.

'I could eat a jaguar,' muttered Grandma. But meat, as usual, was off the menu. There was no question of making a fire either; they'd be spotted from the hotel in a second. So they had to make do with nuts, berries and four packets of crushed Hula Hoops from Abbie's rucksack.

It was pitch dark now – apart from their torchlight, the circular ground lights, the hotel spotlights, the moonlight and the silent scream of stars. And quiet, too, except for the hum of cicadas, the clicking of bats, the rumble of Abbie's stomach, Grandma's snores and the chatter of monkeys reading bedtime stories. Abbie lay in her hammock under her mosquito net and wondered how she'd ever get to sleep.

She was still wondering when she woke up.

'Knock knock.' Perdita's grin shoved through the mosquito net. Coriander was already up, gathering more jungle mix. Abbie's stomach took one look at the berries dropping into the pot and remembered it had an urgent business meeting. She crept into the forest as far as she dared and discovered that palm leaves make the best loo roll.

At breakfast, if you could call it that, Grandma said, ''Ow long do we 'ave to wait 'ere, eatin' monkey nuts?'

'Until we see monkey *business*,' said Coriander. 'Then we go straight back to Puyo and tell the police.'

They sat in their hammocks and took it in turns to peer through Coriander's binoculars.

It was an action-packed morning. At 9.13 two figures emerged from the hotel and lay by the swimming pool. At 10.27 one of them dived in. At 11.48 a window on the second storey opened. At 12.09 it closed.

The biggest thrill came at 1.04. 'The front door!' whispered Perdita, staring through the binoculars. 'A man's

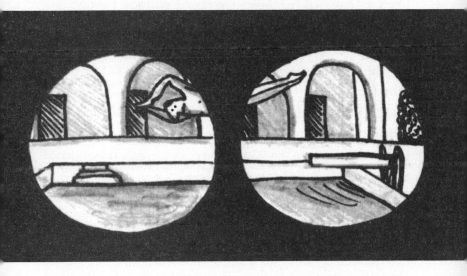

coming out. He's wearing a cowboy hat. He's looking round. He's got bandages on his hands. He's – oh, going in again.'

Lunch was granadilla (orange fruits from a tree) and Digestives (brown biscuits from a packet).

'Well, this is a lark,' said Grandma a few hours later. 'I'm bitten to death, I'm crawlin' with creepies, I've got the runs, the shakes, the sweats. We're never goin' to spot a crime at this rate. 'Ere, Chess – come and fan me face, would you?'

'Chester!' cried Abbie. 'Of course! *He* could slip into the hotel and poke about. He looks like a hairy leaf.'

'Over my dead body,' said Grandma. 'I'm not lettin' 'im out of me–'

But he'd already shot off through the undergrowth.

'Chess,' Grandma hissed, 'come back!'

'Too late!' cried Perdita.

Coriander said nothing – or rather her mouth didn't. But her brown eyes wailed reproach.

'Oh no,' Abbie mumbled. 'What have I done?'

'Only sent me best friend in the world to 'is doom!' cried Grandma.

Abbie bit her cheek. She should have known Chess would jump at the chance to help. And now Klench might catch him, put him on a lead and charge customers a fortune to watch him clean windows.

'Perhaps he return weeth my Carmen,' said Fernando hopefully.

'And 'ow precisely would 'e carry 'er?' Grandma snapped.

Coriander stood up. 'I can't sit here waiting.' She gave a little sob. 'I'll go and get dinner.'

'Me too,' said Perdita. Glaring at Abbie, they headed into the forest.

'Mine's a Big Mac,' muttered Grandma as they disappeared.

They sat in silence. Grandma turned her back on Abbie and made leaf hats for Fernando. Abbie stared through the binoculars, swallowing down tears.

There was a rustle behind. 'Chess?' She wheeled round. But it was only Perdita staggering out of the trees with

166

an armful of papayas. Coriander stumbled behind her with an armful of … what? It looked like a giant woodlouse: a brown dome of overlapping segments.

'Any sign of Chester?' asked Perdita. Abbie shook her head miserably. Perdita dropped the papayas.

Coriander put the ball down gently. She was humming softly, a tune of fat grubs and cosy burrows. Slowly it unrolled into a pointy, jointy–

'Armadillo!' breathed Abbie. Two eyes blinked. Two ears wiggled. The creature uncurled to the length of a cat. 'He's beautiful!'

'He's brill,' said Perdita fiercely. 'I've named him Brillo. We found him in a trap. Set by Klench, I bet.' She bent down and stroked the creature's ears. 'It's OK, Brillo. You're safe with us.'

'So Klench is smugglin' animals again,' said Grandma.

Coriander sucked in her breath. 'The brute. But at least he won't get this one.'

'Doesn't need to,' muttered Grandma. ''E's got somethin' better to smuggle now. My Ches–'

'–ter!' cried Abbie. A hairy ball rolled onto her shoe. She snatched him up and drenched him in kisses. 'Thank goodness!' Tears ran down her cheeks. 'I'm *so* sorry.'

Chester leapt onto Grandma. 'I was beside meself, ducks.'

Then Coriander. 'Don't ever run off again, sweetie.'

Then Perdita. 'I love you, Chess.'

'Hooray you hokay,' said Fernando impatiently, 'but what you find?'

Chester stretched out on Perdita's arm. A crumpled ball dropped out of his curls.

'What's that?' Abbie picked it up and smoothed it out into a sheet of paper. 'Looks like a list.'

Hotel Armadillo
Your junkle pillow

it said at the top. Then:

Price list for disguisink

Scar removink.......$81,500

Nostril closink......$125,380

Eye recolourink......$252,600

Neck shortenink......$368,400

Head squoshink......$802,392.57

For uzzer criminal treatments, please consult our team of top-notch docs – all in glorious surroundinks of natural vorld.

Coriander whistled. 'So that's it – cosmetic surgery for

crooks! Look at the prices. Who could afford those except the rich and infamous?'

'But my Carmen,' squeaked Fernando from the shopping trolley. 'You seen her?'

Chester hopped up and down.

'Where?' said Abbie.

Chester flattened himself on the ground.

'On the ground floor?' Perdita guessed. Chester hopped again.

Fernando swayed like a drunken grape. '*Vamos!*' he yelled. 'Come *amigos*, what we wait for?'

Coriander put her hand in front of him. 'The police,' she said firmly. 'We've got our evidence of criminal activity. *They* must take it from here.'

For a small head Fernando gave a big roar. The startled armadillo leapt three feet in the air and knocked him off the shopping trolley.

'*Estúpido!*' yelled Fernando, thudding onto the ground. 'I roll to hotel myself!'

Abbie picked him up. 'Oh no, you won't.' She popped him on her hammock. 'Klench would just kidnap you along with your wife.'

'I told you,' said Coriander, 'we're going back to Puyo.'

'Not now,' said Grandma. 'It's gettin' dark.'

'She's right, Mum,' said Perdita. 'We can't walk at night. If we set off at dawn we can be there by the morning after tomorrow.'

Lying in her hammock that night, Abbie heard Fernando

sobbing by her ear. She lay on her back and gazed at the stars. Relief and sadness curled through her. Relief that Chester was safe, sadness at spending her last night in the jungle. How would she ever describe it back home? If only she could slice a chunk from this dense, mysterious world. She'd take it with her to touch and smell forever. She opened her mouth and filled up with forest. Her tongue tasted warm, wet darkness. Her nose filled with sweetness and stinks. Her ears rang with clicks, hoots and hisses.

Especially hisses. 'Psssst.'

Abbie sat up.

'Me, I cannot esleep,' whispered Fernando.

'Me neither.' Abbie lay down again.

'What eef police, they take away my Carmen? Because she eellegal trade.'

Abbie opened her mouth then closed it. She hadn't thought of that.

'Chester, he brave. No legs, no hands, no arms, but steell he go.' Fernando sighed. 'If I have legs I creep to her.'

Abbie wriggled her legs uncomfortably.

'Eef I have hands I hug her.'

Abbie jiggled her fingers nervously.

'Eef I have arms I carry–'

'All right!' She sat up. 'I get the point.'

She swung her legs out of the hammock and fumbled for her torch. She was mad. She was stupid. She was ready.

* * *

Klench switched off the lamp on the reception desk. A shriek pierced the darkness. Only at night, when the guests were snoring between their satin sheets, did Carmen come alive to curse her captor. 'Just wait, you brute in suit! My husband, he comeeng for rescue me. Thees I esmell een my nostreels.'

Klench chuckled. Switching off his torch, he reached across the desk and punched her on the nose. 'Sleep vell, head off horror.' Then he went upstairs, changed into his mint-green pyjamas, put on his mint-green bedtime tie and got into bed.

* * *

'You must be crazy.' Greg's eyebrows shot off his forehead, flew to Mars and settled there. Or at least, that's what it sounded like down the phone. Marcus held the receiver away from his ear while Greg banged on. 'Cracked. Bonkers. Off your iPod. No wonder you wouldn't tell me at school yesterday. If anyone was listening, you'd have been arrested.'

'Sssh. Don't let your mum hear.'

'But it's so *dangerous*. People could get hurt.'

'Exactly. And no one'll know it was us.'

'*Us*? You must be joking. Look, I've got to go and finish my breakfast. See you later, dude.' The phone went dead.

Marcus slammed the receiver down. 'Who needs you, anyway?' he muttered. 'Dude.'

18

Together Again

Abbie crept round the circular clearing, keeping well back from the lights. The hotel rose in a floodlit flounce. Light shone from a few windows on the middle storey. The top- and ground-floor windows were dark. She prayed that Carmen was still *on* the ground floor, where Chester had seen her. What if Klench took her to his bedroom every night and popped her on his bedside table for company?

Abbie crouched in darkness ten metres from the entrance. For all its frills and trimmings there was a bleakness about the building. It was the perfect home for Hubris Klench: spotless, fussy and alone.

'Stop esweateeng,' hissed Fernando in her palm. 'I drown.'

'Can't help it,' rasped Abbie. She wished all the water on her hands would flow to her throat, which felt as dry as toast.

She darted across the courtyard between statues of ladies wearing bed sheets. Reaching the huge entrance door she stopped. She took a deep breath. She gripped the handle. *Please be locked, please be locked, please be–*

The door opened. Who needed locks in this lonely spot?

'Bravo!' breathed Fernando.

Her heart punching her ribs, Abbie fished the torch from her pocket. The beam swept round, glinting off the fountains and mirrors of the vast lobby.

'Who there?' squeaked a voice.

Abbie dropped Fernando in terror.

He hit the floor with a gasp, not of pain but of joy. 'My Carmen!' he breathed. 'It ees I, your Fernando.'

There was a squeal. 'My Nando, my Conquiboy! I am here on desk.'

Fernando rolled across the floor faster than an eyeball across an ice rink. Abbie rushed after him, scooped him up and set him on the desk. She shone the torch round.

'Where you?' whispered Fernando.

'Where *you*?' whispered a hairy prune on the desk.

Then three people realised three things:

1. The first hairy prune on the desk realised that the second hairy prune on the desk was her husband.
2. The second hairy prune realised that the first hairy prune was his wife.
3. Abbie realised that Fernando and Carmen had never seen each other like this because, when they were shrunk, their eyes had been sewn up.

'Aaaah,' said everyone, which was one of those sounds you don't have to be English or Spanish or joined to shoulders to make.

There was a shocked silence. Finally, Carmen whispered, 'You look like rotten plum.'

'You no peach melba yourself,' hissed Fernando.

'Why you take so long?' snapped Carmen.

'Why your neck so short?'

'Your breath estink.'

'Your hair honk.'

'For goodness sake,' hissed Abbie, 'let's just get out of here!'

'Eemposseeble,' whispered Carmen. 'I estuck to desk weeth Superdooperglooper Glue.'

There was another shocked silence. Short of carrying the desk, they were stumped.

Unless …

Abbie felt in her pocket – and thanked the Lord for inventors with plaits. 'Matt, you're a marvel,' she murmured, bringing out the pensaw.

With a low hum the blade circled the desk round Carmen's neck. The wood was hard and thick. 'Come *on*,' Abbie muttered. Her heart was flopping like a fish on a deck. Her hands were shaking like a jelly with the giggles. Round and round went the blade, deeper and deeper into the wood.

'Aiee!' shrieked Carmen, dropping out of sight. Abbie shone the torch through the hole. The head had fallen into a drawer and was sitting on a pile of envelopes.

Abbie reached down and lifted her by the hair. 'Gotcha! Let's get out of–'

A light went on. A door slammed. Feet pattered across the floor.

'Vot ze Schnik? Put zat *down!*'

Abbie froze. Hubris Klench was scuttling towards them. He wore a mint-green dressing gown and tie. He was pointing a mint-green gun.

'Vell,' he gasped, reaching the desk and snatching the pensaw from Abbie, 'knock me down viz fezzer! Do I not know you?' Abbie shook her head wildly. But she could see him flicking through his mental photo album. 'Yes,' he cried, 'page eighty-four – you are troublesome girl who spoilt my eefil-doinks last summer. Vot in schnorkels are you doink here?'

'Mmff,' she explained.

Klench nodded. 'Just as I thought. And look at ziss ...' A smile crawled across his face, like a leech making for blood. 'Anuzzer small head.' He leafed again through his mind-album. 'Yes, page eighty-five – you are Fernando Feraldo, troublesome helper of spoilink girl. Vot joy to see you agains. Let me shake you by ze nose.' He gave it a tweak, bringing tears to Fernando's eyes. 'You are most velcomes,' he chuckled, 'to Hotel Armadillo. A little late in evenink, perhaps. But no probs: I have perfect accommodations.'

He waved the gun towards an archway in the wall. 'Please to brink your friends yunk lady.'

Clutching Fernando in one hand and Carmen in the other, Abbie stumbled towards the archway. *Let this be a dream*, she prayed. But the gun in her back and the cruel smell of Klench's soap were as real as the wobble in her legs.

Through the arch he pushed Abbie down a wooden staircase. At the bottom was a door. Klench took a key from a hook on the wall. 'Sveet dreaminks,' he sang, unlocking the door and shoving her through. 'Tomorrow ve decide how to settle old scores.' The door slammed. The key turned in the lock.

'Ohhh,' Abbie whimpered into the darkness.

'Put me down!' squeaked Carmen. 'You pull out my hair.' Abbie set the two heads on the floor. Then she ran her hand over the wall and found a light switch. The bare bulb lit up an empty room with an earthen floor and bare plaster walls. There were no windows, just a tiny air vent below the ceiling.

She sank against the wall. 'What have I done?' she groaned.

'You done great,' said Fernando. 'You find my wife.'

'But no one knows we're here. Klench could leave us to rot and die!'

'So what?' said Carmen. 'I already rotten died.'

'But *I* haven't!' Abbie wailed.

Fernando cleared what he had of a throat. 'May I eentroduce? Carmen, thees Abeegail. She brave *amiga*. Abeegail, thees my …' He couldn't say it. 'Oh, Carmencita, you are sight. What they do to you?'

'You can espeak! My face *your* fault. How many times I tell you, do not esteal gold for Spain? How many times I warn you that Jivaro tribe, they keell us if we raid their land? Oh, you foolish fool. You headstrong head. I eshame of you; I eshame of my country.'

'*Escúchame …*'

'No!' Carmen snapped. 'Never again I leesten to you. And never again I espeak eSpaneesh.' She spun her wooden stand round to face the wall and stuck her nose in the air. 'From now I espeak only Eengleesh that I learn from small Merv.'

Fernando hung his head: not easy when there's nothing to hang it from.

Abbie moaned with rage – at Klench, at Fernando and most of all at herself. What had she been thinking, marching into this web like a fluorescent fly? Mum would never trust her again. Aaaaah – Mum would never *see* her again! She curled up on the floor and sobbed herself to sleep.

* * *

Klench slept fitfully after the night's disturbance. He woke while it was still dark, dressed and waddled downstairs to the lobby. On the bottom step he froze. Mr Hunter was heaving a huge sack through the entrance door. The poacher was doing a great job – sack after sack was coming in between sundown and sunrise – and Klench was glad to leave him to it. The man made him nervous.

And nerves, like most things, made him hungry. When Mr Hunter had crossed the lobby and gone through the door to the kitchen, Klench headed to the lounge for a pre-breakfast snack.

He gulped. It was already full of guests.

'Hey you!' called a voice as Klench headed for the coffee pot. 'We need to talk.' Brag Swaggenham's bandaged hand clamped his shoulder. 'The pain, Tubman. When ya gonna fix it? Ah couldn't sleep a wink.'

The Pittsburgh Pearl Pincher, still blinded by a headband, came up behind him and bumped into a chair. 'Me neither. I'm in agony.'

'Me too,' moaned the man in the chair, whose head was bound in bubble wrap.

Klench turned to the bar. He needed something stronger than coffee. 'Lime soda,' he ordered across the bar, 'extra sour.' The barman, a young man from a nearby village, got squeezing.

A wasp-faced man with a brick on his head staggered up. 'Hey, Klench, this is doing my nut in.'

'But, Mr Gangster Man, your neck is squoshink so nice,' Klench said nervously.

'So's my brain. If you don't cure this headache I want my money back. And my neck.'

'Ad by dostrils,' said a woman with a box round her nose who was sitting on a sofa.

'Pardon?' said the man next to her whose ears were wrapped in cling film.

A little girl on his other side scowled at Klench. 'You're stealing animals from the jungle, aren't you? I just saw that man dragging in a sack.' She stuck out her tongue. 'You're mean. Animals are nicer than people.' And considering that her parents had robbed a hundred and twenty-two banks, who could blame her for thinking that?

Klench smiled weakly at her parents. 'Vot a cute little popsie.' They glowered back. The room filled with whines and whimpers. 'Please, everyones.' Klench clasped his hands. 'You must be patient. You have had major ops. Your vounds vill take time to heal.'

'Don't talk to *me* about time!' shrieked the Pittsbugh Pearl Pincher. 'I've been waiting four days. I need a painkiller – now!'

Voices rose angrily in agreement.

Klench grabbed his lime soda. He drank it in one gulp. Then he pushed past the guests and out of the room.

The barman lifted the empty glass, frowning thoughtfully.

* * *

'Dad, I've been asked to stay late at school today.' Marcus swallowed a piece of toast.

'Why?' Terry Strode-Boylie didn't look up from *The Times*.

'To help some of the others with Maths. Mr Dabbings says I'm better than he is.' Marcus took a swig of orange juice.

Terry glanced up. His light-blue eyes rested on Marcus for the first time in days. 'Really? He's finally realised you out-*class* him, eh?' He scrawled the pun on the sports page to use in his next children's book. 'Good. Don't be too helpful, though. Can't have anyone beating the Boylies, now, can we?'

'No, Dad.'

Terry went back to his paper, muttering, 'Glad to see that teacher's got a brain. I was beginning to think there was nothing but hummus between those sideburns.'

Genevieve popped an apple into Marcus's lunch box. 'What time shall I pick you up, darling?'

'Dunno how long it'll take. It's OK, I'll catch the five-thirty bus home.'

Marcus got up before she could argue. That should just give him time to leg it to the zoo and back.

19

No Escapinks

'Stubborn, reckless and keen on Jammy Dodgers,' said the vicar.

'She preferred Bourbons,' sighed Dad.

Ollie kicked earth into the grave.

'Mind your shoes!' Mum wailed.

'Let him mess,' said Dad, 'we're in mourning ... mournink ...'

'Mornink.'

Abbie opened her eyes. Her lids throbbed. Her nose stung. Her head pounded.

'Your breakfast,' said Klench, who stood at the door with his minty gun. A tray was on the floor in front of Abbie. Next to it stood a bucket.

'You're not going to starve me, then?' mumbled Abbie.

Klench yawned. 'Borink.'

Abbie glanced at the plate of white mush on the tray. 'Or poison me?'

'Dull. I vill dream up somethink more funs. In meantime, zere iss bucket for your ...'

'I know,' Abbie said. 'You *have* held me hostage before.'

Klench chuckled. 'Ah yes. That voss practice. Ziss time zere iss no escapinks.'

Abbie's chin trembled. She'd forgotten how solid he was. A cannonball would bounce off that white suit.

She took a deep breath. 'You can't scare me,' she lied.

'Oh no?' Klench clicked his heels. 'Ve see about zat, my dear.' He marched out.

'Bravo,' said Fernando as the key turned.

'What?' snapped Abbie.

'I mean–'

'He mean bravo you not estarve.' Carmen glared at her husband. 'Say what you mean and mean what you say, head case.'

'Please forgeeve me, darleeng,' Fernando whined. 'Four hundred year too long for angry.'

'Four thousand year too short,' snapped Carmen.

'For goodness sake, stop arguing!' cried Abbie. She drank some water from a bottle on the tray and picked at the food on the plate. 'We have to keep calm. Think straight. Consider our options.'

She did all that. Then she burst into tears.

She sat there for ages, sobbing quietly while the heads bickered their heads off, until–

'Sssh!' Fernando hissed. 'Someone come.'

The door opened. And in tottered the craziest sight. Her cheeks were blotched red. Green feathers framed her sunglasses. Her wispy hair flew in all directions. She wore a glittering blue jacket. She perched on high wooden heels. 'Grandma!' Abbie flew into her arms.

'Thank 'eavens,' breathed Grandma. She hugged Abbie tight. Then she pushed her away. 'What the butternut were you thinkin' of? You've caused no end of trouble!'

Klench followed her in. In one hand he clutched a padlocked box. 'Vunce again ve meet over gun, Madam.' He waved it in his other hand. 'Remember last summer, in Hair Museum, ven I held you hostage so fine?'

''Ow could I forget?' Grandma glared at him with anything but fear. 'And give Chester back *this minute!*' She reached out to grab the box.

Klench sprang back. 'Zat I cannot. I never forget how ziss hairy creature escaped museum and fetched polices.' He wiggled the padlock. 'It vill not happen again, you understand.'

'Understand, my udder! All I know is you're a prize baddie up to your prize baddery. Shame on you.' Grandma jabbed her finger at him.

Klench blinked. A look came into his eye that Abbie recognised from his last encounter with Grandma. Respect. Bullying was clearly a language he understood. 'I am sorry to lock you ups, Madam. I have thought about you much since our last meetink. And I see vunce more you are voman of grits.' Then another look crept into his eye, sly and eager. 'Somethink occurs to me. Viz your boldness and plucks, you vould make fine partner in crime. Perhaps, if you agree to join me in vickeds, I vill consider lettink you go.'

Grandma's jaw dropped.

185

Klench waved his gun. 'Think about it, Madam.' Bowing, he backed out of the door.

Abbie gasped as Grandma's glittery blue jacket rose into a cloud and wafted out after him. Underneath was her old brown cardie.

'Of all the cheek!' Grandma exploded. 'And there go me glad rags too. Well, good riddance!' She shook her fist at the closing door. Then she bent down and patted Fernando. 'At least you're OK, ducks. Now, 'ow about introducin' me.' She cocked her head at Carmen.

'Of course.' Fernando cleared his throat. 'Grandma, thees my wife. And Carmen, thees ... oh, Grandma, why you dress like that?'

'Disguise.' Grandma sat down and broke the crazy heels off her shoes. 'Tried to sneak in as a rich customer so I could rescue you.' She pointed to her blotchy cheeks. 'Fake blusher from a berry. And me blue jacket that just flew away – Morpho butterflies. I smeared me cardie with guava juice and they swarmed on me.' She waved the heels about. 'Branches of teak trees. And *these*,' she tapped the feathers on her glasses, 'I pinched from a parrot.'

'How did Klench get Chester?' said Abbie.

Grandma winced. 'I was wearin' 'im in a new style so that Klench wouldn't recognise me. But the tree sap I used as gel made 'im itch. When I came to reception 'e was wrigglin' all over the place. So Klench just whisked 'im off me 'ead.'

'Oh no.' Abbie recalled how Chester had escaped through the window of the Hair Museum last summer. Now any chance of him flying out the window had – well – flown out the window. 'What about Perdita and Coriander? Did they come with you?'

Grandma snorted. 'Did they monkeys! When we found you were missin' this mornin' I knew exactly where you'd gone. They refused to come lookin'. Said we'd *all* be kidnapped.'

A knife twisted in Abbie's stomach. 'Some friends,' she mumbled, tears pricking her eyes. The people she'd come to trust more than anyone. The girl she'd stuck by at school, the mother she'd admired more than her own – bottling out, too chicken to rescue her.

Grandma patted her arm. 'Don't be too 'ard on them. You know 'ow scared they are of Klench. And they were right. I *'ave* been kidnapped. At least they've gone to fetch the police.'

Abbie sniffed. 'If one of *them* was kidnapped, the other would be here like a shot. But they didn't come for me.'

Grandma planted her hands on her hips. 'No, but *I* did! Let me tell you, missy,' she poked Abbie's shoulder, 'if anythin' 'appened to you, I – I couldn't live with meself.'

Abbie looked at the berry-stained, ex-butterflied old bat. 'I love you, Grandma,' she said.

'Pretty fond of you meself, you pig-'eaded nincompoop.'

Abbie couldn't help smiling. 'Look who's talking.'

'Any road, Perdita and Coriander should reach Puyo tomorrow morning. They'll come and rescue us by police 'elicopter. So by tomorrow evening we'll be safe and sound. Simple as that.'

'Yes,' said Abbie, wishing she believed her. Nothing had been simple on this trip. Tomorrow was miles away. And in the meantime, what tricks did Klench have up his very wide sleeve?

* * *

None, as it happened – just an extremely clean hanky. Sitting in his office, a room off the lobby, Klench pulled it out. 'But Mummy,' he reasoned, 'I like ziss voman. She is stronk and brave like you.'

'How *dare* you!' thundered Inner Mummy. '*No* vun is like me. I am vunder of vorld.'

'Yes, yes.' Klench nodded vigorously. 'I just mean ziss voman too is gutsy. I remember how she told me offs in Hair Museum last summer, vhile I pointed gun at her. She showed much plucks. Imagine – viz such darink she could make fine lady criminal. Please let her join us. Zen ve can train her.'

'Don't be fool, and stop your drool. I can see at glance she iss not eefil-doinks type.'

'But Mums.' Klench gave a little sniff. 'Beink bad is lonely job.'

'Vot you on about? Alvays I am here to chat and boss you arounds.'

'True,' sighed Klench. 'How I ever get rid off you?'

Mummy was just about to cane him on the brain when

there was a knock at the door. 'Vipe your snots and pull up socks,' she hissed.

Klench opened the door. 'Vot you vont?' he barked.

The barman from the lounge blinked in the doorway. '*Señor*,' he said nervously, 'I have idea.'

Klench frowned. 'How dare you disturb me in office, smelly servant!' He started to close the door.

'I can help. With problem of pain.'

Klench stared at him. 'You? You arc junkle man. Vot you know about vunders of modern science?'

'Not me. My uncle. He know wonders of *ancient* science.'

A smile crawled across Klench's face, like a maggot heading for meat. 'You mean your uncle is medicine man?'

The barman nodded.

Klench glanced round the lobby. 'You better come ins.'

* * *

'Marcus! Coo-ee!' Mr Dabbings waved through the window of the zoo café.

Cursing, Marcus went in. Might have known Dabbers would be here. Now he'd have to explain himself.

Mr Dabbings skated across the café floor in his knitted socks. 'What brings *you* here after school?'

Marcus blushed. 'I was just … well, when you said you were helping out, I wondered if I could help too. Just till Perdita and Abigail get back. When *is* that, by the way?'

Wendy looked up from the counter, where she was polishing Mr Dabbings's shoes. 'End of next week, I think.'

Mr Dabbings glanced at Wendy then cleared his throat. 'That's very kind and thoughtful of you, Marcus. But I'm not sure Wendy needs more help.'

It was Wendy's turn to blush. 'No. Bran – I mean Mr Dabbings – is doing a wonderful job. He's knitting winter cosies for my teapots.' She pointed to a pile of wool on the counter.

Mr Dabbings gazed into her eyes. 'And when they're done I'll knit summer ones.'

'Maybe spring and autumn too,' giggled Wendy.

'Ooh, that'll take *ages*,' sighed Mr Dabbings. He tore his eyes away. 'So we're doing fine, Marcus, just the two of us. But thanks for the offer.'

'I didn't mean help in the café. I meant with the animals. Cleaning them out and stuff. Maybe this weekend.'

'Oh, I see. Well, that *is* a nice offer. Especially after your last rather *unfortunate* visit.'

Marcus forced a smile. 'I thought it might, um, help me get over my fear, sir. Forgive and forget and all that.'

'Excellent. You've obviously been practising our Forgive and Forget dance. Why don't we teach it to Wendy now?'

'Um, no thanks. I'll go and find the zookeeper. Do you know where he is?'

'At the hippo pool, I think,' said Wendy.

'Thanks.' Marcus rushed out. He looked back to see Mr Dabbings spinning Wendy in the Kiss-'n'-Make-Up Twirl. Then he ran to the hippo pool, where he found Charlie Chumb scrubbing Hepzibah's ears with a very long brush.

20

Jungle Juice

The cellar door opened. Klench came in with a tray. He bent his little leggies and laid it on the ground. 'Bon appateets.' He waved his gun at the food.

Abbie stared. After her recent diet, it was a feast. There were some kind of sausages with some kind of sauce and some kind of chips. There were two serviettes, folded into paper armadillos, *and* two bowls of chocolate mousse.

'I trust you are OK, madam.' Klench bowed. The smell of pickled gherkins scoured Abbie's nose. His idea of after-shave?

I don't believe it, she thought. *He's trying to impress Grandma.*

It didn't quite work. 'Me – OK?' she roared. 'I couldn't be worse! You're a crime against 'umanity. Let us out this minute!' Seizing her wooden heels, she jumped up and tried to stab Klench. The spikes bounced off his stomach.

He snatched them out of her hand. 'Ah,' he sighed, 'you are feisty girl. Vunce more I invite you to join me in ...'

He trailed off. His smooth face scrunched in concentration, as if he was listening to something in his ear. But Abbie could see no wires.

'She *iss* velcome,' he mumbled. Then he looked at Grandma again: '… in eefils,' he finished.

Grandma put her hands on her hips. 'Join *you*? I'd rather join a troupe of dancin' bears.'

Klench's face fell. His chin collection wobbled. Was it Abbie's imagination or did he mutter something like, 'Go vay, Mums'? Then he cleared his throat. 'In zat case,' he barked, 'zere iss no choice but to proceed viz punishment.'

Abbie's mouth went as dry as Dubai. 'What punishment?' she whispered.

'I have thought up somethink most interestinks.' A smile wriggled across Klench's face like an eel approaching a minnow. 'Somethink to shut you ups so you can never report my eefil-doinks. But not to vorry.' He straightened his tie. 'Ass I said before: no killink. Ven I am done, you vill be free to go.' He turned and marched out, slamming the door.

'What does he mean, shut us up?' whispered Abbie.

''Oo knows?' Grandma sank to the floor. 'But while we're waitin' we might as well tuck in.'

They did. And, considering they were prisoners in a trap they'd walked straight into, locked up by a rogue whose roguery knew no bounds, in a room with nothing but a bucket for relief and two mini heads for company, who resumed their bickering the moment Klench left … it tasted pretty good.

* * *

192

Upstairs Klench scuttled across the lobby. Before he could shut his *prisoners* up, he had to shut his *guests* up. Their moans were growing louder by the hour.

The barman was waiting at the entrance.

'Let us be offs.' Klench pushed him out the door.

* * *

Darkness was falling in the jungle village. The old man looked up from his pot. He peered through the trees. Something was rustling, crunching, crashing through the undergrowth. A tapir? Too clumsy. A peccary? Too pale.

The old man jumped up. He backed towards his hut, blinking. A melon on legs was waddling towards him. At its side came ... was that his nephew Quempo, returning at last from that horrible hotel?

Quempo the barman ran to greet his uncle. Klench hung back. Two naked children ran out of a hut. They pointed and giggled. Klench stepped forward and boxed their ears. More children spilled out of the huts dotted round the clearing. Behind them came men in shorts and women in wraparound dresses.

Klench loosened his tie. Sweat poured down his face. He opened his mint-green briefcase. The curly grey towel that was stuck to the lining wriggled madly. 'Be still, vig of Grandma,' he hissed, grabbing the free end and mopping his brow. Transferring it from the padlocked box hadn't been such a good idea. There was no danger of it escaping – Bitter Albert's Superdooperglooper Glue had seen to that – but the wig squirmed far too much to serve as the soothing facecloth he'd hoped for. Stuffing it back in the case he barked at the barman, 'Hurry ups. Ask old man for medicine to kill pain.'

Quempo translated. The old man shouted back, waving his arms about furiously.

'Uncle angry,' said Quempo. 'He say you steal animals from forest. When he find them in traps he free them. He say animals are food for jungle people, they belong to jungle. Why you take them away? He say jungle not happy.'

'Ooh, poor little junkle,' said Klench rather childishly, even for someone who'd celebrated his last birthday by sending himself a Baked Alaska the size of Alaska. 'You tell *Uncle* that junkle vill soon be vay sad indeed. Becoss I have guest who plans to dig for oil.'

There followed more shouting from the uncle. Then some quiet words from Quempo, which seemed to calm him down. Then some excited chatter between them. Then some nodding and grinning from both. And then …

'Uncle change mind,' said Quempo. 'He say he glad to help you with medicine for pain.'

'Superdoops!' Klench clapped his hands. 'He is vise old codger – I knew he vould see senses. Let us celebrate.' He opened his briefcase again. The village children crowded round, their eyes huge with hunger.

Klench brought out a doughnut. 'Now, kids, you may votch me eat.' He took a bite. The children drooled. Quempo stared. And the medicine man got to work, collecting, crushing and cackling.

***

Two hours later Klench stumbled through the hotel entrance. He was scratched, bitten, filthy, exhausted … and triumphant. He pointed to the pot that Quempo had carried from the forest. 'Pour junkle juice into bottles. Then go and vosh, stinky boy.'

'And same to you,' hissed Inner Mummy. 'You smell like poo.'

Immune to his whimpers of weariness, she made him scrub, lather, rinse and polish all over. Which, for someone with so *much* all over, took a very long time. Dawn was creeping through the trees by the time he laid down his mint-green scouring flannel and fell into bed.

He was woken by a rumbling sound. 'Hush, my friend.' Patting his stomach, he glanced at his bedside clock. No wonder. It was well past lunch time. He rolled out of bed. 'Let us get some foods.' The rumbling grew louder. Klench dressed groggily and waddled to the window. Leaves were shivering and branches swaying on the trees around the jungle clearing. The air pulsed in a rhythmic roar. Klench frowned. Surely not even *his* stomach could cause such a rumpus.

'Ah,' he murmured as a helicopter lumbered into view. 'But strange – no arrivals are due today.'

Inner Mummy's shriek blasted away the last cobwebs of sleep. 'Unexpected guests mean trouble. Call for back-up, at ze double!'

Klench rushed down to the lounge. And five minutes later a welcome team was in place.

The helicopter juddered to the ground. The propellers slowed and stopped. The door opened. Six figures climbed out and dashed across the clearing towards the hotel courtyard.

Klench sprang from behind a statue. 'Not so fasts!' His welcome team leapt from the bushes round the clearing, brandishing an impressive array of personal firearms: pistols, revolvers, even a rifle or two. The visitors were surrounded.

'Hands up,' Klench barked, 'and veapons down. You are much outnumbered.'

Four of the visitors dropped their guns. The fifth dropped the creature she was holding in her arms. And the sixth took one look at Klench and burst into tears.

21

A Fate more Interesting than Death

'When are they *coming*?' Abbie kicked the earthen floor. Sweat trickled down the back of her neck.

It was the following evening. The tension was terrible. All day they'd been waiting for the rescue party.

'Any minute now,' said Grandma.

'You said that three hours ago.' What a day it had been. They'd had nothing to do except listen to Carmen as she unleashed four hundred years of fury on Fernando. 'You husband of hopeless!'

'How many time I must say sorry?'

'Eight thousand five hundred twenty-six. So far you done nineteen.'

'You proud as Peru.'

'You estupid as Spain.'

By seven o'clock Abbie's hope of being rescued was battling with her dread that they wouldn't be. Hope smacked Dread in the face. Dread kicked Hope in the butt.

The cellar door opened. Hope and Dread shook hands. They'd both won. The rescuers had arrived ... but not to rescue.

Coriander fell through the door. Perdita stumbled in behind her. Then came Klench with his minty gun.

'Abbie!' cried the Platts, rushing over.

What Abbie *meant* to say was, 'How could you abandon me?' But their tears and hugs melted her anger. 'I'm sorry,' she mumbled. 'This is all my fault.'

'Never mind the luvvy-doves,' Grandma bellowed, 'where are the police?'

'On safari, Madam.' Klench bowed in the doorway. 'Zey came to arrest *me*, but *I* arrest *zem*.'

'He heard the helicopter,' sobbed Coriander. 'We didn't stand a chance with all those guns.'

Guns, thought Abbie. *Whoever invented them should be shot.*

'At least Brillo escaped,' said Perdita. 'He came all the way to Puyo with us and back in the helicopter. But when we were caught he ran into the jungle.'

'Thank goodness,' said Abbie. She glared at Klench, fury overcoming her fear. 'You'll never get him. He's smarter than you.'

'Unlike policemans.' Klench chuckled. 'Zose four silly sausages are now beink led into junkle. Zey are bound in blindfolds and zeir hands are tied. Much more fun zan killink, no? Zey can play Blind Man's Buffs and Pin ze Tail on Jaguar. Zey vill never make it back to city.'

'You monster!' said Coriander.

Klench smiled. 'Alvays ze compliments. I remember zem vell from our lovely kidnap chattinks last summer. It is good to have you back, my dear.' He turned to Grandma. The sarcasm in his voice gave way to a wheedling tone. 'Madam. I ask vun last time. Vill you join me in life of crimes?'

Grandma rose. She rolled up her cardie sleeves. She pointed her finger at Klench. She gave a look that said it all. Then, just to make sure, she said it all. ''Ear this, you great space 'opper. I'd sooner rob a bank … shoot a president … take the last Smartie from an orphan's *party* pack … than join you in a life of crime.'

Klench shook his head sadly. Abbie could swear he mumbled something like, 'You vin, Mums.' Then he straightened his tie. 'In zat case, I have no choice. You too must be silenced. Tomorrow doctors vill come to perform operation.'

'What operation?' Abbie had spent the whole day imagining what tortures Klench might have planned. She'd pretty much covered them all.

But not quite.

'Brain trimmink.'

A gasp went round.

Klench rubbed his hands. 'Dr Ecclescake has kindly agreed to shrink your grey matters. A simple shavink of temporal lobe to remove a most unhelpful function.'

'What?' whispered Abbie.

'Memory. At least, lonk-term memory. After removal, you vill remember only last three seconds of your life.'

'No!' Perdita clutched her head. 'You're turning us into goldfish!'

'Oh no.' Klench smiled reassuringly. 'Latest research shows goldfish can remember several months. You vill be more like fruit flies, vich, as you probably know,' he nodded at Coriander, 'are most cheerful creatures. So really I am doink you big favour.'

'Why not just kill us and be done?' thundered Grandma.

'Becoss killink is messy and borinks and any old fool can do it. Ziss is more ... creative. And besides, madam ...' Klench sighed, 'I could never kill so fine a voman as you. No, here is vin-vin situation. Vunce you are all adjusted, you vill forget ziss place and my vickeds. Zen you are free to go. You vill be flown to edge of junkle. From zere you can return to civilisation.' He backed out of the door, chuckling. 'Alzough you vill have to ask many directions.'

* * *

Upstairs, Klench crossed the lobby to his office. Unlocking the door, he barged in and collapsed on his tapir-skin sofa. Everything had worked out perfectly. The guests had all received their bottles of painkiller mixed by Quempo's uncle. The prisoners were awaiting their fate more interesting than death. The day had been a triumph of eefil-doink.

So why did he feel so low?

He opened his briefcase and bent towards Grandma's

wig. The grey curls shuddered as he yanked them up and dabbed away a tear.

He hadn't felt this miserable in years. Not since he was five, when Mummy had found him in the garden making a daisy chain ...

'How sveet,' she'd cried, gouging his parting with a fond fingernail. 'A necklace for Mumsie.'

'No,' he'd explained, ''ziss for my teacher, Miss Domestoss.'

'*Vot?*' Mummy had barked. 'How dare you!'

'Vot I done wronk?' whimpered little Hubris.

'You make gift for somebody else!' Mummy spat the last two words as if they were very rude.

'But–'

'Don't you "but" me!' She snatched the daisy chain and swallowed it in one gulp. Then she leaned towards him. 'Remember ziss ...' Even now, forty-seven years later, Klench could smell her vinegar breath ... 'All your presents come to me. Or your life vill GHASTLY be.'

For the rest of the afternoon Mummy had sat in her deckchair feeding Klench slug after slug after slug after–

'Hubes.' Inner Mummy broke into his memory. 'It vosn't like zat.' She sounded hurt.

'Zat's how I remember it,' he snivelled.

'No, darlink. I svollowed daisy chain in *two* gulps. Now, get over it. Vipe your nose and touch your toes.'

Klench stood up. He couldn't even *see* his toes – just Grandma's shopping bag on wheels and the two rucksacks that he'd confiscated from Coriander and Perdita. They sprawled on the floor, unzipped and stinky with jungle. 'Filthy bags. Do not pollute my office!' He opened the door and kicked them out into the lobby. Slamming the door shut, he gave a groan of loneliness. 'I cannot go on!'

'Have snack,' suggested Inner Mummy. 'Just ziss vunce. A bite of bic vill cheer you quick.'

'OK, Mumser.' Klench went to his desk and took a specially imported Chocolate Hobnob from a tin.

It didn't help. His heart still hurt like the blazes. He sat down, laid his head on the desk and cried his little eyes out.

* * *

What a way to spend your Saturday, tramping round in wellies with wild beasts and weirdos. Especially weirdos. Marcus stared at Charlie Chumb. The zookeeper was wheeling a machine towards the tiger cage. It was some sort of box on wheels with a tube coiled round one side. 'Is that a vacuum cleaner?' asked Marcus, hugging himself against the cold.

'Not exactly,' said Charlie. 'It's a ... you know.'

Marcus absolutely didn't.

'A Muck Sucker,' Charlie continued. 'Invented by Perdita's, um, dad. Sucks up the – you know – without me having to go into Silvio's, um ... Just press this, er ...'

Marcus pressed a button on the box. There was a low hum. Charlie uncoiled the tube and threw it over the top of the tiger cage, like a fisherman casting a line.

The mouth of the tube landed by Silvio's paw. The tiger stopped pacing.

Marcus gulped. 'Is it safe? What if he eats it?'

'He won't. It's made of reinforced – you know. You'll be, um ...'

'Fine?' Marcus said hopefully.

Charlie nodded. 'You just pull this, ah ...' He pointed to a lever on the Muck Sucker.

Marcus pulled the lever. Inside the cage, the tube wriggled. He directed it to a pile of dung. With a kissy noise the dung shot up the tube. 'Wow.'

'Well done. I'll be with the, um ... if you need me.' Charlie headed off towards the tapir pen.

Marcus yanked another lever. This was almost fun.

Uh-oh! The tube flipped onto Silvio's back. It sucked at his fur. The tiger growled and turned towards Marcus.

'Yikes!' Jerking the lever, Marcus managed to flick the tube away. But Silvio wasn't impressed. He continued to pace towards Marcus, fixing him with angry yellow eyes. Marcus turned the machine off and backed away from the cage.

'Hey!' came a woman's voice. Marcus looked to his right. *Oh no.* It was that newspaper lady.

'Aren't you the boy who came into my office the other day?' said Corky Shocka. 'What are you doing here? I thought that jumped-up dad of yours wanted to close the zoo down.'

Marcus gulped. *Now what?* 'He, um, changed his mind,' he said feebly.

'I should think so. I come here every Saturday. It's the highlight of my week.' As she turned to go she called over her shoulder, 'Glad to see you helping out, young man. This is a great place.'

Marcus stuck out his tongue at the back of her head. *Yeah, for stinkers and snarlers.* He stamped a furious wellie.

Come on, he scolded himself. *You've got this far.* The supplies were in his rucksack. The plan was going perfectly. He still had a few hours to find the right moment.

He bit his lip. That was the tricky part.

22

Sweet Dreams

Down in the cellar on Saturday morning Fernando was trying to comfort the prisoners. 'Ees not so bad. We lose bad memories too. And we have many, eh, my Carmen?'

'Thanks to you, donkey doo!' she yelled. 'You poop of sheep, you pat of cow.'

'But what about the good ones?' Perdita cried. 'Birthdays and picnics and how to do cartwheels?'

'What about people?' Coriander clutched her two front plaits. 'Oh, Matt, we won't know who you are.' She grabbed Perdita and hugged her tight. They rocked and moaned.

Oh, Mum. Oh, Dad. Oh, Bourbons. Abbie grabbed Grandma and hugged her tight. They moaned and rocked.

* * *

In her bedroom on the first floor, the Pittsburgh Pearl Pincher rocked and moaned *and* moaned and rocked. Five days after her operation and it still felt as if a knife was gouging her eyeballs. She fumbled blindly in her bag for the painkiller Klench had given her. She didn't trust that man an inch – for all she knew it could be poison – but anything was better than this. Her fingers closed round the bottle. She brought it out, unscrewed the cap and drank. Licking her lips, she sat back and closed her eyes. 'Mmm!' It tasted as sweet as revenge.

But whose?

She fell asleep. In her dream, a blurry form appeared. Slowly it came into focus: a white-haired lady wearing a pearl necklace. A second old lady appeared by her side, then a third, then a fourth, until row upon row of old ladies, all in pearl necklaces, stood facing her.

The Pearl Pincher shifted uneasily in her sleep.

The first old lady un-did her necklace and held it up in a U-shape. 'You stole this from me.' She glared at the Pearl Pincher.

'And this from me,' said the second lady, holding up her necklace.

'And this … and this …' echoed the others in a rising tide of anger.

The Pearl Pincher moan-ed softly.

The first lady pulled the clasp off her necklace. She slid a pearl off the string and rolled it in her hand. The others did the same.

'Lift,' said the first lady, raising her fist. 'Aim … fire.'

Pearl after pearl came flying at the Pincher. They slammed into her like giant hailstones. She turned to run. But her feet slipped on the pearls and she got nowhere. They were piling up around her, to her knees, her chest, her chin. They blocked her ears and filled her mouth, almost – but never quite – choking her: an endless burial alive.

The Pearl Pincher screamed in her sleep.

✳✳✳

In the room next door, Brag Swaggenham sat on his bed. His fingertips were throbbing in agony. He leaned towards his bedside table and snagged the bottle of painkiller between his wrists. He pulled off the cap with his teeth, held the bottle between his lips, threw back his head and swallowed. 'Aaah.' Sweetness spread down his throat. He lay back on his bed and dozed off.

He dreamed he was walking through the jungle. Plants crowded on every side: fat vines, spiky ferns and garish flowers with huge, fleshy leaves. Wherever he looked a tree or creeper blocked his view.

'Outta my way.' He kicked a vine that lay across his path. It whipped round his ankles, reared like a snake and strung him upside down. Brag shrieked as the jungle closed in. The ferns bent towards him, jabbing spikes into his face. The flowers

grew brighter, daz-
zling him with their
reds and yellows. Their
fat leaves split into huge
leering mouths.

'I hate ya, nateya!' cried
Brag.

'We know you do,' whis-
pered the mouths. 'We hate you
too. You chop, you drill, you steal,
you spill. You kill, you kill, you
kill, you ki–'

Brag shrieked as the mouths gaped wider
and closer, forever on the verge of swallowing him whole.

* * *

All down the corridor, guests drank the juice, fell asleep and
suffered nightmares of their victims' revenge. The wasp-
faced gangster whined in terror as a rival he'd once stabbed
brandished the knife at him, endlessly about to plunge it in.
The bank-robbing couple screamed as a clerk they'd shot
turned the gun on them and repeatedly cocked the trigger.
The bubble-wrapped man sobbed in despair as the business
partner he'd cheated gave evidence upon evidence in an
interminable trial.

If only Klench had known.

* * *

He opened an eye. How long had he been there, snivelling into his desk? He lifted his head. Oh, how it ached. He gazed at the shelf on the opposite wall. A row of brown bottles, waiting to cure the pain of future guests, gazed back.

Klench blinked. Wasn't his anguish as great as theirs? Didn't his loneliness scream as loudly as any levelled eye or squashed neck? He reached for a bottle, unscrewed it and drank. He leaned back in his chair. His eyelids drooped. He nodded off.

Oh dear. Where do we start?

With a long, long queue. Lining up patiently in his mind were the hordes of people he'd hurt. Why? For sharing the one thing he'd never had. And what was that?

Happiness.

First came the hundred and eighty-four pensioners to whom he'd given Chinese burns just for greeting him in the street. Smiling sweetly, they surged towards him in his dream and pushed him onto his back. Before he could get up, they seized his arms and legs and pinned him to the ground.

Then came Jonty Chuckle, the little boy whom Klench had once seen hugging his dad on the pavement. Enraged by such a show of love, Klench had snatched Jonty's toy rabbit and bitten its ear off. Now Jonty knelt down and gave Klench's ear a never-ending tweak.

Next appeared the army of shop assistants Klench had held at gunpoint just for smiling at him. 'Shut ups!' he shrieked in his sleep as they told jokes he didn't get and roared with laughter.

Then the presidents of two Pacific islands climbed onto his stomach and jumped up and down. Why? To pay him back for the war he'd organised after visiting their sunny, smiley nations.

And that was it. All the happy, skippy, Christmassy folk he'd ever met and maimed – not to mention the animals and birds he'd smuggled – jumped on too, and trampolined their hearts out.

'No!' Klench wailed in his sleep. 'Go vay, happy folks. Go vay, everyone I have hurt.' He slid off his chair. Rolling around the floor, he clutched his ears. But the clapping and cheering, roaring and squawking just grew louder and louder and–

'Enough!' roared a voice.

The dream crowd froze.

Glaring at them was a woman with a face the colour of storm clouds. 'Leave my boy alones. Shoo shoo, ze lot of you!' Inner Mummy raised her arms. The crowd vanished, leaving only Jonty Chuckle still clutching Klench's ear and staring at her in terror. 'You too, vimp!' Jonty blinked and disappeared.

Klench opened his eyes. He rolled onto his front. He pushed himself up. He wiped the tears from his face.

'Stupid boy!' Mummy shouted in his head. 'Vy you drink zat medicine? How dare you be unhappy? Viz mum like me you should be glad. Vot more you vont, ungrateful lad?'

Klench glowered at her with his inner eye. He knew *exactly* what.

'Super pooper-scooping!' shouted a deep voice. Marcus looked up from his shovel. Abigail Hartley's dad was striding up to the elephant pen. 'Thanks a mil for helping out, Marcus. Having a good day?'

Marcus tried to smile. 'Um, yeah. Though I didn't realise there'd be so much …' He nodded at the shovel.

Mr Hartley hooted. 'That's zoos for you. And you've got the cream of the crop there, from Gina. Wait till we tell Abbie. She'll be amazed to hear you're doing this.'

'Mmm.' *That's not all she'll be amazed to hear.*

'Matt! Come and meet Marcus.' Mr Hartley beckoned to a skinny man in a green boiler suit. His black hair was tied in three plaits. He had huge rabbity teeth.

'This is Perdita's dad,' said Mr Hartley.

Duh. You don't say. Marcus gave a tight smile.

'Thanks so much for helping.' Mr Platt looked exhausted. 'There's a lot to do while they're away.' He rubbed a finger over his teeth.

Marcus stared at him. *He's not actually crying, is he?*

'Graham!' A small lady with blonde hair ran up. 'I asked you to … Oh hi, Marcus. I'm Abbie's mum. I've seen you at school. And Abbie's, er, mentioned you a few times. Very nice of you to help.' She frowned. 'Though, I must say, it's quite a surprise. Anyway,' she turned back to Mr Hartley,

'I asked you to put up the picnic table in the ape house, darling.'

'I've been trying to, darling. Can't get the legs down.' Mr Hartley slapped Mr Platt on the back. 'Wondering if you'd do the honours, Matt?'

Mr Platt sighed. 'I was going to play chess with Gina. But OK.'

Mrs Hartley nudged her husband. 'I wanted to give Matt a break, darling. Please try again.'

Mr Hartley nudged her back. 'I've been trying for half an hour. *Darling.*' He winked at Marcus. 'Ask about picnic tables in history and I'm your man. Ask me to put one up and I'm–'

'Useless,' said his wife. 'Oh, by the way, Marcus, please join us for dinner. The zoo closes at five on Saturdays. All the staff eat together at six.'

Marcus stopped shovelling. 'Really? Er, thanks, but my mum wants me home.' He turned back to his shovel.

Yes! He'd found his moment.

23

Klench's Request

Abbie stared at the floor. Not that there was much to stare at, just brown packed earth. She wondered if that's what her mind would look like after the operation: brown packed earth whenever she tried to remember anything beyond three seconds ago.

That got the tears going. They rolled down her cheeks and fell on the ground in dark, fat blotches.

She heard Perdita crying too. Reaching over, the friends hugged. *Friends*, thought Abbie. *We'll forget we're friends. We'll have to introduce ourselves every three seconds.* The tears came faster. She sobbed into Perdita's shoulder.

'Quiet!' said Carmen.

Abbie looked up. 'I can't help it,' she sniffed. 'The thought of–'

'I mean leesten.'

Holding her breath, Abbie heard the tiniest noise. A scraping, rustling sound coming from Carmen's direction.

Coriander looked at Perdita. 'Recognise that?'

214

Perdita sat back and wiped her eyes. 'Woodworm. The hairy harp of Hibernia.' She turned to the others. 'Mum brought the harp back from Ireland and stood it in the corner. Took us ages to work out what the noise was.'

Coriander looked round. 'It must be coming from your stand, Carmen. That's the only wood in this room.'

'Aiee, I am eenfested! Worms they climb my neck and eat my brain.'

Fernando rolled onto Carmen's wooden plate. 'Come, worms. You eat my Carmen, you eat me too.' He kissed her on the mouth: a smeary smackeroo. 'Remember, wife, you are love of my life.'

Carmen blinked at him. Her lumpy lips trembled. 'I suppose,' she admitted at last, 'you love of mine too.'

Life, thought Abbie. Her own hurtled before her. Hot chocolate on Friday nights. Racing Mum along the beach in Cornwall. Pinching chips from Ollie's plate. Dad's historical dinners: medieval gruel, pease pudding not so hot. Cuddles from Winnie; puddles from Minnie. Even Marcus and his insults. Oh, to be in the playground right now, insulting him back.

Her chest ached. Memories. They made her who she was. Without them life meant nothing. *She* meant nothing. Why had God bothered making her at all? Why hadn't he put his feet up and watched *Masterchef* instead?

The door opened. Klench appeared, gun in hand.

Abbie gasped. Forgetting her misery for a second, she stared at him. What on earth had happened? His face was red. His jacket was buttoned up wrongly. His shirt hung loose underneath. And, most shocking of all, his parting was wonky.

'Madam.' Klench turned to Grandma. His squeaky voice was softer than usual. 'I need to talks. I offer you vun last chance of freedom.'

Her eyes went heavenward. ''Ow many times do I 'ave to tell you, I will never, not in a month of *bundays*, join you in–'

'I know, I know.' Klench sighed. 'Ziss I am no lonker askink. Now I am requestink your helps.' He leaned forward and whispered, 'You see, I have problem in brain.'

Grandma snorted. 'You're tellin' me. All that villainy – must be somethin' skewy up there. Why are you whisperin'?'

'Because my problem is snoozink. But she vake up any moment.' Klench talked quietly and quickly. 'You see, my mums has come back from dead. She sits in my mind and orders me abouts. She is super-smart, viz many degrees in crime. She is also tough and bold like you. Lonk story short – I believe you can help me send her packink from my head.'

Grandma frowned. 'And 'ow on earth would I do that?'

Klench twiddled the buttons on his jacket. 'By givink me lessons. Teachink me how to stand up to her, give her vot for. You are expert in vot for.'

Grandma sniffed. 'You mean I'm a bully?'

'No no.' Klench shook his head wildly. 'I mean you are brave and fine.'

'Oh.' The corners of her lips twitched upward.

'Grandma!' Abbie jumped up. 'Don't be fooled. He's just trying to flatter you. You know you can't trust him an inch.'

Klench wiggled the gun in frustration. 'Zat is point. You cannot trust me becoss of my mums. Vunce you help me get rid of her, I vill be super-trusty bloke.'

''Ang on a mo.' Grandma stood up slowly, shaking her head. 'Are you tellin' me that your wickedness is your mother's fault? That she's to blame for all your crimes?'

Klench nodded so hard that his parting changed shape. 'I knew you vere clever cookie.'

Grandma put her hands on her hips. 'Clever enough to know that you're talkin' *poppytwaddle*! I don't care what your mother's like. I don't care what she says or does, whether she's in your brain or your boots. You're a grown man. You – and you alone,' she jabbed a finger at him, 'are responsible for your actions. You 'ear me? Stop blamin' your baddery on someone else.'

Klench sank back against the door. 'But, madam.' His voice was whiny. 'If you met my mums you vould ...'

A look of fear came into his eyes. Fear and distraction. He gazed past Grandma, shaking his head and muttering, 'Go back to sleep, Mums. I am busy.'

He blinked back at Grandma. 'So, madam. You refuse to help me.' There was a tremble in his voice. 'Fair enoughs. Zen ve proceed viz op. Tomorrow you vill all say goodbye to today.'

* * *

Up in the lounge all the guests who'd drunk the jungle medicine were sprawling in addled agony.

'The pain's even worse!' Brag lay on a couch. 'Not just ma fingers but ma branches – ah mean arms. And ma stems – ah mean legs.'

'Feels like pearls are ramming into my eyes,' wailed the Pincher, her head in her hands.

'I'll pay everything back,' groaned the bubble-wrapped head. 'Just let me go free.'

Klench came in. He'd tucked in his shirt, redone his buttons and straightened his parting. He was back to professional neatness. Only his voice betrayed uncertainty. 'Please to quiet, folks,' he bleated, almost timidly. 'I vill go back to junkle man. He must have made simple mistake. He vill redo painkiller and all vill be sorted.'

'Oh, gimme a break!' cried a lady whose arm already had three.

* * *

Down in the cellar Carmen, too, was crying. 'Owee! Get off. You never free me from stand. Woodworm, they comeeng to eat my brain.'

Abbie stopped twisting. She couldn't detach Carmen's neck. And the scratching was getting louder.

'Shhh.' She put a finger on Carmen's lips. Another sound, faint but chirpy, was growing in time to the rhythmic scraping. A sound you'd almost call–

'Singing!' Abbie moved Carmen aside and put her ear

to the ground. She sat up and scrabbled at the dirt with her fingers. 'Come on,' she yelled. 'Dig!'

* * *

It was getting dark. People were trickling out of the zoo exit.

At the gate Charlie Chumb shook Marcus's hand. 'You've done a great day's um … Sure you won't join us for … you know?'

Marcus humped his rucksack over his shoulder. 'No. I told Mum I'd be home by five-thirty.'

'Well, thanks for all your hard, ah … And do come again any, um …'

'Thanks.'

And no thanks. Marcus headed out of the gate. He turned left and dived behind a tree as Charlie disappeared back into the zoo. Taking out his cell phone, he rang home. 'Mum? We're watching a movie. And Greg's mum's doing pizza. Can I stay?'

'Fine by me, love,' came his mum's voice. 'You won't need dinner then?'

Marcus's stomach growled. He was starving. 'Maybe a snack. Greg's dad said he'll drop me home.'

'Enjoy the film, dear.'

Marcus looked at his watch. Four fifty-two. The last visitors trickled towards the exit.

Marcus rushed up. 'I forgot my jumper,' he said through the gate. On the other side, a lady was dragging a little boy to the exit.

'I wanna stay in the zooooo,' whined the boy.

'Look, Otis.' The lady pointed at Marcus. 'There's the boy who was shovelling doo-doos.' Otis stopped to stare. The lady clicked the gate open and held it for Marcus.

'Thanks.' Marcus ran inside.

'Wanna shovel doo-doos,' wailed Otis as his mother pulled him out.

Marcus crept past the entrance pond and along the path. It was dark and deserted. He took off his rucksack and pushed it into the bushes at the side. Then he followed and crouched down. Clutching the heavy rucksack, he waited.

24

Stick Around

Everyone with hands dug madly, spraying up earth from the cellar floor. Everyone without them shouted, '*Olé!*'

The hole grew deeper. The singing grew clearer. The scratching grew louder, faster, closer. Then a shout, a snout and–

'GAV!' yelled Abbie. The little silver gadget popped up, doing a jig on the head of–

'BRILLO!'

Box and beast emerged from the hole. Abbie kissed Gav on the screen.

Perdita threw her arms round Brillo. 'You darlings! You heroes! You superstars!'

'So *that* was the scratching sound!' said Abbie.

Carmen whooped. 'My brain eet safe from wooden worms.'

'Grab your partners,' sang Gav, 'give a cheer,
    I'm the one who led us here.
    Tracked down Brillo, steered his snout

Through the ground, then up and out,

Waited underneath the floor

'Til that lout reeled out the door.'

Everyone who could clapped. Everyone who couldn't glared at Gav for having legs.

'Amazing!' said Coriander. 'But how did you escape, Gav? You were turned off in my rucksack.'

'Which Klench took when we were captured,' said Perdita. 'Did *he* switch you on?'

Gav's eye winked on the screen. 'Not on purpose, no sirree. Only accidentally.'

'How?' said Abbie.

Gav demonstrated with a new dance:

'Kick that rucksack, switch me on,

Slam that door – and bye, I'm gone.'

Abbie grinned. 'Wow. So you ran out of the hotel. But how did you find Brillo?'

Gav rolled his screen eyes.

'I'm a Sat Nav, I could find

a wart upon a whale's behind.'

Abbie shook her head in wonder. 'So you knew where to find us, too. Amazing.'

'Not so amazin' when Klench comes back and finds us 'avin' a coffee mornin',' said Grandma. 'Come on, let's skedaddle.'

Easier said than done, thought Abbie. The tunnel was about half a metre across – impressive, when you considered that Brillo had dug it single-clawedly. But was it impressive enough? She looked doubtfully at the two biggest bottoms in the room.

As if reading her thoughts, Coriander said, 'I'll go last. Then I can push you through, Grandma.'

And who'll push you *through?* thought Abbie. But she said nothing. It was wonderful to see Coriander back to her brave old self. Besides, what choice did they have? So into the tunnel jumped:

Brillo to lead the way, then
Gav, to sing them out through the darkness, then
Perdita holding Carmen, then
Abbie holding Fernando, then
Grandma who heaved and huffed and
Coriander who pushed and puffed.

'You OK, Mum?' shouted Perdita from the front.

'Ye-he-hess.'

'You OK, Grandma?' called Abbie.

'Ye-he … no. I'm stuck. Can't move.'

'You must,' gasped Coriander. 'You can. You have to.'

'Yoo hoo!'

They froze.

'Out – now!' squeaked the voice. 'Or bullets vill up bumsies.'

'Mum!' screamed Perdita. 'Back out!'

Everyone shuffled backwards. Well, not quite everyone. Brillo and Gav had scuttled on through the tunnel.

Free again, thought Abbie. *Lucky jammers.*

Behind her Klench was giving instructions. 'Callink all doctors. Down to cellar schip-schnap.'

Everyone backed out of the tunnel and sat on the floor. Klench stood in the doorway. He held his gun in one hand and a walkie-talkie in the other. 'And brink equipments. Over and out.' He waggled the gun wearily at the prisoners. 'You leave me no choice.'

Something had changed. Abbie could see he was putting on a brave bad face, but the quiver in his voice and the tremble in his chins spoke of a new insecurity. 'Since you insist on escapinks, I vill proceed viz op right now.'

Three figures appeared in the doorway. They wore white lab coats.

Terror flooded Abbie's chest. *This is it. We're fruit flies.*

The doctors came in. The first, a man with banana-pale hair, carried an electric drill. Then came a woman with a pot in her gloved hands. The third doctor had dark hair and a scalpel in his breast pocket.

Klench pointed at Abbie. 'Start viz Miss Meddle.' Screaming, she clutched her head and backed against the wall.

The woman doctor stepped forward. 'First we'll Superdooperglooper Glue your hands together. Don't want them interfering with the skull opening, do we, Dr Banoffee?'

'Ooh no, Dr Ecclescake.' The pale-haired man wiggled the drill playfully.

'Don't you dare!' Perdita jumped up and blocked the woman's path. Coriander tried to grab the drill. Grandma stamped on the dark haired doctor's foot

Klench fired the gun. The bullet hit the wall a centimetre from Abbie's ear.

'Stop!' she yelled. 'I'd rather be dim than dead!'

Dr Ecclescake turned to the dark-haired man. 'Would you do the honours, Dr Squidgychocolatelog?'

'With pleasure, Dr E.' He grabbed Abbie's hands. He held them out, palms up.

Dr Ecclescake shoved Perdita aside. Coming towards Abbie, she flipped back the pot lid.

She took a paintbrush from her pocket.

She plunged it into the pot.

She removed it.

She brought it forward and ...

Shrieked! Something leapt at her chest. The pot and

brush flew from her hands. Glue splashed onto her nose. 'Aaagh!' Panicking, she ran for the door. She banged into it. Her nose stuck fast.

'Brillo!' cried Perdita. 'You're back!'

'Vot ze Schnik?' squealed Klench as another armadillo jumped up and whacked him in the chest. The walkie-talkie fell from one hand and smashed on the floor. The gun dropped from the other. Abbie snatched it up.

A third armadillo leapt out of the tunnel. And a fourth. They flew at the other two doctors. Abbie gasped as more armadillos appeared. They must have been behind Brillo in the tunnel, helping to dig – and he'd run back to get them! Ten, eleven, twelve … they knocked the doctors down and piled on top of them, scratching and clawing.

Gav the Nav scuttled out of the tunnel. 'Turn around upon the floor,' he sang. 'Stop that villain at the door!'

Abbie wheeled round to see Klench trying to shut them in. But Dr Ecclescake was wedged in the doorway, her nose firmly glued. Klench gave up and scampered off up the stairs.

Gav ran about, cheering on the armadillos. 'Gouge their faces, claw their heads. Tear those wicked docs … to … shreds.' His voice trailed off. His screen went dead. All the leaping and dancing had run his battery down.

Coriander scooped him up. 'We need to get out of here,' she cried, 'before Klench comes back with the other guests. They're armed and sure to help him.' She turned to the armadillos. 'Run, my darlings.'

'No!' yelled Grandma. 'We need 'em 'ere to keep the docs down.'

'No!' Coriander yelled back. 'Klench'll put them in cages and smuggle them to China.' They glared at each other.

Now what? thought Abbie. *They're both right.* She looked frantically round the room. *Of course!*

Handing Grandma the gun, she ran over to the glue-pot that Dr Ecclescake had dropped. Coriander hummed a run-for-your-lives sort of tune. And, as Grandma trained the gun on the doctors, the armadillos slipped off and dived back into the tunnel.

Abbie and Perdita dragged the bleeding, dazed men to the door. 'I hope you're right-handed,' she said, lifting Doctor Banoffee's limp left arm.

'Mwaaah,' he moaned into the floor. She painted his fingertips with glue. Perdita did the same to Doctor Squidgychocolatelog.

'What are you doing?' Doctor Ecclescake whimpered down her stuck nose from the top of the door.

'Keeping you three out of the way.' Abbie nudged the doctor's legs aside. She glanced nervously at Perdita. Together, the girls stuck the glued fingertips to the bottom of the door. The two doctors groaned, their heads lolling forward.

'Let's go.' Abbie took the gun from Grandma and led the way upstairs. Perdita picked up Carmen and followed. Then came Grandma with Fernando and Coriander with Gav the flat Sat Nav.

At the top Abbie looked across the deserted lobby. The entrance door was open. 'Make a run for it,' she whispered.

A hand grasped her shoulder. 'Chester.' Grandma's face was thunder.

Abbie gulped. 'Of c-course.' How could she have forgotten him – especially after launching him into danger before? She glanced round the lobby. He could be behind any of those doors – or upstairs – locked inside that box. She took a deep breath. 'We'll search the ground floor first. Keep together. I'm the only one with a gun.'

What did I just say? She looked at her hand, clamped round the mint-green handle. Was she actually in the Amazon jungle, holding a gun, defending six human(ish) beings and a flat Sat Nav from a hotel full of hoodlums? *Yikes.* She almost dropped the gun. *Get a grip. Think cool. Think calm. Think headline.*

GUTSY GIRL CRUSHES CRIMINAL CARRY-ON.

It sounded good. She tiptoed across the lobby towards the glass doors of the lounge.

* * *

All of which left time for Klench to whip round upstairs.

'You need help from guests and guns,' barked Mummy, 'to stop zat lot before zey runs.'

'I know,' he snapped. 'I vosn't born last Vensday.'

'Don't be cheeky, Chubby Cheeks.'

He blew an inner raspberry. How would he ever be rid of her? Blinking back furious tears, he barged into the first bedroom on the landing.

'Who's there?' came a weak voice. The gangster was lying on his bed with the brick still on his head. He turned his squashed face towards the door.

'I need your gun,' squeaked Klench. 'Ve are invaded by law-abidink persons viz snouty friends.'

'Can't find it,' groaned the man. 'Can't find anything. My eyes have closed up. Oh, the agony.'

Klench slammed the door and ran along the corridor. In the next room he found the bank-robbing couple moaning in armchairs. The woman was clutching the box on her nose and the man was clasping his cling-filmed ears. Their daughter sat on a bed jabbing a DS. She glared at Klench and picked up a book from the bedside table.

'I need your mumsie and dadsie's gunsies,' he gasped, trying to sound like a cuddly uncle. 'Vizzout delay ... Oww.' The book slammed into his shoulder.

'That's for trapping animals!' yelled the girl. She reached for the table again and grabbed a vase of flowers.

Klench shut the door as the vase sailed towards him. He ran down the corridor and hammered on the next door. The Pearl Pincher raised her head from her desk.

'Give me your gun!' ordered Klench. 'Ve have enemy in our middles.'

Still blinded by bandages, the Pincher groaned. 'No idea where it is.' Cursing, Klench rushed out and banged on the next door.

'Yeah?'

'Mr Brag,' gasped Klench, 'if you do not help, ve face much arrestinks.'

Brag rose slowly from his chair. A thousand wasps were stinging his fingertips. 'Take mah gun,' he drawled wearily, nodding towards a drawer. 'Ah can't use it. But ah'll do what ah can. No one's gonna nab Brag Swaggenham.' He followed Klench out with more of a stagger than a swagger.

* * *

Marcus rolled over in bed. His heart was hammering. His breathing was quick. The tiniest sound roared in his ears: the tick of the bedside clock, the distant growl of cars. He'd never get to sleep. He sat up and switched on the light.

Has it worked? Is she out there, lumbering through the night?

He got out of bed, went to the window and drew back the curtains. Where was she? What was she doing? And what on earth would happen tomorrow?

25

Attack

'Where can Chester be?' whispered Coriander.

Not in the lounge. Not in the games room, the TV room, the restrooms or restaurant. And not in the kitchen. The only person there was a young man in a brown uniform He was putting scraps of rotten fruit and peel into a bowl. When Abbie burst in with the gun, he dropped the bowl and threw up his hands.

He looked so scared that she couldn't help saying, 'Sorry to trouble you. I need to find Chester.'

'Sorry?' His dark eyes widened. 'Never here I hear this word. Klench *never* say sorry. He *love* to trouble me. You not with him?' It was more a plea than a question.

'Of course not. As if! Please, just tell me where Chester is and I'll go.'

But he shook his head when she described the patch of grey hair locked inside a box. 'I never see this creature.'

'Oh.' Her face fell. 'Thanks.' She turned to go.

'Wait.' He blinked nervously. 'Please – you have gun.

You come help me.' He pointed to a door at the back of the kitchen.'

'I can't. I have to find Chester before Klench finds us. I'm sorry.'

She backed out of the door, leaving him shaking his head in wonder and murmuring, 'Sorry? She say *sorry*?'

Out in the lobby Perdita was trying one last door. It was locked.

'Oh no,' breathed Abbie. They'd have to look upstairs – and risk running into Klench and the guests.

Heart pounding, head throbbing, she led them all across the lobby and climbed the first step. Her sandal sank into mint-green carpet, soft as moss. The heat, the dread, the roar in her head – she knew how an egg must feel entering boiling water.

Up the next step … and the next. She gripped the banister. Her sweaty palm cooled on the golden rail that curved up, then round to the right, in a great showy arc.

Around the bend she froze. Klench was at the top of the stairs, brandishing a gun. Beside him stood a tall thin man in a cowboy hat. It wasn't the moment to drop her gun in terror.

She dropped her gun in terror.

Quick as a cat, Klench darted downstairs and whisked it up. 'Dearie me,' he squeaked. 'Vot butterfinkers. But so kind to return my gun.' He threw it to the cowboy, who caught it in his diamond-studded teeth. His bandaged hands hung limply at his sides.

'Back down to lobby, you lots,' barked Klench.

No! Abbie turned and stumbled after the others, Klench following closely behind. She'd messed up again, for the bazillionth time on this trip. Tears of rage and shame blurred her vision as she lurched down the stairs.

The stairs? Since when did stairs move? She blinked through her tears. Since when did they chatter and squeal and … 'Aaagh!' … trip her up? She wheeled round.

A black monkey with impossibly long limbs shot up the stairs and snatched the gun from a startled Klench. It leapt onto the banister then reached up and grasped the chandelier above his head. Hauling itself up, it hooked its tail round the frame and hung upside down. Klench shrieked and tried to grab the gun from its hand.

'Spider monkey!' gasped Coriander. She began to hum: a sharp, high tune of attack. The monkey smacked Klench in the face.

Another monkey streaked past Klench and up to the landing. It wrapped its skinny arms round the cowboy's knees. 'Aark!' he yelled as his legs were yanked forward. He fell onto his back.

The gun flew from his mouth. The hat sailed off his head. The monkey jumped on his stomach.

The dangling monkey dropped the gun it was holding.

'Ha!' Klench bent down and scooped it off the carpet.

'Watch out!' yelled Perdita. But she didn't mean the gun. Abbie felt a rush of air as dark wings beat above her. A massive grey bird landed on Klench's head, clasping his ears with brutal talons. He screamed and danced on the stair, trying to shake the bird off.

'Harpy eagle!' cried Coriander. 'The more he wriggles, the more it'll think he's dinner.'

The monkey, seeing its chance, dropped from the chandelier. It snatched the gun again from the bird-bound Klench and threw it upwards. The weapon lodged with a tinkle amid the glass baubles of the light. The monkey turned and ran up to the landing, joining its companion on top of the cowboy. They held him down, whooping and beating his chest with their leathery fists.

Abbie yelped. Two furry brown creatures, like long-legged guinea pigs, scooted past her. They caught Klench's trouser legs in their teeth. He kicked them off. They came back for more and Klench ran for the landing.

'Go agoutis!' cried Coriander. She brandished Gav in the air.

The cowboy wriggled out from under the monkeys. He hitched the gun that had flown from his mouth between his wrists. Rolling onto his side, he manoeuvred the handle to his mouth and clamped it between his teeth. No matter how the monkeys pummelled his back and shoulders, they couldn't dislodge the weapon.

Until he screamed. The gun fell out as a huge hairy spider crawled onto his face. One of the monkeys whipped up the weapon from the carpet and threw it down the stairs. Abbie caught it.

'Where the blinkers are they comin' from?' yelled Grandma as more tarantulas scuttled onto the cowboy.

Gun in hand, Abbie ran downstairs. Rounding the bend, she stopped and stared.

The servant from the kitchen stood on the far side of the lobby. He was holding open the door to the kitchen. He waved at Abbie as animals and birds streamed through. Some were heading out of the hotel entrance into the jungle. Some were scurrying round the lobby. And others were making for the stairs. At the front flew a green parrot with a red face. Then came a snouty creature that Abbie recognised as an anteater and a grey, pig-like creature that she didn't. At the back scampered two spotty cats that could only be jaguar cubs. And at the front *and* back, stretching right across the lobby, was an … an …

'An … aconda,' she breathed.

From thin head to pointy tail it must have been longer than Perdita, Coriander and Grandma put together. It was already flowing up the stairs in a silent, green, gravity-flouting river. Abbie backed against the banister and edged upstairs crabwise, level with its head. Around the bend the others too pressed back, speechless, to let it pass.

The monster reached the landing. It paused, flicking its tongue at the screaming crooks. Then calmly it reared and slid round Klench's knees. Lazily it slipped beneath the cowboy's calves. And gently, almost lovingly, it hoisted him upright. One by one the other creatures let go. They scurried or flew down the corridor that led off the landing, leaving the snake to squeeze the villains in its cold embrace.

'Stop huggin' me!'

'Stop squoshink me!'

'Breathe in, can't ya?'

'Use aftershaves, can't you?' And, as the snake encircled their vast combined middles … 'He-he-*help*!' they chorused.

'Madam!' Klench screamed, catching sight of Grandma. 'In ze name of your loveliness, stop ziss!'

'I can't!' Grandma covered her eyes. 'Do somethin', Coriander. We can't let 'em die.'

Coriander gripped the banister. She pressed her lips together. 'No,' she said at last. 'We can't.'

Her low, smooth hum of enough-is-enough stopped the snake. Curving back its upper body, it fixed the two villains with glittering amber eyes.

Chester, thought Abbie. It was now or never. Grasping the gun with both hands, she crept across the landing past the snake-bound baddies.

The spider monkeys were dancing down the corridor, opening doors on either side with their clever fingers.

Abbie peered into the first room. A man lay on a bed. A brick was strapped to his head. The harpy eagle perched on

236

his stomach. He was crying like a baby. Not too much of a threat there.

In the next bedroom a man and woman whimpered in armchairs as tarantulas crawled over their chests. A little girl sat on the floor. A spider on her lap was jabbing a DS with a hairy leg.

The girl looked up. 'Hi. Who are you?'

'Uh … Abbie.'

'Are your mum and dad here?'

'No. Are they yours?' Abbie pointed to the box-nosed, cling-film-eared grown-ups.

'Yup. And they're getting what they deserve,' she said. 'Wanna play *Nintendogs* with us?'

'Er … not right now, thanks.' Abbie closed the door.

In the next room a woman stood in front of a mirror. The green parrot held the end of a bandage in its beak and was flying round her head, unwinding it. Her eyes underneath were bruised and bloody. The left one was higher than the right.

'No!' the woman sobbed. 'All that pain and they're *still* wonky!' She sank to the floor. The parrot perched on her head, dug in its claws and squawked unsympathetically.

Shaking her head in amazement, Abbie backed into the corridor. A man rolled out of his room. 'Get off!' he wailed, trying to escape the agoutis that gnawed at the bubble wrap round his head. The plastic came off, revealing a tiny face, wrinkled as a raisin.

A girl rushed out of another room. The jaguar cubs were swiping at her plaster cast arms. 'Ow!' she screamed. 'I give up!' She sank down on the floor. All along the corridor, guests staggered out, trying to escape the creatures that were nibbling, pecking and biffing them.

The spider monkeys rushed from room to room, emptying drawers and ransacking wardrobes. With a little musical prompting from Coriander, they collected all the guns they found and threw them into the corridor. Abbie gathered up the weapons and handed them out to the others, who were still watching Klench and the cowboy on the landing. There were plenty of guns to go round. Everyone took two except for Coriander, who still had Gav in one hand; Carmen, who said don't talk to her about guns; and Fernando, who said don't talk to him about hands.

The bank robbers' daughter came out of her bedroom. 'Good job,' she said to Abbie. 'I never liked that lot. 'Specially my parents.' Which seemed to Abbie a very sad thing to admit – although the girl didn't look bothered at all. 'I'm Dollarine.' She held out her hand. Abbie shook it. 'And this is Maisie-Lou.' The tarantula on her shoulder held out a leg. Abbie waved politely. 'Ooh, by the way,' said Dollarine. 'You'd better watch out. There's a nasty man round here who's been trapping all these animals. I don't know where he's gone.' Abbie glanced nervously down the corridor. But there was no time to look for him now.

Grandma and Perdita herded the guests downstairs, with the help of the jungle creatures who scampered, flew and crawled alongside to keep them in order. Abbie stayed on the landing with Coriander and Dollarine. The little girl watched wide-eyed as Coriander hummed an uncoiling sort of tune. Slowly the anaconda unwrapped its prey and glided downstairs. Klench and the cowboy followed, with Abbie and Grandma's guns at their backs. Not that the baddies were much of a danger now. Wild-eyed and whimpering, they fell rather than walked down the stairs. Last came Dollarine, her eyes wider than ever, carrying Fernando in one hand and Carmen in the other.

A line of staff stood against the far wall of the lobby. They cheered as Klench appeared at gunpoint.

He and the cowboy joined the other bedraggled guests in front of the reception desk. The spider monkeys swung from the lobby chandeliers, reaching down to whack the crooks on the head. The agoutis pulled off the cowboy's boots and chewed them down to their golden toecaps. The harpy eagle flapped its wings in one of the fountains, spraying the guests. And the jaguar cubs scratched patterns on the floor. When they'd had enough, the creatures headed through the entrance door, back to their beloved forest – all except the anaconda, who formed a calm, impregnable fence in front of the guests.

One of the staff members came up to Abbie. 'I did good, yes?' he said with a shy smile. It was the young man from the kitchen.

She beamed back. 'Oh, yes. Though what exactly *did* you do?'

He explained how the sight of her with a gun had given him the courage for what he'd dreamed of doing, but hadn't dared, since the hunter had started his dirty work. When Abbie left the kitchen, the young man had crept down to the wine cellar. Checking that the hunter was asleep before his night shift, he took the gun that lay under the bed and … 'I shoot him.'

Abbie gasped. 'You mean he's–'

'Still asleep.' The youth grinned. 'I stun him with dart gun, like he stun animals. Serve him right. Then I take keyring from under his pillow and open all the cages.'

Two other staff members came forward to help the young man go down and tie up the hunter. And when Perdita explained about the doctors glued to the door, another four hurried off to sort them out.

''Ang on.' Grandma slid her glasses down her nose and glared round the staff. ''Ow come you lot are so keen to 'elp all of a sudden? Why didn't you stand up to Klench before?'

Another young man stepped forward. 'We scared of him,' he said sheepishly.

'Why didn't you leave, then?' said Coriander. 'Go back to your villages?'

The man chewed his lip. 'There is no future for us in jungle. We want to find work in city.' The other servants murmured in agreement. 'But we have no skill. Here we can learn hotel work. So we must put up with mean boss. At least …' He stared at the ground. 'At least, I think that at first. But when I see how he trap animals and help criminals, I ashame.' He looked up at Coriander. 'Then I angry. So I take him to my uncle.'

Everyone stared as Quempo the barman explained how his uncle had concocted a brew that would give the crooks nightmares and weaken their strength.

'But not enough. Only when you appear with gun can we defeat them. For this we thank you from bottom of heart.' He began to clap. The rest of the staff joined in while the Platts and Hartleys shuffled and blushed and said, aw, it was nothing.

The applause died down.

'Now what?' mumbled Abbie. It was one of those awkward moments – you know the sort. You're standing in a hotel lobby in the Amazon jungle pointing a gun at the world's top criminals and you haven't a clue what to say next.

Luckily someone did.

'Chester!' roared Grandma. 'Where is 'e?' She waved her two guns at Klench. 'You give 'im back this minute or there'll be fireworks!'

* * *

Charlie Chumb tugged his earlobes. 'She can't just have … you know.'

'But she has!' Matt wailed. They were standing on the bridge over the hippo pool. Inflatable crocodiles were bobbing between the bubbles. Hepzibah wasn't.

Ollie and Abbie's mum and dad rushed up.

'Got here as soon as we could,' Mum gasped.

'The zoo barrier's smashed in two,' said Dad. 'She must

have barged straight through. When do you think she left?'

Matt rubbed his teeth with a frantic finger. 'Could've been any time last night after we closed.'

'But why?' said Dad. 'She's got everything she needs here.'

'She seemed so happy,' said Mum.

Matt shrugged miserably. They stared at the pool in silence.

'Marcus?' said Ollie.

Everyone looked at him.

'But he came to help,' said Dad.

'And he left long before Hepzibah – you know,' said Charlie.

'I was just *saying*,' said Ollie.

'Even if he wanted to let her out,' said Dad, 'how could he? Small boy, big hippo – you think he dragged her on a lead? I don't think so.'

'She's got nothing to leave *for*,' wailed Matt. 'She's got everything she needs here.'

'Have you reported it?' said Mum.

Matt shook his head. 'If this got out, there'd be hell to pay.'

Mum laid a hand on his arm. 'A hippo's got out. There *will* be hell to pay.'

* * *

The little girl pointed towards the playground in Bradleigh Park. 'Look, Daddy, there's a new rock.'

'Don't be daft, Frankie. You don't get *new* rocks. Rocks are very, very old. Rocks were formed millions and millions of–'

'It moved, Daddy.'

'Don't be silly, darling. Rocks don't move. Not unless there's an earthquake. That's when plates in the earth slide against–'

'It's got a tail, Daddy.'

'Don't be ridiculous, sweetie. Rocks don't have tails. Rocks are made of–'

'It's yawning, Daddy!'

'For goodness sake, Frankincense. Rocks don't …' His jaw dropped. The new rock shambled off across the park, wiggling its tiny tail.

26

Safe, Sound and Bound

It was a long night at the Hotel Armadillo. So long it turned into day.

First came the Great Chester Rescue. With two guns at his back, Klench led Grandma to his locked office. He took a key from his pocket and opened the door. His briefcase lay on the desk.

'Chess!' Grandma yelled when Klench snapped it open. The hair wriggled madly. Grandma jabbed Klench with the gun. 'What've you done to me budwig?'

'I am sorry, Madam,' Klench mumbled. 'He is Super-dooperglooper Glued.'

There was nothing for it but to cut Chester's curls. He leapt onto Grandma's head, restoring her to hairy splendour, apart from a short patch over her ear.

Then came the crooks' confinement. Klench and the guests were herded into the TV room at many gunpoints. They were joined by the three doctors. What a sorry sight. Two of them were scratched all over and their lab coats shredded. Abbie felt a pang of guilt as she spotted the wooden discs attached to the fingertips of their left hands.

'We have no choice,' explained one of the staff. 'We must saw through door to free fingers.'

The third doctor had tears trickling down her cheeks. They made pretty patterns round the disc that was stuck to her nose.

'Oh dear,' said Coriander. 'Do you think that'll ever come off?'

'Maybe she can burn it,' suggested Perdita – which led to even prettier patterns.

Last to be bundled inside was the hunter, bound and snoring.

Six staff members volunteered to guard the TV room. Winking at each other, they turned the TV on. It was a game show with a prize of a million dollars, which must have been a fraction of the fortune the guests would lose now they were headed for prison. Carmen and Fernando perched on top of the telly. Whenever a guest began to doze off, the heads burst into a dire Spanish duet. It was wonderful to see such harmony in their disharmony.

Next came the Grand Gav Revival. A staff member plugged him into a socket in the wall. When his battery had recharged, Coriander switched him on.

Gav's mouth yawned onto the screen. 'My, that sleep was mighty sweet. Just the ticket for my feet.'

'And I've got just the job for them,' said Coriander. She popped the little box on the ground. 'How about you go and rescue those policemen from the jungle?'

'Clap those hands and tap those toes,

I'll be back before it snows.'

Which, in the Amazon, was a pretty safe bet.

Gav scuttled out of the hotel and into the night. Exhausted, the girls staggered upstairs to catch some sleep. Dollarine and Maisie-Lou invited them to share their bedroom. The girls collapsed on the double bed, too tired to wash. But with Dollarine on the floor thumb-wrestling the tarantula, it was impossible to sleep. Abbie and Perdita gave up and went downstairs.

Coriander and Grandma were in the lounge. The anaconda was there too, draped several times over several sofas. Quempo was behind the bar, pouring fruit juice into glasses from a jug.

'Quempo's been telling us how Klench has been treating the staff like slaves,' said Coriander, 'working them to the bone, paying them a pittance.'

Quempo handed the glasses round, then gave the jug to Coriander. She took it over to the anaconda. The snake plunged its head inside and downed the juice in one.

Abbie took a sip of juice. Liquid sunlight poured down her throat. 'Will you go back to your village now?'

'No.' Quempo took a bright red fruit from a bowl. Picking up a knife, he peeled it. The skin spiralled down in a single perfect strip. 'Now at least I have skill.' He grinned. 'I will go to city and find job. But I never work for such bully boss again.'

'Bully,' echoed Grandma. 'Makes you wonder.' She slurped her drink thoughtfully.

'Wonder what?' Perdita frowned.

'That business about 'is mother. I mean, if 'e really thinks she's in 'is mind, orderin' 'im about, then you've got to feel a *teeny* bit sorry for 'im.'

'Grandma!' Abbie banged her glass down. 'Just because he admires you, there's no need to swallow that claptrap.'

Coriander nodded. 'You said yourself he's responsible for his own behaviour.'

'I know. It's just ...' Grandma shook her head. 'You can tell 'e believes she's there, the way 'e keeps mutterin' to 'imself. And if she brought 'im up badly, and she's still controllin' 'im, then …'

Everyone stared at her.

She stared back defiantly. 'Then I could weep for the poor flabber.'

* * *

Dawn was trickling into the sky when Abbie heard singing.

'Two to the left, two to the right

Home again by morning light.'

Everyone rushed into the lobby. Through the door tripped Gav. Behind him stumbled four policemen.

'Brillo!' cried Perdita. The armadillo scuttled in after them, his claws rattling on the lobby floor. She scooped him up into her arms.

'Found him waiting by a tree,' Gav explained. 'He came too and set them free.'

The policemen's hands had indeed been untied and their blindfolds removed. Their uniforms were ripped and their faces swollen from bites and stings. They stared round the lobby, then at Gav.

'I dream we are rescued by box on legs,' mumbled the chief policeman. Abbie recognised him as the officer from Puyo station: the one who'd refused to investigate their story.

'Perhaps we have jungle fever,' giggled another officer. They collapsed on the lobby floor.

Quempo fetched some juice and fruit from the kitchen.

When the policemen had drunk and eaten and felt a little more normal – though they couldn't stop gawping at their strange rescuer – they headed out to the police helicopter, still standing in front of the hotel. The others watched from the entrance as it stumbled into the sky like a huge clumsy bird and flew off to fetch reinforcements.

When it had gone Coriander yawned. 'Better get some sleep. We've got a long day ahead.' They went upstairs. Avoiding the second bedroom, where Dollarine and Maisie-Lou now lay snoring, everyone headed down the corridor to catch a few hours' sleep.

Later that morning they gathered in the kitchen. The staff had prepared a wonderful breakfast of specially imported Frosties and milk followed by specially imported croissants with Ecuadorian chocolate spread. When they'd eaten their fill, the Hartleys and Platts went into the TV room to check up on the prisoners.

What a miserable crowd. Dripping bloody bandages and crumbling plaster casts, they lay on the floor, staring into space.

Klench sat alone in a corner. Seeing Grandma he staggered to his feet. 'Madam, have mercy on me. Imagine vot police vill do. Perhaps zey lock me avay for sixteen lifetimes. Perhaps zey chop me up and feed me to pensioners.'

'Don't be daft,' Grandma snapped. 'I'm seventy-three and I wouldn't touch you with a bargepole. You'd be tough as old turnip.'

'But others are not so kind. You know how I admire you,

madam. Now I am captured I am no danger. Have pity on me.'

'You mean like all the pity *you've* 'ad for all the people you've wronged?'

'But …' Klench widened his piggy eyes as if trying to convey a secret message, 'I have told you of ze power behind my crimes.'

'So?' Abbie burst out. 'What difference does it make?'

Klench scowled. 'Alvays you butt ins. *So*,' he turned back to Grandma, 'now I am no threat, perhaps you vill consider helpink me.'

'Don't listen to him!' cried Coriander. 'Remember all the things he's done.'

''Ow could I forget?' Grandma folded her arms. 'But you'd be no lavender bag yourself with a mother like that.'

There was an uncomfortable silence. Everyone stared at the floor – except the Pearl Pincher, who stared at the floor with her right eye and the wall with her left.

'Madam!' Klench clasped his hands. 'I understand I must be punished. Since takink junkle medicine I begin to feel bad for my vickeds … yes I *do*, Mums,' he muttered to himself. Then, to Grandma again, 'I vish to change my vays. But I cannot do it alones. Teach me to stand up to *You Know Who*.'

Pity shone in Grandma's eyes. Compassion glowed from her nose. Chocolate gleamed on her chin. 'What can I do?' she said. 'They'll chuck you in prison and throw away the toothbrush after all you've done.'

Klench pressed his hands together as if in prayer. 'You are voman of mettle and kind as petal. I know you vill find a vay.'

It was a very thoughtful Grandma who wandered back to the kitchen for a cup of specially imported Earl Grey tea.

While the others waited in the lounge for the police to return, Abbie went to the reception desk. She picked up the phone. *Hang on. There'll be so many questions.* She replaced the receiver. Better leave it till they were back in Puyo. Then she could email Mum and Dad.

* * *

'No phone calls, no emails. It's been a whole week!' Mum pressed her fist against her mouth.

'They must still be out of reach,' said Dad. 'Probably just held up. You know what these jungles are like.' He tried to sound light yet loving, caring yet casual.

It didn't quite work. Mum burst into tears.

'Just trying to help,' Dad murmured, wiping his own eyes. He put his arms round her and said soothingly, 'I know, love, it's a nightmare.'

Ollie patted Mum's arm. 'Don't worry. Teacher says most big jungle animals are harmless. Only a jaguar would eat Abbie and–'

Mum wailed.

Ollie rolled his eyes. 'I was *going* to say – and jaguars are shy.'

251

Dad put his arm round them both. 'I'll give Matt a ring. See if he's heard anything.'

But down the phone came nothing but moan. 'My wife, my daughter, my hippo ... where *are* they?'

* * *

At Bradleigh police station Sergeant Bolt leaned over his desk. He took a pen and stuck it behind his left ear. He stuck another one behind his right ear. He stuck one up each sleeve, one down each sock and one in each nostril. 'Eight,' he murmured. 'Same as last time.' He found another pen and stuck it in his left earhole. 'Ha!' Removing the pen from his left sleeve, he jotted down his new record for biro body-storage spots.

He sighed. The nostril pens whooshed across the room. Sunday was the pits. Nothing ever happened. No hold-ups, no showdowns, no car chases or murder cases. Not that they happened from Monday to Saturday either. It was just that he felt it more on Sunday. That was because it was the day of his favourite TV show, *Cop on to This*, in which ace detective Aubergine Frisk solved extraordinary crimes with his mind-blowing powers of–

The phone rang. Sergeant Bolt snatched the receiver. '*Brad*-leigh Police Station. Can I help you?'

There was a muffled sound.

'One moment, please.' He pulled the pen out of his left ear. 'Could you repeat that?'

'I said there's a hippo in the park.'

Sergeant Bolt lowered the receiver and wiggled a finger in his ear. Was the pen lid stuck inside? 'I'm sorry, sir,' he said into the mouthpiece, 'I thought you said–'

'I *did*. My Frankincense spotted it early this morning. I've phoned eight times but there was no answer.'

Sergeant Bolt blushed. That was because he'd been watching Aubergine use his staggering gifts of–

'You still there?' said the voice.

Sergeant Bolt cleared his throat. 'Can you please inform me of the exact location of this mammalian individual?' Nothing like a few big words to hide your boo-boos.

'By the playground in Bradleigh Park. But that's not much use. It left ages ago.'

Sergeant Bolt put the phone down. It rang again.

'Oi,' came a woman's voice. 'Bleeding great pottymus wandering down me street half an hour ago. Thought you oughtta know.'

'Where exactly did it–?' The line went dead.

Another call. 'Twenty minutes ago … Primrose Mall … heading for the river.'

And another. 'You won't believe this, officer. I'm at the river. I was just feeding the ducks and–'

'I'll be right there.' Sergeant Bolt slammed the phone down. He scooped up his car keys and toy gun – a real confidence booster – and ran out to the police car. Then, sirens wailing and gun-caps loaded, he sped off to the river.

27

Goodbyes and Hellos

After lunch at the Hotel Armadillo (specially imported pizza and chips) the police returned. A huge helicopter shuddered down, sending leaves and monkeys flying.

Inside the aircraft the head policeman rubbed his forehead. It was on fire. Must be the jungle fever. After flying all the way to Quito to fetch a bigger helicopter and extra men, he felt worse than ever. He fished a bottle from his pocket. The doctor he'd seen this morning had prescribed one pill a day. He swallowed two. Then he clambered out of the helicopter.

He stopped. He stared. He shook his head. The weirdest crowd was tottering towards him.

A man without a neck.

A woman with wonky eyes.

A tall man in a cowboy hat with bandages dripping from his hands.

A burger-on-legs in a grubby white suit and a mint-green tie.

Three figures in white coats, one of whom had a circular wooden nose.

An old lady with a wig that bounced on her head.

A little girl with a tarantula that danced on hers.

An anaconda that glided off into the forest.

And bringing up the rear – Santa Alba and her blessed Chihuahua! – that crazy little box on legs.

The head policeman lifted the pill bottle and poured the lot down his throat. Giggling with a sudden and inexplicable joy, he stumbled forward and began the arrests.

Abbie and the Platts lingered at the entrance with the hotel staff. After hugs and cheers from the young men, they headed for the helicopter. Brillo scuttled after them.

Halfway across the clearing Perdita stopped. She bent down and lifted him into her arms. 'Pleeease, Mum. He'd have a great life. Dad could make him a sandpit or clockwork bugs to chase.'

'But there are real bugs here,' said Coriander gently.

Brillo nuzzled Perdita's face with his snout. 'You see? He's saying he wants to come.'

Or maybe, thought Abbie, *he's saying goodbye.* 'How could we take him on the plane?' she said.

Perdita sniffed. 'If we can take two shrunken heads, we can take an armadillo.'

Coriander laid a hand on her shoulder. 'Darling,' she said gently, 'we must let Brillo decide.'

The armadillo wriggled across into Coriander's arms. He lay still for a moment then reached towards Abbie. She kissed his ears, drinking in his earthy smell. He slipped to the ground, rubbed against Perdita's leg and shot off into the forest.

Perdita stared after him. 'Bye, brill Brillo,' she whispered. Abbie squeezed her hand. They walked slowly towards the helicopter.

The pilot agreed to drop them off in Puyo so they could collect their luggage. Abbie also wanted to visit Antonio Monio again to thank him for his help in finding Carmen. Maybe that would cheer the poor man up. Meanwhile the helicopter would fly on to Quito with the VUPs (Very Unpleasant Prisoners), then return to Puyo to collect them tomorrow morning.

Grandma asked to sit in front with the head policeman. The VUPs sat behind them, handcuffed and guarded by the other officers. Abbie, Perdita and Coriander sat at the back.

The helicopter roared into the air. Abbie saw Grandma talking to, or rather shouting at, the head policeman. *What's she on about now?* Abbie couldn't hear a thing above the racket of the engine. Whatever it was, the head policeman was nodding wildly – though it wasn't clear if he was agreeing with Grandma or trying to dislodge Gav, who was hopping on his head.

Abbie gazed out of the window. The forest canopy stretched below: a bubbling, endless lid of green. *But underneath*, she thought, *it's all so fragile.* Somewhere down there lay Quempo's village, and who knew how many others, all with mums, dads, uncles and children. Perhaps some of them knew nothing of the outside world, of ice-cream or blue eyes or socks.

I hope that's true, thought Abbie. *The Earth needs its secrets.* This delicate immensity must be one of the last. She hugged her rucksack and prayed it would stay that way.

The rucksack wriggled.

Abbie opened the flap. 'You OK?' she whispered.

'More air,' hissed the bag. 'We sweat like peegs down here.'

'I'll leave the top open,' said Abbie. 'But don't let the police see you. You're illegal, remember?'

Half an hour later the helicopter touched down outside Puyo police station. When the propellers had stilled, Abbie, Perdita and Coriander climbed out.

'Come on, Grandma,' called Abbie.

'I'll stay put,' Grandma shouted from her seat. 'This nice chap's agreed to take me on to Quito. I've got some business to see to.'

'What business?'

Grandma tapped her nose. 'See you tomorrow.' The helicopter door closed.

'Come back!' Abbie cried.

Grandma waved. The engine started up.

'She can't do that!' wailed Abbie. 'She'll never manage on her own.'

'She's not on her own.' Coriander patted Abbie's arm. 'She's got Gav to direct her and the police to look after her.'

'And *she* can look after Dollarine,' said Perdita, 'while her parents are being locked up.'

Abbie sighed. 'I s'pose so.' Though young Dollarine seemed quite capable of looking after herself, especially with a spider the size of her sandal in tow.

When they'd waved the helicopter off, Abbie, Perdita and Coriander went into the police station. The officers who'd been rescued from the jungle were waiting for them with handshakes and party cakes.

'How we ever can thank you?' said the first officer, handing round slices of passion-fruit pie.

The second officer raised his glass of guava juice. 'A toast …' he said.

'… To dancing box,' finished the third officer.

A snort of disgust came from Abbie's rucksack. She jabbed it with her elbow. 'Er, thanks for the cakes,' she said loudly. 'We should be going now.'

A safe distance from the station she opened her bag. 'Numpties! You nearly gave yourselves away.'

'I never say notheeng,' came Fernando's voice.

'Wasn't me,' insisted Carmen.

'You liar lady.'

'You cheatie boy.'

'I love you, my Carmen.'

'I love you, my Nando.'

'Could've fooled me,' Abbie muttered. 'You never stop arguing.'

'You argue too,' said Carmen, 'eef you been through what we been through.'

'Good point,' said Coriander. 'It's amazing when you think about it. Death, decapitation, desertion – and they're *still* devoted.' She reached into Abbie's rucksack and patted the shrunken heads. 'You're a great advert for marriage, you know.'

Abbie stopped. 'What did you say?' She stared at Coriander. 'Now *there's* a thought. I wonder if …' She shook her head. 'Nah.' It was a potty idea.

So potty it was worth a try.

'Come on!' she cried. Grabbing Perdita and Coriander's hands, she ran down the road. Not towards the hotel. Towards a bar by the river.

* * *

You'd think he hadn't moved for a week. Antonio Monio was slumped over the same table in Bar Tipitopitapas. 'Oh oh,' he moaned when Abbie tapped him on the shoulder.

'Oh oh,' he groaned when she introduced Perdita.

'Oh oh,' he sighed when the shrunken heads were popped on the table.

'Oh *no*!' he cried when Abbie told him her idea.

* * *

Mrs Monio opened the door. Seeing her husband she tried to close it.

But Abbie shoved past Antonio and jammed her foot in the door. 'Please,' she said, 'we're here to help you. Let us in.'

Mrs Monio frowned. 'Who you?'

'It's a long story,' said Abbie.

A very long one. Four hundred and thirty-two years to be precise, plus twenty-six minutes for insults. But that didn't matter. By the time Fernando and Carmen had finished their tale, Mrs Manuela Monio's eyes were shining.

'Such love,' she whispered. 'Such strong hearts.' Not strictly true. But for once neither Carmen nor Fernando corrected her by explaining their hearts had conked out centuries ago.

Carmen nodded. 'You see? Eef we estay together, so can you.'

Antonio Monio reached his hand across the table. 'Take me back, Manuela. Weeth golden Inca box we can buy another hotel, oh oh.'

She blinked at him. 'But not een backside of beyond – you promeese?'

He banged the table. 'New York, Paris, London … Monio Metropole, here we come!'

'Oh oh,' breathed Manuela, clasping her husband's hand.

* * *

'Graham, quick!' shrieked Mum. Dad ran over to the computer and stood behind her.

'Oh,' he breathed. 'Thank goodness.' He put his hands on Mum's shoulders and read.

Email: hartleyhome@yahoo.co.uk
Subject: safe and sound

Hi Mum, Dad and Ollie,
   I'm writing this from the hotel in Puyo.
We've had the most amazing adventure in
the jungle. Can't go into it now, except to
say that we've found Carmen. And can you
believe it, Hubris Klench has been arrested!
   Carmen is the crossest, bossiest shrunken
head you've ever met. She's always arguing
with Fernando, which apparently means they
love each other to bits. Are grown-ups weird
or what?
   Hi Ollie. Tell your class we've stroked an
anaconda, tickled a tarantula and met the
coolest armadillo in the Amazon.
   I'm off to bed now. We're flying back to
Quito tomorrow – by helicopter! Can't wait to
see you on Thursday.

   All my love, Abbie XXXX

Mum kissed Dad. Dad kissed Mum. They both kissed the
screen.

* * *

'HA!' Terry Strode-Boylie punched the air with his fist. 'Victory!' He jumped up and waved the Monday paper above his head.

'What, dear?' Genevieve put her coffee down.

Terry smacked *The Bradleigh Bellow* on the table. He jabbed the headline.

HIPPO HOP - ZOO FACES CHOP

special report by editor Corky Shocka

A runaway hippo could spell THE END for Bradleigh Zoo. Sunday strollers were STUNNED by the sight of Hepzibah Potts shambling round the town yesterday. The mud-mad monster CRASHED through the zoo barrier some time between Saturday evening and Sunday morning, when her escape was discovered by Charlie Chumb. The DISTRAUGHT zookeeper was at a loss for words.

'It's … er … we can't, um … she'd never … ah …' he told *THE BELLOW*.

Zoo owner Matt Platt agreed. 'Why would she run away? She has a wonderful life here,' he snivelled. 'Something must have tempted her out. It's a complete mystery.'

The WANDERING WOBBLER was finally arrested by Sergeant Bernard Bolt of Bradleigh Police. 'I found the mighty miscreant immersed in the river west of Bradleigh Park. Her owners were contacted immediately. Upon their arrival, the offending mammal returned willingly to her pool of origin in the zoological gardens.'

While the police are sure that Ms Potts has a WHALE of a life at the zoo, her escape is forcing them to RETHINK its FUTURE.

'Hippo today – who knows what tomorrow?' said Sergeant Bolt. 'Without fences we could face all manner of wildlife on the streets. Much as it grieves me, we have to consider closure.'

'How about that, Marcus?' Terry banged the table. 'Your shame avenged. Once that disaster area's shut down we'll stand tall again.' He stood tall. 'Revenge is sweet.'

'Look, Dad.' Marcus pointed to the bottom of the article.

BUT WE'LL FIGHT THIS, won't we, readers? Join *THE BELLOW*'S BATTLE to keep the zoo open. I'm sure you love visiting as much as I do. So put your names where your hearts are – and sign our petition below.

Terry snorted. 'Who's going to sign a pesky petition? No, I guarantee it's curtains for the zoo. Don't you feel great, m'boy?'

'Yes, Dad,' said Marcus, feeling completely, utterly and 158.74% the opposite.

28

The Middle of the World

Abbie needn't have worried about Grandma. She'd had the time of her life in Quito. 'I've been treated like a princess,' she said, tickling Chester.

It was Monday lunchtime. They were sitting in the canteen at Quito police headquarters. For once the plans had gone smoothly. The helicopter had collected Abbie, Perdita and Coriander from the hotel in Puyo and flown them to the capital.

Grandma had spent the previous night at the Chief Superintendent's home. 'They couldn't do enough for me,' she said. 'Mrs Super washed all me clothes. And the Chief bought me that.' She pointed to a brand new shopping trolley in the corner of the canteen. '*And*,' she produced a card from her pocket, ''e gave me this.' She passed it round.

'A lifetime's free bridge jumping, anywhere in Ecuador.' Abbie giggled. 'Aren't you the lucky one?'

'Not just me. Gav got an award for rescuin' the policemen.'

The little box jumped from Grandma's lap onto the table. He bowed. A medal was stuck to his screen. 'Clap your hands for Gav the Fleet,' he crowed, 'Order of the Natty Feet.'

He skipped across the table. Omelette and potato flew everywhere.

'For love of Maria,' yelled Abbie's bag, 'turn off thees beeghead!'

Wiping egg off her T-shirt, Abbie was glad to oblige.

'Course,' said Grandma, 'it's the least they could do. We've really put the Ecuadorian police on the map. All them top villains caught red-'anded.'

'What'll happen to them?' said Perdita. 'Will they stay in Ecuador?'

Grandma shook her head. 'They're bein' flown back to their own countries to stand trial. At least ...' She paused. 'Most of 'em are.'

Coriander put down her fork. 'What do you mean?'

'Well, that cowboy chap – they 'ad to let 'im go.'

Perdita smacked the table. 'Why? He was about to wreck the rainforest!'

'No proof,' said Grandma. 'The police thought at first 'e was Brag Swaggenham, a notorious oil baron 'oo once burned down an island in Indonesia. So they 'ad Brag's fingerprints faxed from Jakarta. But the prints didn't match this chap's. So 'e's free to go. And ...' She cleared her throat. 'There's someone else, too.'

'Who?' said Coriander faintly.

'Well …' Grandma pushed potato round her plate. 'A man 'oo's committed most of 'is crimes in England. A man 'oo's robbed more banks, smuggled more animals, traded more weapons, done more Chinese burns in *our* country than anywhere else in the–'

'Grandma,' said Abbie, 'what have you been up to?'

'Ahem, well, I might've asked the Chief Super to phone Scotland Yard. They were thrilled to take Klench. Said it's only fair 'e goes to prison in the UK.' For a woman who'd leapt off a bridge, tramped through the jungle and risked her life for her granddaughter, Grandma looked surprisingly nervous.

'And?' said Abbie sternly. 'What aren't you telling us?'

Grandma's cheeks went plum. 'Well, there's prisons and there's prisons and there's …'

Then it all tumbled out … 'Bradleigh prison. And I thought if Klench went there I could visit some time, and help 'im learn to stand up to 'is mother, 'coz whether she's really in 'is mind or not, 'e believes she is, and what sort of chance does 'e stand with a woman like that, so if I don't do somethin' Klench'll never be rid of 'er, and 'e'll never change, and 'e'll just carry on with 'is wickedness forever, and …' Grandma took a breath. She looked at Abbie, who looked at Perdita, who looked at Coriander, who looked back at Grandma, who said, 'Look–'

'It's OK.' Coriander raised her hand. 'I understand.' She took a deep breath. 'As long as he's locked away, what does it matter if he's nearby? And you're right. It's worth a try.

Maybe with your help he *can* become a new man. Kind.'

'Caring,' said Perdita.

'Considerate,' said Abbie.

'Cute,' said Grandma. Everyone stared at her. That was pushing it.

'What about Dollarine?' said Abbie. 'Where will she go when her parents are in prison?'

'To live with 'er grandparents,' said Grandma. 'Apparently they run a centre for abandoned pets in California. Dogs bought for Christmas then dumped in January. Pythons that frighten the neighbours, aardvarks that dig up the lawn – that sort of thing.'

Perdita clapped her hands. 'Perfect! Maisie-Lou will love it.'

After lunch the Chief Superintendent invited them all to stay at his house until they flew back to England. But Abbie whispered to Grandma that Fernando and Carmen would have to hide in her handbag, which was no way to spend the last two nights in your country of shrinkage. So the visitors declined politely.

The Chief Super insisted on giving them a lift to the Hotel Cóndor where they'd spent their first two nights in Ecuador.

'Come again to Ecuador,' he said, beaming at the hotel entrance. 'You always welcome at my home. And who know – thanks to these arrests, perhaps next time I president.' He puffed out his already puffed-out chest. He smoothed his already smooth hair. He shook them by the hand. He kissed them on the cheek. He bowed. He saluted. He cleared his throat and sang the Ecuadorian national anthem. Then he marched off picking his nose.

* * *

Over breakfast next morning Coriander suggested that they visit the equator. Fernando and Carmen, who'd been shrunk before its discovery, were thrilled to learn that their country of conquerage sat slap-bang in the middle of the world.

When they arrived at the monument, the heads insisted on having their photo taken. That was easier said than done amid a crowd of tourists. But at a quiet moment Abbie popped Fernando on one side of the yellow line that halved the world and Carmen on the other.

'I love you from north to south,' shouted Fernando.

'I love you from top to bottom,' declared Carmen, which, even when you *have* no bottom, is a lovely thing to hear.

Then Gav ruined it all. Coriander had switched him on, feeling it was only right to take his photo too. He capered either side of the line like an electronic Rumplestiltskin.

'Turn around and touch your toes,

Hold your partner by the nose.
If you want the *real* equator
Follow me – or see you later.'
He skipped off along the paved avenue.

Abbie glanced at her guidebook. Gav was right. 'Modern data shows that the equator is actually 240 metres north of the marked line,' she read.

Trust him to spoil the fun. She waited till he returned from the real equator. 'That's enough of your lip,' she said firmly, switching him off.

Email: corkyshocka@bradleighbellow.net
Subject: Letter from the Equator

I can't believe it's our last day in Ecuador.
I know I haven't written for a while, but
we've been busy having the adventure of
several lifetimes. If I told you about it, you'd
never believe me. So here's a game to help
you work it out for yourself. Use the words
to piece together what happened to us in the
jungle. Send your answers to *The Bradleigh
Bellow*.

Armadillo
Crooks
Tarantula
Superdooperglooper Glue
Mint-green

Disguise

Ecclescake

If you find it really hard, here's a clue.

It's really hard.

So hard that Grandma Hartley-Absinthe will award the winner a lifetime pass for Ecuadorian bridge jumping.
Good luck!

* * *

On Wednesday morning it was a sad yet happy Mr Dabbings who stood before the class. 'Bad news and good news, lads and ladles. Which do you want first?'

'Good' shouted the left half of the class and 'Bad' the right.

The teacher wagged his finger. 'Eeny meeny miny mitch. Knit one, purl one, drop a stitch. OK. Bad it is.' He placed his palms flat on the desk and leaned forward. 'I'm afraid,' he said slowly, 'the zoo is definitely going to close down.'

A gasp went round.

'But what about the petition?' cried Claire. 'The whole school signed it.'

It was true. Even Marcus had scrawled his name to avoid suspicion. Greg had given him the funniest look. In fact, Greg had given him the funniest looks ever since Monday's news about the hippo's escape. And he'd steered clear, too.

Mr Dabbings sighed. 'We tried, kids. But the problem is no one knows *why* Hepzibah walked out. So no one can be sure it won't happen again – with her or another animal.'

'Why don't they put them all in cages, then?' asked Rukia Zukia, whose middle name should have been Sensible but was actually Lukia. 'Like other zoos. Then it can stay open.'

Mr Dabbings shook his head. 'No can do. The Platts don't want it to be like other zoos. They insist their animals must be as free as birds.'

'But they're animals,' said Craig, who wasn't the sharpest Frube in the tube.

'What I mean,' said Mr Dabbings patiently, 'is that Mr Platt refuses to run a zoo where the animals are locked up. And he refuses to sell it to anyone who'd do that, which is basically everyone.'

'Hey, sir,' shouted Henry, 'how d'you know all this?'

Mr Dabbings shifted from one sandal to the other. 'I've been, er, spending some time at the zoo. Which brings me to the *good* news. Wend–, I mean Miss Wibberly, and I are …' He held up his left hand. On the fourth finger sat a knitted green band.

'ENGAGED!' roared the class.

'Pure cashmere wool,' he said proudly.

'I thought only ladies wore engagement rings.'

'It's a statement, Terrifica. Of our equality, unity and harmony.' Mr Dabbings sighed with joy. 'All big words, kids, which basically mean that I'll be doing the dishes. There'll be an announcement in *The Bradleigh Bellow* tomorrow.

You're all invited to the wedding, 25 December.'

'But that's Christmas Day!'

'Indeed, Henry.' Mr Dabbings beamed. 'We chose that date to show that *every* day of our marriage will be like Christmas.'

* * *

Mrs Strode-Boylie picked up a dirty sock from Marcus's floor. She sighed. Just like his dad, expecting her to clear up after him. She really should get them to tidy their own messes. But whenever she'd suggested it, their sulky silences made it easier to do it herself.

She made her way through the T-shirts and trousers on the floor and picked up Marcus's waste-paper basket.

She took it downstairs to empty in the kitchen bin. It was packed tight. She wiggled the contents out. Broken pencils, a comic, two apple cores, a tightly crumpled white paper bag. Another crumpled bag. Another one … and another …

Genevieve frowned. Bag after bag was stuffed in the basket. And at the bottom was a pile of white crystals. No! Was Marcus sniffing something? Or injecting? Or pouring it into his ear or whatever they did these days? Her heart racing, Genevieve smoothed out a packet on the kitchen table.

She breathed out with relief.

Licking her finger, she tasted a few crystals to check. Yes. Thank goodness. Sugar.

Odd, though. Since when was Marcus addicted to sugar?

Eighteen one-kilo packets – hardly a bedtime snack. Terry would have a fit. Imagine the headline:

BY GUM! DENTIST'S SON NEEDS DENTURES

Genevieve frowned across the table. Talking of headlines … her eye caught the front page of Monday's *Bellow*. Terry had ordered her to frame the article about the zoo closure.

She gasped. A crazy thought had popped into her head. So crazy it couldn't possibly – Genevieve chewed her lip – be true. She'd go and knock it straight on the head.

She went into Terry's office. She switched on the computer and Googled 'hippopotamus'.

'No!' She tried another website. 'No!' And another. She put her head in her hands. Then she went to the hall and dialled the Fniggs' number.

No, Mrs Fnigg told her, Marcus hadn't come round last Saturday, and was everything all right?

'Fine,' Genevieve whispered. 'Thanks.'

She put down the phone and burst into tears.

29

Zoo Blues

'Abbie!' Mum and Dad waved madly across the barrier in the Arrivals area. Ollie had already wriggled underneath and was hurtling towards her. He crashed into her arms. Dad swung his legs over, ran up and smothered her in a hug.

Mum scuttled round the barrier and shoved through the stream of arrivals. 'Sorry!' she snapped, sounding anything but. 'It's my daughter.'

Abbie put down her rucksack, held out her arms and hugged them all. Grandma removed her top teeth, scraped off a toffee then hugged them all.

'We've missed you so much,' Mum sobbed, laughed and gasped all at once. 'We were so worried.'

'With good reason,' said Grandma. 'This young lady's been a right 'andful. Frightened the life out of us, worried the pants off us and – oh yes – 'elped save our bacon.'

'No, Grandma, *you* did.' Abbie laughed. 'We'll tell you all about it after that lot untangles itself.' Matt, Perdita and

Coriander were blocking the gangway with a muddle of cuddle.

When Dad offered to pull Grandma's new shopping trolley for her, she swatted him away. 'Get your paws off. I won't 'ave any Tom, Dick or Graham draggin' me Saco Supremo. Top of the range, you know,' she added so proudly and loudly that a passing grandpa heard thunder in his hearing aid.

Abbie, too, refused to let Dad carry her rucksack. 'You'll disturb the happy couple. They're fast asleep.'

'Esleep? How we esleep when you bang us about like the jumpeeng beans?' shrieked a voice.

Abbie led everyone to a quiet spot and lifted Carmen out. 'Mum, Dad, Ollie, Matt. meet Mrs Feraldo.'

'I happy to hello.' Carmen twitched her nose. Dad gave a little bow. Mum gave a little curtsey. Matt gave a little sigh.

Abbie stared at him. He had his wife and daughter back. So why did he look as dismal as dishwater? 'Are you OK, Matt?' she asked gently.

'Y-yes.' He rubbed a finger over his teeth and glanced at Dad.

Dad put his arm round Abbie. 'Let's get to the car, darling. We're dying to hear about your adventure.'

Which they did: or at least the bare bones. Travelling home in the Hartleys' car, Abbie and Grandma told their story. Mum, Dad and Ollie listened, enthralled.

In the Platts' van, driving behind them, there must have been a different story. Because when they all arrived at the zoo, Coriander jumped out and rushed through the entrance gate.

'What's happened?' said Abbie.

Perdita couldn't speak. Tears were streaming down her face. She ran after Coriander.

Mum laid a hand on Abbie's arm. 'There's been an … incident, darling.' Then Dad explained all about Hepzibah's escape and the zoo having to close.

'NO!' Abbie yelled. She too rushed into the zoo.

Everyone gathered by the hippo pool. Charlie was there, gazing at Hepzibah as she wallowed in bubbly bliss, immune to all the fuss.

'We can't imagine why she, um …' Charlie's huge ears wiggled wretchedly. 'Not like her at all. And she's back now, happy as – you know. No sign of wanting to, um … again.'

'How *could* you, Heppie?' yelled Perdita.

'Ssssh.' Charlie put a finger to his lips. 'Please don't make her feel, um … It wasn't her fault. She was just – you know.'

'No, I *don't*!' Abbie cried.

'Nor does anyone else,' said Matt. 'We have no idea why she walked out. And we can't risk it happening again. Hepzibah's not used to town life – the crowds and traffic. If anything startled her she might panic. Someone could get killed. *She* could get killed.'

'So?' cried Perdita. 'Build cages, then! Anything's better than closing the zoo.'

Coriander clutched Matt's hand. Her face was white. 'No. We can't do that. The whole point of this zoo is to give the animals as much freedom as possible. We can't lock them up now. They'd feel so betrayed.

Everyone knew that was true. But no one would admit it. So they gazed in silent misery at Hepzibah's giant yawn.

The homecoming was ruined. Abbie didn't even smile at Wendy's poster in the café window.

Welcome back and i know it's terrible but at least there are buttons to polish, and a wedding to look forward to

Underneath she'd added:

(mine)

Abbie hardly tasted Dad's welcome dinner of Bourbon lasagne followed by Jammy Dodger soufflé. And, in her distraction, she stepped on the welcome-home anaconda which Ollie had made by threading fifty-nine toilet-roll tubes on a piece of string and draping them round the house.

For once, though, Ollie didn't cry. 'It's OK,' he said, squeezing her hand. 'I'll feed it a tapir. That'll make it fat again.'

Which didn't help one bit, because tapirs made Abbie think of the zoo, which made her think of the not-much-longer zoo.

There was no question of school the next day. Abbie and Perdita spent the Friday 'recovering from their flight', which meant moping round the zoo, crying a lot, having hugs and emptying the café of chocolate bars.

'Mum says we can keep Clement and Persephone,' said Perdita, stroking the tortoises' shells.

'Gee whizz. Aren't you the lucky ones?' sighed Abbie. 'Nothing personal,' she added, as Clement's eyes shone in a way that reminded her of boyfriends being dumped on TV soaps.

'And Mackenzie can stay too.' Perdita tickled the claws of the parrot, who refused to leave her shoulder.

Big deal, thought Abbie. *That means you'll only have to get rid of the tiger, the ostriches, the penguins, the eagle, the chameleons, the zebras, the porcupines, the seals, the giraffe, the crocodile, the elephant, the orang– NO!* The thought of losing Vinnie, Winnie and Minnie to a jungle adaptation centre in Borneo got her sobbing for the eighteenth time that day.

'Sorry.' Abbie wiped her face with her sleeve. 'I just can't bear to think of the orangs.'

That set Perdita off. She began to howl. Mackenzie

shrieked. Then Abbie howled, Perdita shrieked and Mackenzie wailed. Then Abbie shrieked, Perdita wailed and Mackenzie howled. It was like Rock, Paper, Scissors for the Very Distressed.

'Anyway, how *do* you send an animal home?' Abbie sniffed. She imagined wrapping the giraffe in brown paper, addressing the parcel 'African Savannah' and then discovering that Alphonse didn't fit in the post box.

She pictured putting Silvio in a crate and writing 'Indian Jungle: Handle with Care', by which time the tiger would have chomped through the box.

She thought of packing Gina's suitcase with brushes to paint the forests of Thailand, only to find that the ellie exceeded the airline's luggage allowance.

By five o'clock Abbie had had enough. She'd hugged all the huggable animals and waved to all the unhuggable ones. She'd spilled enough tears for a bath and filled up with more chocolate than a vending machine.

'I'd better go home,' she sighed, standing by the penguin pool.

'OK.' Perdita was fitting a pair of goggles round a penguin's head. 'See you tomorrow.'

Abbie turned to go. 'What the …?' She gasped. 'What's *he* doing here?'

Walking towards them, with his head bowed, was Marcus Strode-Boylie. A lady with dark curls led him by the hand. A carrier bag hung from her arm.

'Hello,' said the lady, whom Abbie recognised as Marcus's mum. 'You're Abigail and Perdita, aren't you?' Her pretty face was grim. 'I wonder, dear,' she looked at Perdita, 'could I have a word with your parents?'

'Sure.' Perdita smiled as cheerfully as a girl who's about to lose her home, plus all her furry and feathered friends, can smile. 'Hi, Marcus.'

He stared at the ground.

'Thanks for helping out while we were away,' said Perdita. 'Dad told me.'

Abbie gawped. *Marcus helping out? Penguins might fly!* The penguin tried to and fell flat on its beak.

'The goggles are for swimming, not flying, you jackass.' Perdita helped the penguin up. 'Not the smartest birds,' she explained to Mrs Strode-Boylie. 'Come with me.'

Coriander and Matt were standing by the hippo pool with Mum and Dad. Hepzibah was in the water, her mouth agape, while the Platts cleaned her teeth with very long brushes. Mrs Strode-Boylie stopped nervously at the edge of the grass.

'It's OK,' said Perdita. 'Heppie won't come out. At least …' She bit her lip.

'I know,' said Mrs Strode-Boylie. 'That's why we're here.' Taking a deep breath, she stepped onto the grass. Then she turned the carrier bag upside down. Eighteen flattened paper bags fell out. 'Marcus,' she said, 'tell them why their hippo went walkies.'

* * *

Corky Shocka's fingers flew across the keyboard. She hated working on Saturdays – tried to leave it to the weekend staff – but this story broke all the rules. She'd even cut short her weekly zoo visit to rush to the office.

Corky finished typing, sat back and read over her article. It couldn't even wait till Sunday. She'd print a:

Special Saturday Edition

HIP HIPPO HOORAY! THE ZOO CAN STAY

The Bellow reveals the whole sweet tooth

Bradleigh Zoo is saved! Thanks to a STARTLING CONFESSION, the mystery of the wandering hippo has been solved. *THE BELLOW* can reveal that hefty Hepzibah Potts was lured from her home by nothing more fancy than humble household SUGAR! Some SICK TRICKSTER left a trail of the treat along the path by her pool. Smelling her NUMBER ONE NOSH, the hungry hippo gobbled her way out of the zoo. The ROTTEN RUSE was rumbled on Friday when the culprit came clean.

And thanks to the admission, Police Sergeant Bolt says the zoo can now stay open. 'After extensive discussions with the proprietors, we are satisfied that precautions can be taken to prevent further abscondings,' he said. Which to you and me, readers, means IT WON'T HAPPEN AGAIN.

Why not? Because zoo owner Matt Platt is already at work inventing a SNEAKY SNACK-TRACKER. 'All visitors will be scanned at the entrance by a special camera that detects food,' he said. 'Any treats will be confiscated. So there'll be no more escapes and no need to lock the animals up.'

But WE want to lock someone up, don't we, readers? Yes indeed – the LOUSY LOUT who poured the sugar out. Who's behind the PESKY PRANK? Someone with a grudge? Someone seeking revenge on the Platts for a past insult? Who could it be?

'I'm afraid I can't tell you,' said Matt Platt.

'Mum's the word,' said his wife, Coriander.

'It wouldn't be fair,' said their daughter, Perdita. 'He's only a boy.'

Only zookeeper Charlie Chumb was prepared to spill the beans – or should we say sugar? 'It was, um – you know,' he said.

* * *

There are several skills you don't need to become a Massively Successful Dentist. Among them are modesty, humility and losing well at Monopoly.

One skill you *do* need, however, is basic maths. Which is why Terry Strode-Boylie soon put two and two together to make roar.

'MARCUS!' He smacked the Special Saturday Edition of *The Bellow* on the table. 'COME. HERE. THIS. MINUTE!'

30

Missing

Abbie should have been happy. The zoo was saved and Marcus was disgraced.

But she was furious. Fuming. Spitting mad. Well not actually spitting – it was Saturday evening and she didn't want to waste her dinner on the tablecloth – but certainly mad.

'*Why* couldn't we tell Corky it was Marcus who let Heppie out?' She stabbed a sausage. 'He deserves to have his name splashed all over *The Bellow*.'

'Over *The Bellow*, over *The Bellow*,' squawked Mackenzie, 'name him and shame him, the smelly young fellow.'

Hear hear, thought Abbie. Thank goodness Mum had chosen the bird house for their dinner spot. At least the parrot saw sense.

'Look,' said Dad, 'even if we *had* told Corky, she couldn't name Marcus in the paper. He's a child. It's against the law.'

'So was letting Heppie out,' said Abbie. 'He should pay for his crime.'

'Pay for his crime, pay for his crime,' echoed Mackenzie, 'no doubt about it: the boy should do time.'

You tell 'em, Mack. Abbie threw him a pea gratefully. He rolled it on his tongue.

'I'm not sure it *was* a crime,' said Matt. 'Remember, Heppie wasn't fenced in. That could be a bit of a grey area in the law.'

'Anyway,' said Mum, 'this way the Strode-Boylies owe us one. Genevieve promised that if we don't go round telling people, she can keep her husband quiet. Otherwise he'll be so mad he'll find another way to close the zoo down.'

'So Marcus gets away scot-free? That's outrageous!' said Abbie.

'Outrageous, unfair, disgraceful, unjust.

The boy needs to pay for his deed – it's a must.'

Amen. Abbie threw Mackenzie a sprout. He caught it in his beak and swallowed it whole.

'I bet he *will* pay,' said Perdita. 'His dad's bound to punish him. So we shouldn't go blabbing at school either. That would make it unbearable for Marcus.'

Mackenzie cocked his head:

'I hear what you're saying – annoying but true –

When you put it like that, I agree with your view.'

'Traitor!' Abbie threw a baked potato and knocked Mackenzie off his perch. She stood up from the table and stormed off.

Grandma found her later by the porcupines' bouncy castle. Abbie was throwing tennis balls at a turret.

'That's it, my girl. Get it out of your system,' said Grandma.

'It's so unfair!' Abbie snapped. 'Marcus nearly ruined our lives.'

Grandma nodded. 'Certainly did.'

'And now he's got away with it.'

'True.' Grandma tutted.

'Like he always does.'

Grandma sighed. 'So it seems.'

'And I can't even *tell* anyone!'

'Oh, I wouldn't say that.'

'What do you mean? You heard them at dinner.' Abbie lobbed a ball at a battlement.

Grandma folded her arms. 'You could tell Marcus.'

Abbie blinked. 'What?'

'Tell 'im exactly what you think of 'im. Get it off your chest. It'll do you a power of good.'

Abbie's eyes widened. 'You mean at school? Wow.'

'Somewhere private, mind.' Grandma shrugged. 'Just a thought. Chew on it.' She pottered off.

Abbie gazed after her. It was a great idea … but how to get Marcus alone? If anyone overheard, and word got out, she'd be in the poop.

She threw another ball. '*Now* what do I do?' she said, as a porcupine speared it on one of his spines.

***

Nothing, as it turned out. When she and Perdita walked

into the classroom on Monday, Marcus wasn't there. Nor was anyone else.

'Are we early?' said Perdita. 'Or late?' She frowned round the room. 'According to that thing,' she pointed at a knitted sundial on Mr Dabbings's desk, 'it's either midday or night-time.'

Abbie guessed that woollen sundials don't cast the best shadows. So she looked at her watch. 'It's ten to nine. Where is everyone?' Her heart sank. She'd actually been looking forward to school. Not just to shout at Marcus. She'd also dared to hope that the class might welcome them back. At the very least, you'd think they'd celebrate Saturday's article in *The Bellow* about the zoo staying open.

'Perhaps they're on a school trip,' said Perdita. 'Had to leave early.'

'Then why didn't Mr Dabbings tell us? He could've left a message with Wendy.' Abbie scowled. She'd never water his classroom herbs again.

♫ 'FOR … *THEY'RE* TWO JOLLY GOOD FELL-OWS!' The class burst through the door. They were singing, clapping and playing all manner of papier maché instruments.

Terrifica tooted through a paper trombone.

Behind her came Henry on cymbals. 'Smash! Wallop! Clang-ang-ang!'

Claire trilled through a newspaper flute.

Rukia plucked a floppy banjo.

Ursula tapped a tissue-paper triangle. 'Ping!' she yelled, though it was drowned out by Snorty's nose percussion.

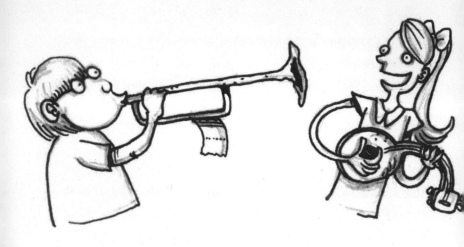

'Welcome home!' they shouted, crowding round the girls.

'How was the trip?'

'You're so brown.'

'Fantastic news about the zoo.'

'We missed you.'

Abbie grinned, though her insides were blushing. How could she have doubted Mr Dabbings? Or the class? She still hadn't got the hang of being, dare she say it, *popular.* Everyone grinned back.

Everyone except Marcus. She looked round. He still wasn't there.

The others were tying bells round their ankles for the Welcome Home Frolic.

After she and Perdita had been wrapped in ribbons like human maypoles (who cared if it was December?) Abbie went up to Greg Fnigg. 'Where's Marcus?' she said.

Greg shrugged. 'I dunno. Off sick I s'pose.' He blinked at the ground.

And suddenly Abbie knew. 'You know, don't you?' she said.

'Know what?' Greg blushed.

'*You* know. About the You-Know.'

'I … no. Oh no.' And then it all came out. How Marcus had told Greg his plan. How Greg hadn't taken it seriously until Hepzibah's escape. How he'd been in agony ever since, not even confiding in his parents. How he was worried about getting into trouble for covering up Marcus's crime. And how he was even *more* worried about Marcus.

'I've phoned loads of times,' Greg said, his face all pinched from the strain of not crying. 'But his dad won't let me talk to him. I bet he's having a dreadful time.'

Abbie snorted. *Here we go again. Everyone's on Marcus's side.*

'Look,' Greg went on, 'I know he's been horrible to you. And I have too. I'm really sorry. I should never have gone along with him. And maybe it's no excuse – but things aren't easy for him at home.'

Abbie glared at him. Skinny, snickery Greg Fnigg, all tea and sympathy. 'It *is* an excuse!' she yelled. 'It's nothing *but* excuses!' She stomped off. Marcus Strode-Boylie was the pits of the planet, the U-bend of the universe – and she was going to tell him so.

It was easy enough to slip back into the classroom at lunch break. Perdita was in the playground handing out Incan toothpicks. Mr Dabbings was in the staff room knitting Wendy's wedding bouquet. Abbie ran along the corridor into the empty classroom. She crept up to Mr Dabbings's desk and opened the top drawer. Taking out the class register, she turned to the page of pupils' contact details. She scribbled down Marcus's address on a scrap of paper. She slid the book back in the drawer. Then she hurried out and along the corridor. At the school office she asked to phone home. After a quick 'Hi-Mum-I'm-going-to-the-zoo-with-Perdita-after-school-I'll-catch-the-bus-home-see-you-around-six-love-you-bye', she ran back to the playground, arriving just in time to pull Henry Holler's toothpick out of Ursula Slightly's arm.

Abbie's heart hammered through the rest of school. When the home bell rang she jumped up from her chair. 'Do me a favour,' she said to Perdita. 'If Mum phones, pretend I'm at the zoo with you. See you tomorrow.'

'What are you …?'

But Abbie was already out of the door. She ran to the cloakroom, threw on her coat and rushed out of school. Ten minutes later she was on the bus to Bradleigh's smartest suburb.

* * *

Marcus pulled the pillow off his face. There was a knock at the door.

'Yes?' he said, sitting up and wiping his nose on his sleeve. *Please let it be Dad, please let it be Dad, please let it be–*

290

His mum crept in. She was carrying a glass of milk and a chocolate bar. 'Give me the wrapper when you've finished, darling. Don't want your dad finding it.'

'You mean he might look in my bin. Like you did.'

Genevieve blushed. 'I had to, darling, you know that.'

Marcus hugged the duvet round his knees. 'Is he still mad?'

'I'm afraid so. We need to give him time.'

'Why? I was trying to close the zoo down. I thought that's what he wanted.'

Genevieve sighed. 'Yes, but he's worried that if word gets out it was you, the family name will be ruined.' She ran a hand through Marcus's hair. 'Look, this'll all blow over. We just need to give him time.'

'He's *had* two days.'

'Mmm. But you know what he's like. Best keep out of his way for now. How about going back to school tomorrow? Better than lying here all day.'

'No.' Marcus pulled the duvet up to his chin. 'What if everyone knows it was me who let the hippo out? What if Greg or Abigail or Perdita have told them?'

Genevieve shook her head. 'They won't. Their parents promised.'

Tears rolled down Marcus's cheeks. If only his mum knew how horrible he'd been this term. Abigail Hartley would be itching for revenge – and this was her chance.

31

Payback

Abbie stared over the gate. The lawn was huge and perfectly mown. *Bet they've got a gardener.* In one corner was a pond with a fancy rockery. *Bet there are goldfish.* In another corner was a trampoline. *And that's just the front!*

As for the house, it was enormous. There were windows everywhere, French doors at the bottom and skylights in the roof. A huge glass conservatory stuck out on the left. The garage on the right would make a decent home in itself. The Strode-Boylie Jaguar was parked in front.

He's loaded, thought Abbie. *Rolling in it. Stinking rich.* Marcus had everything he wanted. Why couldn't he leave her and Perdita alone? By the time she'd opened the gate and crossed the lawn she was radiant with rage. She rammed her palm against the doorbell. It rang, loud and long.

The front door opened. Dr Strode-Boylie loomed in the doorway. He wore a V-necked sports jersey, the same light blue as his eyes. Below the left shoulder an embroidered lion roared.

'Yes?' He arched a silver eyebrow.

Abbie couldn't help stepping backwards. 'I – I'm Abigail Hartley.'

'I know. Daughter of that writer foo– fellow.'

'I've come to see Marcus.' Abbie cursed the quiver in her voice. *I'm not scared*, she told herself, *I'm furious. I'm not scared, I'm furious. I'm not scared, I'm …* 'Aah!' He was closing the door.

Abbie shoved her hand through. 'I know what Marcus did,' she said quickly. 'And if you don't let me in, I'll tell everyone at school.'

Dr Strode-Boylie stopped. Something flared in those pale eyes. Uncertainty? Fear? He cleared his throat. 'You'll, ah, do no such thing, young lady. Now go home and mind your own business.'

'It *is* my business.' Abbie's voice was louder than she intended. 'Marcus has spent the whole term bullying my friend Perdita. Just because she comes top in Maths and Geography and–'

'*What*? My son is top of the class. He comes first in everything.'

'That's not true. Perdita's beaten him in every single Maths test.'

'Are you accusing my son of–?'

'Ask him yourself,' squeaked Abbie.

Dr Strode-Boylie turned his head. 'Marcus!' he roared into the hall. 'Here, now!'

Marcus must have been listening because three seconds

later he appeared behind his dad. His face was white, his eyes red. His hair was rumpled, his shirt crumpled. He stared at Abbie, miserable as mumps.

She swallowed. This was her moment of power and payback. Her chance for revenge, to right all the wrongs Marcus had done.

She took a deep breath – and let him have it. 'How can you be such a bully? Pushing people around, cheating and shoving your way to the top, doing anything to win, blaming everyone else if you don't? How can you,' she yelled, 'ruin your son's life?'

Because the truth was staring her in the face. The truth she could no longer ignore, that she'd glimpsed at the school gates, through the window of a Jaguar, in Maths tests and running races. The truth that a frightened boy would stop at nothing to win his father's love.

The boy took a step back. The father took a step forward.

'How. Dare. You,' Dr Strode-Boylie whispered, 'Speak. To me. Like. That. I. Am. A Massively. Successful. Dentist.' He bared his teeth as if to prove it.

'And I,' came a voice, 'am. A Massively. Fed-Up. Wife.'

Mrs Strode-Boylie appeared behind Marcus. She seized his hand and pushed out of the door past her husband. Out on the porch she threw her arms round Abbie. 'Thank you. Thank you. Thank you.' She hugged her tightly.

She wheeled round. 'You,' she jabbed Dr Strode-Boylie in the chest, 'have just heard' (jab) 'what I've never dared' (jab jab) 'say. *You*,' she pushed him backwards, 'are an Impossible

… Unpleasable … Ridiculous … PLONKER! Nothing is *ever* good enough for you – your massive success, your flashy car, your meek little wife, your wonderful son. Don't you see? Marcus would do *anything* to make you happy! Even close down a zoo, if that's what you want. How *dare* you punish him!'

Dr Strode-Boylie went as pale as pasta. His eyebrows bunched; his forehead scrunched. His shoulders shivered; his lips quivered. 'B-b-but,' they managed, 'the shame. The family na–'

'The family name, the family name!' Mrs Strode-Boylie clapped her hands to her ears. 'I've had enough of the family name. Stuff the Strode-Boylies, long live the Strod-boils!' She ran across the lawn and leapt onto the trampoline. 'Strodboil!' she yelled, jumping up and down. 'I married a Strod-boil! A silly, snobby Strod-boil!'

Next door's lawnmower went silent. A car slowed down in the road. And four slugs stopped their game of lawn tennis to stare at the loopy leaper.

* * *

'I wish you could've seen her,' said Abbie that evening. She was on the sofa in the sitting room. 'You'd think she'd won the lottery.'

'I wish I could've seen *you*,' said Mum. 'I can't believe you spoke to Marcus's dad like that.' Abbie couldn't tell if there was pride or dismay in her voice.

Dad came to the rescue. 'Not a moment too soon. Just what that pompous twit needed. Well done, my girl.'

'I'm not so sure about that.' Mum frowned. 'He's a powerful man. I don't fancy going to any dentist in Bradleigh now.'

'Yippee!' Ollie danced round the room. 'No more fillings.'

Mum sighed. 'I mean we'll have to go somewhere else.'

'Fillin's,' said Grandma. 'Waste of time. Better to pull your teeth out and get falsies. *I* 'aven't seen a dentist for three years.' She grinned proudly, revealing a sliver of chicken wedged between her top dentures. 'Mind you, I'd like to 'ave seen *this* dentist. Bet 'e was a sight.'

'Not for long,' said Abbie. 'He ran inside and slammed the front door. But Marcus stood there like a bomb had hit him.'

'A good bomb or a bad bomb?' said Ollie.

Abbie rolled her eyes. 'When did you last see a *good* bomb?' But to tell the truth it wasn't such a daft question. She recalled the confusion on Marcus's face – amazement, fear, anxiety and hope – as his mum had jumped off the trampoline and run to her son. Mrs Strode-Boylie had waved at Abbie and led him off round the side of the house.

'What a performance!' Grandma chuckled. 'Sounds better than *Suds*. 'Ere, talkin' of which ...' She tapped her watch.

'We'll leave you to it, Mother,' said Dad. Abbie followed him out. She'd never understood what Grandma saw in her favourite soap, about daily life in a launderette.

* * *

Klench finished his plate of cold chicken. 'No puddink?' he said.

The Ecuadorian guard took the plate. 'This jail,' he said, 'not five-star restaurant.' But looking at the roly-poly inmate huddled in the corner of the cell, he felt a twinge of pity. In his bright prison boiler suit, Klench looked like a lonely orange.

Lonely? Klench *dreamed* of lonely. 'Go vay, Mums!' he cried when the guard had gone.

'But I can help you escapes,' she cooed. 'Ve'll make a plan, my captive man.'

Klench clapped his hands to his ears. 'Never mind prison. I vont to escapes *you*!'

32

No One to Hate

Abbie didn't know what to expect at school next morning. Would Marcus be friendly or furious? Grateful or hateful? Would he even come?

He did. But he slunk in late, after the class had greeted December the eleventh.

Mr Dabbings looked up from his desk. 'Welcome back, Marcus. What was wrong with you?'

'A bug, sir.'

Mr Dabbings nodded. 'Some nasty bugs going round. I don't mean the actual *bugs* are nasty. They just make us *feel* nasty. The bugs *themselves* are probably kind and thoughtful. Remember, kids, germs have feelings too.'

All morning, when she wasn't thinking of Ten Ways to Respect a Dandelion, Abbie kept glancing at Marcus. But he was always bent over his book or talking to Greg.

'Do you think he's mad at me?' she whispered. She'd told Perdita all about her visit to his house.

Perdita shrugged. 'Dunno. Depends what happened after

you left.'

Abbie dreaded to think. Had she made things worse?

At break time Perdita tried to cheer her up. 'It was brilliant what you did,' she said as they stomped round the playground to keep warm. 'You stood up for Marcus. And his mum loved it, even if his dad didn't.'

'That's the point,' said Abbie. 'His dad'll be furious. Maybe he'll take it out on Marcus.'

'Hi.' Greg appeared in front of them. And behind him – for the very first time in the history of behinds – came Marcus.

'Hello,' said Perdita. Abbie stared at the ground. Feeling sorry for Marcus was one thing, *admitting* it to him a whole new packet of Pringles. 'I …' she said.

'I …' he said.

'You first,' she said.

'You first,' he said.

'Sorry,' she said.

'Sorry?' he said. '*I'm* the one who's sorry. For everything.'

Abbie took a deep, grateful breath. *So* that's *why he's been avoiding us. Out of shame.* 'Well, I'm sorry too,' she said. 'I know things have been, um, hard for you.'

Marcus blushed. 'It's fine.'

Wow, thought Abbie, *whatever's happened at home, he still won't complain about his dad.* She felt a grudging admiration.

Marcus turned to Perdita. 'Look. Letting your hippo out – it was all my idea. You mustn't think anyone else helped me.'

She glared at him. 'I don't.'

He kicked a stone wretchedly. 'It was a terrible thing to do.'

'You're telling me.' She nodded fiercely.

'You probably won't forgive me.'

She shook her head. 'Probably not.' Then she whacked him on the arm. 'Because I already have! Here.' She held out a tiny package. 'Have an Incan toothpick.'

* * *

What a strange day. Abbie kept expecting Marcus to trip her up, or put her down, or at least smirk. Strangest of all was the PE lesson, when he chose her and Perdita for his Rounders team. Even Miss Whelp looked surprised, her eyebrows doing high jumps.

Along with her own amazement, Abbie felt … what? Not exactly disappointment, more a kind of bewilderment. There was no one to loathe any more, no one to blame for a bad day at school.

As the day wore on, though, she began to get the hang of not hating Marcus. It was actually quite fun. Being enemies had been such hard work, like trying to make a jigsaw from pieces that didn't fit. Because when you decided to hate someone – *really* hate them – you had to hate every single thing about them: the colour of their hair; the way they threw paper aeroplanes into the bin; the tone of their voice.

And the truth was that Marcus's hair was the happiest of yellows. His aeroplane aim was to die for. And he had a good voice. Whenever it was his turn to serenade the classroom herbs they had a growth spurt.

Abbie had arranged to go to the zoo after school with Perdita. They'd booked a volleyball match with Winnie: the ape's mighty arms could easily handle two opponents. As the girls headed through the school gates to the bus stop, Abbie felt a tap on her shoulder. She turned round.

'Hey.' Marcus was smiling. *Not a bad smile*, thought Abbie, *without the sneery bits.*

'My mum asked if we can give you a lift.' Marcus pointed to the small, blue, distinctly un-Jaguarish car parked by the pavement. Mrs Strode-Boylie waved at the girls from the driver's seat. Next to her, staring at the floor, sat the Massively Successful Dentist.

Abbie gave Perdita a look that said, *Hang on. What if he yells at us? Or kidnaps us? Or zaps us with a dento-gun and turns us into toothpaste?* But Perdita was already striding towards the car. Biting her lip, Abbie followed.

To her relief, Marcus's mum smiled as they got in. 'Hi, girls. Glad we saw you. We're popping over to the zoo anyway. Aren't we, *dear*?' The MSD nodded into his tie.

All the way to the zoo Mrs Strode – sorry, Strodboil – hummed a happy tune. Her husband sat in silence.

The car pulled up at the zoo. Abbie and Perdita got out. They waved to Charlie, who was feeding the ducks at the entrance pond.

'Well I'll be …' he gasped, dropping his loaf as Marcus followed the girls through the barrier.

Behind them came Mrs Strodboil. She was guiding a silver-haired man by the elbow. 'Hello, Mr Chumb,' she said. 'You haven't met my husband. He's a Massively Successful Dentist, you know. And a Massively Kind one, too. Aren't you, sweetness?'

The MSD winced.

'Which is why he'd like to offer a free dental checkup.'

The MSD whimpered.

'To all the animals.'

The MSD whined.

'Starting with the carnivores.'

The MSD wept.

'Otherwise,' she nudged her husband playfully, 'I've explained that Marcus and I will be packing our bags and visiting my parents. For a very long time.'

* * *

'This little piggy vent to Bradleigh,' murmured Klench. In a few days he'd be on the plane to England, prison and the woman of his dreams.

'No!' cried the woman of his nightmares. 'I vill not let her visit.'

'How you stop her?' shouted Klench. A spider heading for a breadcrumb in the corner dropped her bag in alarm.

'I'll find a vay, you great soufflé,' muttered Inner Mummy.

33

Deck the Walls

Friday didn't feel like the last day of term. Maybe that was because the class had spent the week making wedding decorations, so it seemed like they were already on holiday. Or maybe it was because the children had arranged to meet at the zoo the following week. Perdita had invited them all to help prepare the café, the venue for the wedding service.

Wendy insisted on spring-cleaning over the weekend. 'Everything that *can* sparkle *will* sparkle. And,' she added wisely, 'there's a sparkle in everything.' By Sunday afternoon Abbie had to agree. Even the tea bags on the counter gleamed.

'Now,' said Coriander, taking Wendy's elbow, 'off we go. You're not allowed back before Friday.' She led Wendy out of the café to discuss hairstyles for the orangs. The options for Winnie, of course, were endless.

On Monday at ten o'clock the children gathered in the café.

'OK, team,' said Terrifica, who'd organised a rota, 'seating and cameras today. Henry and Jeremy, you clear the tables.

Claire and Rukia, you can arrange chairs. Snorty, you're in charge of microphones – no crackle, please. Greg, Marcus and Craig, you can help Mr Platt set up cameras round the zoo. Then the animals can watch the ceremony and the guests can watch the animals.'

'What about me?' squeaked Ursula. She ended up checking that all the chairs were 7.62cm apart, which was pointless because Rukia had already done it.

On Tuesday everyone brought in decorations. They were a mixture of Christmas, wedding and plain weird.

Greg brought tinsel, which he draped over the counter.

'They'll love that,' said Abbie. 'Green for Mr Dabbings, sparkly for Wendy.'

Marcus brought twelve boxes of dental floss. 'Mum ordered Dad to bring them from his surgery,' he said. 'It makes great string.'

Rukia cut the floss into lengths of 12.54cm. Jeremy tied them to his holly angels. Henry hung them from the ceiling. With their wonky leaf wings and red-berry eyes they looked more like drunkards than God's holy choir.

Snorty brought polystyrene bells that sniffed instead of chimed.

Claire had made a banner that said:

Congratulations to the happy cuple

in dried lentils.

'Wow, that must have taken ages.' Abbie kicked Perdita before she could point out the mistake.

Ursula stuck a Christmas star on the window, though no one saw it because it was made of cling film.

Craig brought nibbles.

'Those aren't decorations,' said Terrifica, 'they're sausage rolls. They'll never last till Friday.'

'Good point,' said Craig and nibbled them all up.

Wednesday was flower arranging. Even though the wedding was still two days away, there was no danger of the flowers wilting because Mr Dabbings had knitted them.

'No real ones,' he'd insisted. 'Think how it must feel, kids, to be wrenched from the soil.'

Thursday was Christmas Eve. The children gathered in the reptile house to wrap their joint present.

'Do you think they'll guess what it is?'said Claire.

'Not if we add some knobbly bits,' said Abbie. That was easy, as they were covering the gift in tinfoil.

'Wendy'll love the packaging as much as the present,' said Perdita.

It took all morning, not just because of the size. The chameleons kept scuttling out of their playground and getting caught in the wrapping.

'Oh no. I've taped Hue to the front again.'

'That's not a ribbon. That's Toney.'

There was a nasty moment when Henry opened the sliding door and ran into Edie's cage. 'Look at me!' he cried, sitting on her back and waving his arm like a rodeo rider.

'Off!' barked Perdita, as Edie opened a grumpy eye and an even grumpier mouth.

Everyone left after lunch. Abbie and Perdita waved them off from the zoo entrance. 'You've done a brilliant job,' Perdita called. 'See you tomorrow.'

'I'll be off too,' said Abbie. 'I promised Mum I'd help decorate the cake.'

'That'll be fun,' said Perdita.

'I'm not so sure,' said Abbie as Dad drew up in the car. 'Mum's really nervous.'

She needn't have worried. At home she found Mrs Strodboil in the kitchen with Mum. Hearing about the cake from Marcus, she'd phoned to offer her help. Abbie wowed at the sculpted masterpiece.

'When you're married to a dentist you get to know toothpaste.' Mrs Strodboil laughed. 'It's very similar to icing.'

'So can I clean my teeth with icing?' asked Ollie, licking a spoon.

Mrs Strodboil smiled. '*Apart* from the sugar.'

The cake had three layers separated by little white pillars. The bottom layer was a replica of the classroom. Tiny pupils sat at their desks. At the front stood a teacher with sideburns holding a guitar. The second layer was a replica of the zoo café. A lady in an overall was dusting a teapot. On the top layer a pair of knitting needles leaned against a huge button. Every single thing, from sideburns to duster, was made of icing.

* * *

Klench sat in the aeroplane, practising compliments for Grandma. 'Your eyes are as brown as chocolate mousses. Your skin is softer zan old boots.'

The policemen sitting either side exchanged a knowing look, as if to say, *Solitary confinement – always drives 'em nuts.*

34

Hitched

Thank goodness it was a cloudy day. If the sun had been shining Abbie would have gone blind. Because a star had landed in the café.

From top to toe Wendy dazzled. Her veil glittered with silver sequins. Her dress was ablaze with bling. Studs and buttons, balls of silver foil and even a few teaspoons were sewn on with silver thread. Her train gushed behind like a waterfall.

By the bride's side walked her stand-in dad. Sergeant Bolt stared ahead, the buttons of his police uniform nearly popping with pride.

The bridesmaids walked behind holding the train. Minnie wore a saucepan on her head. Winnie's hair was tied with dozens of silver chewing-gum wrappers.

The groom was waiting at the café counter. He wore a knitted green suit. Bells hung from his jacket sleeves. They tinkled as he took his bride's hand. They turned to the counter to face the vicar of St Brad-on-the-Tussock.

The Reverend Bulbs had a round face, smooth like an onion bulb and shiny like a light bulb. 'Dearly beloved ...' he said. And the service began.

The best bit was the vows. 'I, Branston Chickpea Dabbings, take you, Wendy Wanda Wibberly, to have and to hold, to love and to polish, till death us do part.'

'I, Wendy Wanda Wibberly, take you, Branston Chickpea Dabbings, to have and to hold, to love and herb-relish, till death us do part.'

The best man stepped forward – except that he wasn't a man and he didn't exactly step. (Wendy had refused to have a best man: '*You're* the best man, Brangles. I won't have anyone stealing that title.') Sporting a silver bow tie, Vinnie shuffled up and held out the wedding rings.

Abbie caught her breath. She'd been worried about this bit. Mr Dabbings would want knitted rings and Wendy would want shiny ones. Things could get messy.

Phew. Mr Dabbings slipped a glittering band of gold onto Wendy's finger, and Wendy slipped a knitted band of gold wool onto his.

Everyone clapped. Abbie looked round. There wasn't a dry eye in the café. Mum's face was striped with mascara. Dad was snorting into a hanky. Ollie was wiping his nose on Mum's sleeve. Coriander's cheeks shone. Matt's windscreen wipers raced across his glasses. All round the café pupils blinked, parents dabbed their eyes, policemen sniffled and Grandma insisted it was 'just a cold'.

There wasn't a dry eye in the zoo, either. On the wall

above the counter Matt had projected a huge screen that was split to show all the animals watching the wedding from their quarters. In the elephant area Gina's eyes watered. In the spider sandpit tears trickled down the tarantulas' legs. In the tiger cage Silvio brushed his whiskers dry with a paw. And in the reptile house Edie shed fat crocodile tears.

Perdita sat beside Abbie. 'Look,' she said, pointing to the back of the café. Abbie gasped. Who'd have thought? Corky Shocka, the hardest hack in town, was blowing her nose on yesterday's *Bellow*.

Corky stood up. 'Ladies and gentlemen, boys and girls, apes and, er …' Mackenzie swooped into the café wearing a tartan top hat … 'parrots. The bride and groom have given me the honour of holding the reception at my family farm. So please come and join us for a whopping great knees-up.'

Everyone spilled out of the café. The children threw confetti made from leaves. 'Dead ones only, kids,' said Mr Dabbings. 'We don't want to hurt them, now.'

At the zoo entrance stood the wedding carriage, a wooden cart draped with tinsel. Everyone oohed. Because at the front, in a silver harness, stood Hepzibah. It had been Coriander's idea. 'We know she loves to wander. And this ties things up perfectly – no hard feelings and all that.' Because guess who was leading the procession to the farm?

In front of the cart, in Corky's open-top car, sat Marcus. Corky got into the driver's seat. Mackenzie flew onto her head. Then, when the other guests had found their cars, Marcus stood up. He waved a stick of sugar cane in the air. Hepzibah lumbered forward. And they were off.

At the farmhouse a feast awaited. Mum had organised a buffet in the huge dining room. Corky's farming family had helped, which was just as well because there weren't just humans to feed.

'Fruit over here,' said Corky's thin brother, Forky. He led the orangs and a gate-crashing pig to a tray on a bench.

'Hay over here,' said his friendly wife, Talky. She steered Hepzibah and a wandering sheep to a bale on the floor.

'Seeds over here,' said their pale son, Chalky. He guided Mackenzie and a random chicken towards a bucket in the corner.

Abbie ate till she ached. There were sausage rolls, profiteroles, schnitzels and pretzels. There were pizza slices, lemon ices, cream cakes and milk shakes, ginger ales and cocktails, fizzes and whizzes …

Whizzes? Those were in Abbie's stomach as she decided against a fourth chocolate meringue. 'I think I'm going to be sick,' she whispered.

'Wait till after the speeches,' suggested Perdita helpfully.

Mr Dabbings stood on a sofa. 'Ladies and gents; blokes and blokinas; kith, kin and kids. I'd just like to say a few words about my new wife.'

Forty minutes later he was still banging on about the richest jewel in the nose-stud of life, the brightest berry in the bramble of being …

'Can't someone shut 'im up?' said Grandma in what was meant to be a whisper but came out a shout.

Mr Dabbings stopped. There was an awkward silence.

Corky saved the day. 'And now,' she cried, jumping up, 'let the barn dance begin!' Everyone rushed to the barn. And everyone danced – which was no mean feat for those with no mean feet.

Because there were Fernando and Carmen, kitted out in their finest gear. Fernando wore a conquistador helmet that Ollie had made from a silver Chinese takeaway box. Carmen wore an Elizabethan ruff that Dad had made from loo paper. Wrapped round her stand, it hid her disaster of a neck. Abbie picked up Fernando and grabbed Perdita by the hand. They teamed up with Snorty and Henry, who couldn't take their eyes off the shrunken head.

Charlie Chumb played a note on his fiddle. And the Dashing White Sergeant began.

'Circle to the left, circle to the right – Great to see you here tonight,' sang a familiar voice.

'Gav!' shouted Abbie, dropping Fernando in surprise. The head bounced on the floor.

Gav the Nav laughed. 'Watch your step – I mean your head –

Gav has risen from the dead.

Matt recharged my battery

In time for this fine jamboree.'

He capered off as Abbie scooped a furious Fernando off the ground.

You wouldn't believe who was dancing with whom.

There was Corky with Sergeant Bolt. He was shouting off-the-record police gossip in her ear. 'Don't tell a soul,' he warned, after describing the Superintendent's earwax sculptures in a voice that shook the barn.

There was Coriander with Marcus and Greg. The boys were gaping as she recalled the time she put highlights in a hyena's hair to cheer him up after his wife ran off with a jackal.

There was terrified Matt, being whirled, twirled and tremendously hurled by Terrifica Batts and Jeremy Boing.

There was the Reverend Bulbs welcoming Ursula into his circle. She looked so thrilled to be asked, her cheeks shone almost as brightly as his.

There was Mrs Strodboil swinging Carmen. They were having a blast complaining about their husbands.

And there – ohmygoodness, fetch the camera – was Dr Strodboil whizzing with Winnie. Or rather, being whizzed. 'I'm a Mazzively Zuggzezzful Dennis, ya know,' he was shouting. She looked at him adoringly. Then she gave him the biggest, sloppiest, on-the-lippest kiss in the history of dental surgery.

And there were Mr Dabbings and Wendy, spinning round in wedding clothes and shiny green wellies. They only had eyes for each other.

After three rounds of Dashing White Sergeant, two Eightsome Reels and a Flying Scotsman, in which Mackenzie flapped round the barn, Gav called for quiet.

'Drop your partners, take a break
Time to cut the wedding cake.'

There was a tense moment when Winnie actually *did* drop her partner. Luckily he was too dizzy to care.

Everyone stood at the barn entrance.

'Oooh,' they gasped as Mum and Mrs Strodboil brought in the cake.

'Aaah,' they sighed as the newlyweds lifted the knife.

'Ouch,' they squealed as an iced pupil was sliced in two.

When cake had been handed round, the guests wandered

outside. Sergeant Bolt linked arms with Corky. He was telling her how he'd once gone to the cinema wearing a blue shirt and watched a film in which – 'Can you believe it? *Brad Pitt* wore one too!' Mrs Strodboil came out with Fernando on one shoulder and Carmen on the other. Winnie gave Dr Strodboil a piggy back. Mum and Dad held hands. Matt and Coriander held plaits. Perdita held Gav. Ursula followed the Reverend Bulbs, whose face made an impressive torch. And Snorty shared a joke with the gate-crashing pig.

Last came the newlyweds. Marcus, Terrifica and Henry disappeared round the corner and returned with the class's present.

'Ohh,' sighed Wendy, stroking the silver foil.

'Oh ho!' cried her husband, unwrapping it.

He lifted his bride into the gleaming wheelbarrow. Amid whoops and cheers, the happy couple squeaked off into the night.

Abbie peered through the darkness. A figure was sitting on the edge of a water trough. A curly wig jigged on its head.

'What's up, Grandma?' Abbie perched next to her and took a bite of cake.

'Oh, just thinkin'.'

Abbie followed her gaze upward. The sky was dazzling. You'd think the stars had been specially polished. 'What about?'

'Our new neighbour.'

Abbie stopped chewing. In the excitement of the wedding she'd forgotten about Klench. 'He's got so much to thank you for, Grandma. Without you he'd be stuck in some jail in – in wherever he comes from – with no one but his mum to boss him around.'

Grandma patted Abbie's knee. 'And without *you*, young Marcus would be stuck in 'is bedroom with no one but 'is dad to boss 'im around. We're quite a team, you and me.'

Abbie looked at the muddy-trousered, barmy-haired old boot and couldn't think of higher praise. She squeezed Grandma's hand. 'Be careful, won't you? Do you really think you can help him change?'

Grandma shrugged. ''Oo knows? But I've got to try. For me own peace of mind.'

And you'd better succeed, thought Abbie, her cake suddenly tasting of cardboard. Because if not, who knew what eefil-doinks might escape once more onto the streets of Bradleigh?

Have you read the first book in the series?

When Squashy Grandma's teeth get stuck behind the radiator, Abbie meets the Very Odd Job Man, Matt Platt, and his daughter, Perdita. Drawn into a hair-raising hunt for Perdita's missing mum, Coriander, Abbie is helped along the way by Fernando, the heartbroken shrunken head of a Spanish conquistador, and Chester, a helpful patch of chest hair.

But waddling in the shadows is the white-suited, burger-shaped Hubris Klench. Abbie soon discovers that finding Coriander is one thing, but saving the world from Klench's 'eefil doinks' quite another.

www.mercierpress.ie
Leabharlanna Poibli Chathair Baile Átha Cliath
Dublin City Public Libraries

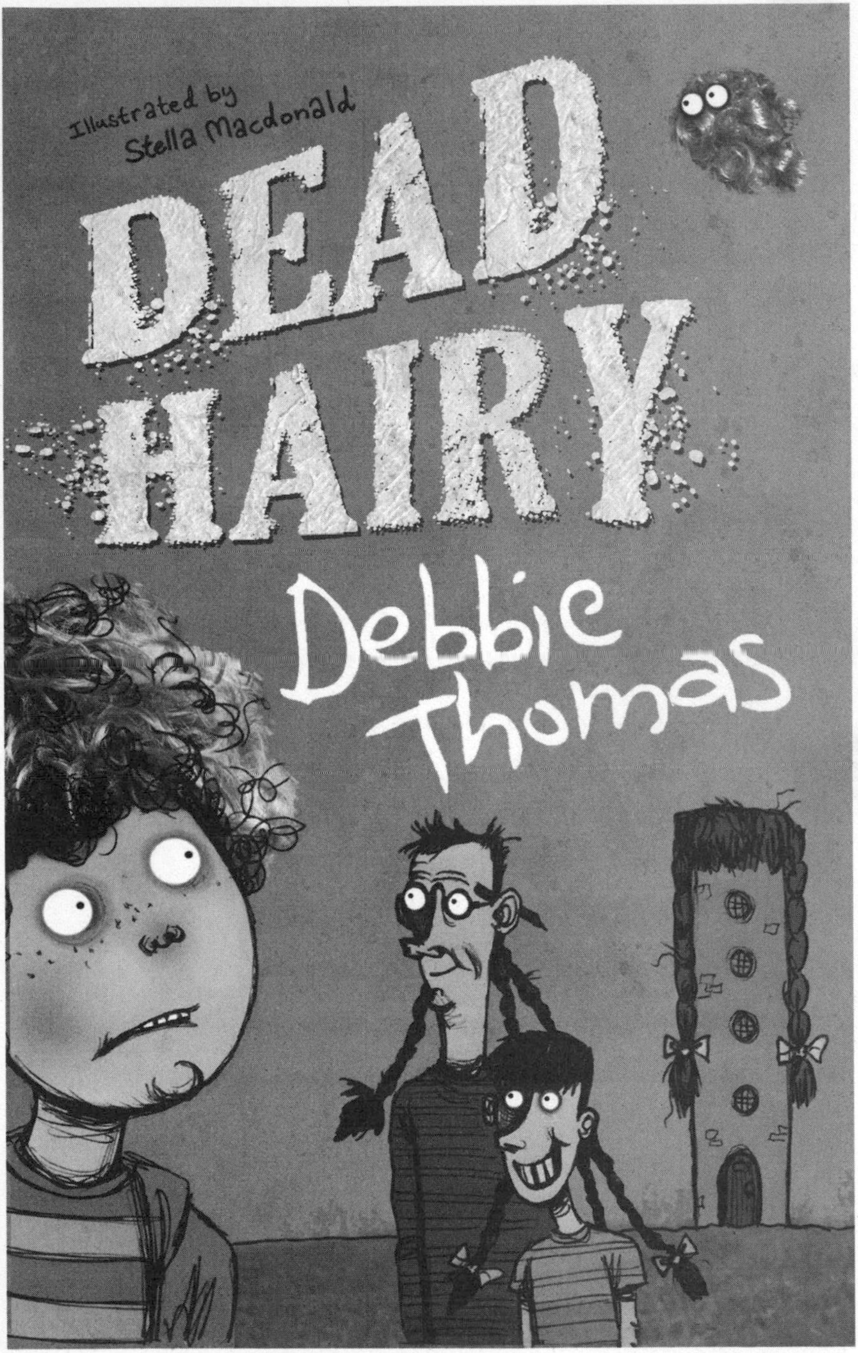

Illustrated by
Stella Macdonald
DEAD
HAIRY
Debbie
Thomas